THE JOURNAL
OF
CALLIE WADE

DAWN MILLER

POCKET BOOKS

New York London Toronto Sydney Tokyo Singapore

This book is a work of fiction. Names, characters, places and inci-
dents are products of the author's imagination or are used ficti-
tiously. Any resemblance to actual events or locales or persons,
living or dead, is entirely coincidental.

Originally published in hardcover in 1996 by Pocket Books

POCKET BOOKS, a division of Simon & Schuster Inc.
1230 Avenue of the Americas, New York, NY 10020

ISBN: 0-671-52101-2

First Pocket Books paperback printing December 1998

10 9 8 7 6 5 4 3 2

POCKET and colophon are registered trademarks of
Simon & Schuster Inc.

Cover design by Gina DiMarco
Handlettering by David Gatti

Printed in the U.S.A.

This book is dedicated to my great-grandmother

Nellie Mae Harper
1898–1978

*This is for you, Grandma. For all the love
and patience you selflessly gave.
I miss your laughter.*

Part One

❦

Independence, Missouri
1859

"Home is where your heart leads you."
—Amanda Wade

Callie,

Happy birthday, honey. I know this little journal isn't much of a present, but it was all I could manage, being that I can't get around too well lately. The peddler I bought it from says it's real quality as far as these books go. Well, I hope you make good use of it.

Your loving mama

Tuesday, April 12

What you can't duck, you best welcome. That's what Mama used to always say, anyway. I guess today is as good a day as any to remind myself of this, as Pa came home with the news that we will be joining a wagon train for California. There is a man in town, Pa says, that will give us a good amount for the farm. The spring rains have come again, and although Pa doesn't mention it, I know he fears another failed crop.

I suppose I should have fought the idea, should have begged Pa not to take us so far from our friends and home, but I couldn't seem to find the salt to do such a thing. Even as he sat across the table from me this evening, holding on to that tattered piece of a Mormon Way-Bill he'd bought for a map, my mind wanted to shout out at him and tell him going West was a mistake. But there was such a light in Pa's eyes, a kind of hope that I hadn't seen since Mama passed on, and I didn't have the heart to take that away from him.

"Callie," he said to me, "I won't lie to you. It ain't goin' to be easy. But I think maybe we can save Rose."

It scared me, him talking that way about Rose, but I knew he was only speaking the truth. I saw it in my brother Jack's eyes, too. We hold our fear in about Rose, her being the baby and all. But it's there just the same. She's nearly nine and a little slip of a thing . . . so painfully frail. There are times, when I watch her sleep at night, that I imagine her being a *real* rose, and with each ragged breath she takes, another petal falls from the flower.

One year—that's all it's taken for this disease to rob Rose of her strength. There isn't a night that goes by that I don't pray for some kind of miracle, *anything* to take away the dark smudges beneath her eyes, to erase the painful determination on her little face while she strains to keep ahead of the sickness. I don't think I'll ever forget the day Doc Hughes told us that Rose was a "lunger," leaving Pa standing in the swirl of dust from his wagon, holding a bill for his time and not much hope.

But now Pa thinks there might be a chance, that Rose could get better out West. Our neighbor, Mrs. Jensen, told me she's heard talk of folks like Rose who have traveled out there and found health.

But what if she can't make it?

I wish there was someone I could talk to, someone who would understand. If only Maggie was still in Independence. Why she let her pa force her into marrying that man from Blue Mills, I'll never know. But then, there's a lot that doesn't make much sense anymore.

Sometimes I feel I'll go mad keeping all these feelings locked up inside of me. But there's no one to turn to. So, instead, I give my life to these pages, my hopes, my dreams—and my fears.

God grant us the strength to make this journey.

Friday, April 22

The wagon train we're to join put me of a mind of a restless child—pulling and tugging to break free—as we came up on it this morning. The entire hillside moved and changed with the endless blanket of wagons and teams; men staking down tents, cattle bawling, women trying to keep close watch of both fires and children. Some of the newcomers were seedy looking. I'd held Rose tight to me as I watched their children pile out of the mud-specked wagons, their little bodies caked with a good month's worth of dirt and filth.

"Ain't as bad as it looks," came a voice, and I saw a stream of tobacco shoot past the running board of our wagon. Before I had a chance to think, there was a thin, wiry old mulatto dressed in buckskins offering me a hand down. "If yer of a mind ta talk ta the captain, he'll be back in a few," he said, turning to Pa. "Name's Stem. I'll be helpin' ta guide ya folks west."

I was surprised at the strength of the old man's grip as he helped me down, then Rose, smiling at us.

"He looks like them pictures of Moses in my Bible stories, Callie," Rose whispered, " 'cept for that wooden leg." I had to grin in spite of myself.

It was hard to tell how old he really was. The gray hair that fell almost to his shoulders did remind me of Moses in a way. He had a face that had known weather and enough wrinkles to put him anywhere between fifty and forever—and forever was more likely. He studied both Pa and me for a moment, taking measure of us I suppose, then turned and led the way through the tumble of children and dogs that ran up and down the rows of tents and wagons.

Just as quickly as he'd appeared, the old man was gone, limping back through the throngs of people. Pa, Rose, and I were left standing before an angry-looking woman hunched over a dying fire. The woman peered over at us and straightened up. She was incredibly tall, with a wide girth and a hard face that seemed stretched taut by the severe bun that held her brown-gray hair.

"Imagine you're lookin' for the captain. I'll have my son find him," she said to Pa, then moved away before he could answer, her eyes sweeping up and down the rows. "Zachariah Koch!" she bawled loudly, "you go fetch the captain for these folks, y'hear?"

I saw a slender young man with fair hair pause and glance in her direction, and his countenance gave me a start. There wasn't anything exactly odd about his appearance—just the *look* he gave his mother before he walked away that chilled me.

I didn't have much time to ponder this, as the woman had turned back to us and I felt Rose suddenly clutch at my leg, peeking out from behind my skirts. The woman got a real pinched look on her face. "I'm Della Koch, the preacher's wife. Most of us round here have learned to pull our own weight," she said with a questioning glance to Pa. Her gaze then fell on Rose. "Can't none of us afford to pull anyone else's."

Pa stood a little straighter, and I saw that the preacher's wife had annoyed him, hinting about Rose like that.

"I'm a farmer by trade," Pa said evenly. "And I'm

good with my hands. 'Magine I can help to build the rafts and such when the time comes. My son, Jack, he's been learnin' to smith, and Callie here . . ."

"Already got a blacksmith," was her answer, and she pointed to her left. "That's Quinn McGregor over there." We all turned to where she pointed. I saw a young man a little older than Jack, maybe twenty-three or twenty-four years old. The cotton shirt that stretched across his broad shoulders was drenched in sweat, his dark head bent over an anvil in concentration. He must have sensed us watching, for he looked right at me with great, serious eyes, pale blue in color, and then returned to his work.

"Folks say that his ma and pa died of the cholera back East in Pittsburgh just before he came here," the preacher's wife supplied. "We made sure he slept apart from the rest of us for a good spell to be sure he wasn't carryin' the sickness. Put him to work soon after that. He's helped build more'n a few wagons. But he's got a queer turn to him, never says a word to anyone. Irish," she snorted. "Well, I always say blood will tell."

The captain of the train picked that moment to show himself, and I don't think any of us had ever been more relieved. "Let's talk," he said to Pa, pushing his hat back to reveal a sparse tuft of brown hair. Rose and I followed close as they walked across the camp together, Captain Belshaw rattling off the endless list of supplies we'd need to make the journey: ". . . flour, sugar, salt, dried food, bacon, and coffee, maybe a cask of whiskey if yer inclined. Don't forget medicines, for gawd's sake . . . three-yoke team for the wagon." My head should have been swimming with it all; instead, I found my thoughts turning again and again to Quinn McGregor.

It was the haunted look in his eyes—a look that reminded me so much of Pa the day we buried Mama—that kept coming to me. I thought of him during the ride back to the farm, over dinner, and while I was cutting out some muslin shirts for Pa and Jack and finishing the coat for Rose. I guess I saw some of myself in him too. Although I still have Pa, Jack, and Rose, I know what it's like to lose someone you love.

Later—*Blood will tell*—that preacher's wife rankles me.

Monday, April 25

Sometimes I don't understand myself. Only two days ago I was annoyed at that preacher's wife, and here I've gone and behaved just as poorly.

Quinn McGregor was standing on our front porch when I came up from the field this afternoon, my hands wet with the wild greens I'd picked for our noon meal. I noticed right off he looked a little different from when I first saw him—tamed in a way. His shirt and pants, although faded, were clean, and I saw when he took his hat off that his hair was still sort of damp, curling over his collar, black and shiny, like he just bathed.

"Your Pa's hired me to do some work for him," he said as a manner of explaining, which angered me some—not that he'd been hired—but that Pa and Jack hadn't thought to mention it to me, which seemed to be happening more and more lately.

He was staring down at me, and I felt my cheeks grow hot. I saw something like a shadow of a smile go across his face then.

"Name's McGregor, ma'am. Quinn McGregor," he said. He held out his hand, and I dried mine against my skirt and took it. Of course I knew who he was. I couldn't have forgotten those eyes if I wanted to, tinged with sorrow as they were. There was a gritty strength about him, too. I saw that plain, standing as close as I was. I started to grow uncomfortable after we'd stood there for a moment, like he'd held on to my hand too long, and I pulled it away.

"Callie Wade," I said. "My pa and brother are in town. They'll be here shortly, if you care to wait down by the barn." I turned away, then stopped myself. I had been rude, dismissing him like that when I knew deep down it was Pa and Jack that had irritated me. The two of them leaving me out of the plans they made—plans that meant as much about my life as theirs. I tried to summon my manners, offering him Pa's chair on the porch and a cool drink.

"I believe I'll just wait at the barn," he said quietly.

Even though his expression hadn't changed, I saw a difference in his eyes, a sort of dignity that didn't speak of foolish pride, but of something else, something I couldn't quite put my finger on, and I felt as if I had shamed him in some way. The smile, if there had been one, was gone. Before I could muster an apology, he had walked off toward the barn, his back straight and rigid, like a wall.

*   *   *

Later—Mama always said I could be real snappish when I was unsure of things, most of the time blaming it on the red hair I'd inherited from Grandma Wade. I figure she wasn't too far from the truth, on account of how I was feeling when Pa and Jack strolled up to the porch a while ago. As soon as Jack heard Quinn McGregor was here, he headed on down to the barn.

"Why didn't you mention hiring him on?" I said to Pa as he started to walk away.

"He's a good man, Callie," Pa said, taking my words wrong. "He ain't askin' for pay, just for enough materials to get his own wagon in order. Besides, every wagoner in town is busy, includin' McCurdy, and we don't have time to wait. What's got into ya anyway, gal?"

I didn't answer. Instead, I let the door smack shut as I went into the house. From the parlor window, I watched Pa hurry down to the barn.

Even from a distance I couldn't help but notice the ease in the way Quinn McGregor pitted his strength against the large hickory bows set to hold the wagon canvas, his almost effortless swings of the hammer as he put them in place. I listened for a long while to the steady thud, over and over until I finally shut the window. But the sound leaked through anyway, muffled but regular, making sure I wouldn't forget we were leaving.

Tuesday, April 26

Weary today. I feel so much older than eighteen, at least a lot older than I felt only a month ago. They say that with age comes wisdom and virtue, but I have to admit I haven't felt a lick of either this day. I wonder if I'll turn out like those bitter, pruned-up spinsters that Maggie and I used to laugh about.

Oh, well, at least my work is almost done: I've finished the clothing for us all, the double canvas for the wagon, the bedding, and the linen food sacks. But then, planning what we're to bring is easy—compared to deciding what we have to leave behind.

For all its flaws, I'll miss our farm. Not because it's the only home I've ever known, but because of the memories that it holds within these walls. If the old house could speak, I think I might hear the whispers of our lives, of Mama and Pa's marriage, of births, of friends and laughter, and . . . of death. So, what do I take with us, which treasures am I to pack, which remembrances of our childhood here and of Mama? And what do I give away?

From my place by the window, I can see Pa kneeling underneath the old willow tree that shades Mama's grave; so lonesome a figure, he seems. I feel an awful tightness in my throat as I watch Pa's hands reach out and slowly touch the tiny grave of the little boy they never had a chance to name.

Maybe Pa is right, maybe we will have a new chance at life in the West.

But, oh, the price.

Wednesday, April 27

Rose met me in the kitchen late this afternoon, filled with questions. I had no doubt she'd been near the barn where Quinn McGregor had been working. She's taken a liking to him, and it seems, he's taken with her as well. But then, most people can't help but fall in love with Rose.

"Which way is California, Callie?" she'd asked, all breathless, and I put down the sacks I'd been stuffing with dried fruit and pointed in the general direction.

"Are we really going?" she asked then, and when I told her yes, she nearly hooted with joy. "Pa says that I will get well out there, Callie. He says soon I will be able to run and jump and play just like all the other children." Rose giggled. "Pa says he'll have to lasso me to keep me down."

I watched her out of the corner of my eye as she scooped up some green coffee beans filling one of the sacks. I sometimes think of her as a little elfin creature. Although Mama and I were small in size, Rose is nothing else if not downright *tiny*. Her hair's dark, like Pa's, with only a bit of red, and her eyes are

thoughtful most of the time, like she was waiting on
something none of the rest of us can quite see.

"You know, I bet you will get well out there," I
said as cheerfully as I could manage. "Pa ain't ever
been wrong yet."

If a heart could break, I think mine did when I saw
the hope that bloomed in her eyes.

I listened to the slow shuffle of Rose's shoes as she
made her way to the front yard. *Let her dream real
big dreams, God,* I prayed.

Thursday, April 28

Well, the day has faded off and I've got no one but
myself to blame for how poorly I'm feeling. I
should've fought Pa on leaving, but I didn't, and now
it's too late. Pa was paid for the farm this morning,
and we set out for town to purchase supplies. For
some reason, the crowds seemed bigger than usual to
me: mountain men and bullwhackers, Shawnees smok-
ing their shuck-rolled cigarettes, all lined the walks.
Smithies and wagon shops rang with the sound of iron
against iron, and freight wagons careened down the
streets as merchants hawked their goods. I felt as if I
would smother. When Jack glanced over at me and
winked, all I could manage was a weak smile.

Jack and I have stuck together since kids; we were
both young enough to cling to each other when Mama
died, yet still old enough to know pain. Lately, I feel
as if Jack's passed me by somehow. Even though he's

only two years older than me, he's a little more hard about things, and a lot more sure of this trip than I am.

When we finally reached the front of the mercantile, it was Jack that struck up a conversation with a group of men. They were part of about six wagons that were leaving today, heading for Oregon, they said.

I noticed that one of the wagons, if you could call it that, was filled with no less than five children. The young girl tending to those children took me around to the back of her parents' wagon, and I was filled with pity seeing their meager load—which, to me, didn't appear as if it would last them one month, let alone see them through the six or eight months I've heard it can take to reach Oregon.

When the train finally pulled out, the men shot off their guns and hollered their cheers for the new territory, and I saw Jack wave them on, his eyes dancing with the prospect of riches and Indian fighting. For the men, these journeys seem to hold such adventure.

But what of the women?

I will take to my grave the face of that young girl's mother as their wagon passed us. So haunted it was. Never once did she look back or wave to her friends and family that called after her. Instead, she stared straight ahead, her eyes lit by a desperation that I felt so deep that I turned away.

As I stepped up into our wagon, I glimpsed the figure of a man leaning against the large buffalo sign that stood in front of Mr. Jones's hotel, and I realized it was Quinn McGregor. His eyes met mine, shifting away from the women, the children—families. He didn't smile or wave. But there was a feeling of understanding that seemed to pass between us.

The dust in the street kicked up as the men and their wagons rolled on. By the time everything had cleared, he was gone. I wondered for a moment if he had been there at all. But the memory of his face, the understanding I had seen had been too real, and I pondered if I was better for knowing that—or worse.

Later—Jack just came in the kitchen. "Pa and I've been talkin', Callie," he said, standing over me as I was throwing lime and salt into one of the water barrels filled with eggs. "He says once we get through Kansas and Nebraska we might just lay over in Salt Lake. He heard we can pick up work for a spell there. Then if Rose is up to it, we'll move on to California."

"We'll go if we're ready, Jack," I said, the memory of that woman's desperation giving me a strength I didn't know I had. "Or we won't go."

Friday, April 29

Pa had the wagon backed up to the door by the time I finished getting dressed this morning. Not long after Mrs. Jensen had brought Ruthy over to play with Rose, we went about loading everything: our pots and pans, the humpbacked trunk for clothes and linens, Mama's Bible and some keepsakes tucked underneath, Grandma Wade's good dishes she left to me buried in barrels of flour, only a few pieces of furniture. The rest, Pa told me quietly, had been sold to the new owners. I stood firm on taking Mama's rocker, and Pa finally relented, his eyes telling me he understood.

By afternoon there wasn't much left but the bedding, which we planned to sleep on for the night, Pa figuring we could head for the rendezvous in the morning. I picked up the broom and headed for the door, when Jack peeked out of the window.

"Good idea, Callie," he said. "Ain't nothin' left but what that broom can catch, now."

For the first time all day, I stepped into the house and looked around, really looked. I saw nothing but space and the leftover dust from Pa's and Jack's shoes. I felt torn by the emptiness, as if a part of my life would never be the same. And afraid, too, that maybe my memories wouldn't be enough or that I might forget the times shared between these walls.

Outside, I could hear Pa and Jack laughing over something, and I couldn't help thinking how odd it was that men didn't feel the loss the same as women. To them, a home was no more than where they ate or slept. I wasn't mad, just saddened that it had to be that way.

I must have been pretty worn out from the packing, because I didn't know I'd even fallen asleep until I woke up from the thud of Jack's boots hitting the porch.

"Where've you been?" I asked him, and he sat down next to me with that slow, easy smile of his. "Charming" is what the ladies in town called it, but I wasn't much in the mood to be charmed.

"Town," he supplied finally. "Preacher's son near lost his pants playin' cards." Jack tipped his hat back as he took a long drag off of the cheroot. "Almost broke his neck, too. Fool drunk took a spill down the steps of the tavern."

When he said that, I nearly groaned out loud. I'd had a bad feeling Jack'd take some unsuspecting soul at a game of cards. His "talents" are well known about these parts, but not to those passing through. I recalled the look in Zachariah Koch's eyes that day at the rendezvous, and I felt a chill of fear. *Oh, Jack, why the preacher's son?* But just as quick I could hear Jack saying: *Why not?*

As much as Pa teases me about inheriting Grandma Wade's sass, I often wonder if Jack won't be the one to carry on that old woman's legacy.

"Well, I hope you'll be up to handling them oxen come morning," I sniffed. "Specially if you're still feeling the liquor." Down by the barn, one of the milk cows bawled loudly, as if the idea of the trip had put her out as well.

"Don't you worry none about me. I can hold my own," Jack said in a voice loud enough to wake the dead.

"Best hush, lest you want Pa to come out here."

"I'm a man now, Callie. Pa ain't got any hold on me."

I wanted to smack Jack right then. But I knew deep down that the way I was feeling wasn't because of Jack and the rest of the men spending their final evening at the local tavern. It was more that he didn't seem to mind none that we were leaving our home—that we would be leaving behind all of the sights, smells, and sounds that reminded me so much of Mama. Like the little cherry tree she planted in the yard just before she passed on and the sassafras—and even the pawpaws that grew down by the river that we used to collect together right before the first frost.

"Now, what are you lookin' so down in the mouth about?" he asked. "Hell, I'll give Zach his money back if it'd make you happy."

"It's not that, it's Mama," I told him, and for only a moment I saw pain in Jack's eyes, then it was gone so quick I wondered if I'd seen it.

"Mama's dead, Callie, and we're alive— You'd do good to remember that," he said, his voice a little harsh. "Don't you see, this is *our* chance. I'll be damned if I end up like Pa—scratchin' at the dirt like some chicken to make a livin'. I've got dreams, Callie. Big ones. There's fortunes to be made out West. One of these days I'm goin' to have enough money to set us all up good, you mark my words."

And he believed every single word. But then, Jack had enough grit in him to think he could—and maybe he would.

"There's no promise that we'll make a *fortune* out there, Jack," I said.

"There's no promise there'll be a tomorrow either, but we work for it just the same, don't we? Things ain't good around here no more. If nothin' else, think of Rose. Doc Hughes's done said that she won't get any better here. Out there . . . well, she has a chance, too. Don't you think Mama would've wanted that?"

Jack's hand rested on my shoulder, and I thought of Rose as she was that afternoon in the kitchen, dreaming of being like the other children, of running and jumping and playing. I felt ashamed, thinking only of myself. I covered Jack's hand with my own. "I suppose I'm scared is all."

"We're all scared," Jack said, and I felt his hand drop slowly from my shoulder.

When I looked over to Jack, his handsome face appeared older somehow. I wondered for a minute if it was only the shadows playing tricks on his features. But I guess deep down I knew it wasn't, because most of what he'd said to me was true. It just took me a while longer to admit it.

Somewhere along the way, without my knowing it, Jack *had* become a man. And I was proud of him.

"It's going to be a long day tomorrow," Jack said, helping me to my feet.

Off in the distance the lone cry of a whippoorwill sounded in the night, and I turned and followed Jack into the house.

Later—Rose has got her face pressed to the window in the parlor tonight. She says that our new covered wagon looks as pretty as a pearl, shining in the moonlight as it does. I tell her I'm busy when she asks for me to come see.

Saturday, April 30

Maggie came to bid me good-bye. I don't think I've ever before been as surprised as I was seeing her standing at our door this morning. She told me she'd been in town with her pa and old man Todd and had begged them to let her come say good-bye to me.

It made me mad that she had to *beg*. What did they

take her for, a slave? I could picture her pa waiting down the road a piece, just to make sure I didn't carry her off West with me. I admit, now, the thought did cross my mind.

Pa can be hard at times, but he's fair. Maggie's pa is plain hard. I haven't found it in my heart to forgive him for making her marry old man Todd, either. Jack and I suspect it was because of Mr. Todd's money. Everyone knows he's rich—richer than God, Jack likes to say. Funny thing is, Maggie's never given a fig about money.

I didn't mention any of this as time was short.

While Pa and Jack were yoking the team, we walked together through the rooms of the house, our voices loud in the emptiness, bouncing off of the walls and reminding me of the sounds of our childhood together. We talked about old times, about the dreams we had; sitting in the back of Mrs. Harper's classroom whispering of seeing the world, of the adventures we would live and I would write about . . . the handsome men that would fight for our attention.

"Do you ever think of those times, Callie?" she asked, and when I told her I did, her face was so wistful I wanted to cry. "I do, too," she said.

There were so many things I'd wanted to ask her: Was she happy? Was old man Todd good to her? But then, Jack was standing at the door, telling us that Pa was ready to pull out. Maggie linked her arm in mine, and we slowly walked across the yard together. "So, who's this Irishman that hired out to your pa?" She'd asked casually, and I have to say, it didn't surprise me that Maggie knew of Quinn McGregor. Ever since we were kids she'd had a knack for finding out things.

"No one *you* need to worry about," I told her, and she grinned.

"I'm not worried."

Without knowing it, we were standing next to the wagon. When Maggie hugged me tight, I felt like everything was laid bare. Like we were borrowing against a time that had already passed and I was holding my foot against the door to a part of our lives that was shutting fast. I knew Maggie felt it, too.

"I'm so scared," I whispered to her, hoping Rose couldn't hear.

"Amanda Wade was the strongest woman I knew," she said to me. "You remember that, Callie, because you take after your mama more than you think. Remember what she always used to tell us? 'The good Lord don't give nobody more than they can carry.' I kind of imagine she'll be looking after you all from heaven now. That is, if she ain't too busy handing out advice." We both laughed.

"Callie," Pa called from the wagon, "we're ready to go."

The ache of loneliness that Maggie's presence had soothed for a while flowed through me once more. So little time. But is there ever enough time to say good-bye?

"I love you, Mag," I said finally, pulling myself up into the wagon.

"You write me, Callie, you hear?" Maggie called to me as Pa hawed to the team.

I could only nod, tears smarting my eyes as our wagon lurched forward.

Long after we were settled in for the night at the rendezvous, I sat inside our wagon, hugging the friend-

Dawn Miller

ship quilt Maggie had made me tight to my chest.
When I closed my eyes jut right, I could still hear
the echoes of Maggie's laughter, dry and somehow
comforting, and still feel the warmth of her embrace.

If we never meet again in this lifetime, old friend,
at least our memories will endure.

Part Two

Along the Santa Fe Trail, Missouri and Kansas Territory

"When things get rough, remember:
It's the rubbin' that brings out the shine."
—Amanda Wade

Sunday, May 1

As soon as first light stretched against the sky, we began to break camp. How often over the last few weeks I'd pictured the scene in my mind, lying in bed at night. But my imagination had failed to do it justice.

People were everywhere, pulling up tent pegs, loading and reloading their wagons, men fighting to yoke oxen or mules, as the sharp smell of camp smoke mingled with the early haze. Some folks I recognized from that first day; Preacher Koch making his rounds; his wife, Della, so close to his back Jack swore there was a puppet string; Stem, his lanky body dressed in full buckskin as he limped after Captain Belshaw, checking folks' supplies and turning away the ones who didn't have enough, making sure there were enough willing hands to spell the drivers when the need came.

Down the rows of tents and wagons the word was passed that we would be pulling out soon.

Not long after, the line of wagons began to form, awkward and disjointed at first as several of the unseasoned teams balked. Then came the call to move out. Pa cracked his whip, walking alongside of the team, and Rose and I took one last look back as the wagon jolted forward. When we'd passed Hickman's mill, I felt a fear I'd never known rise up in me as my last tie to home faded out of sight.

On and on we moved down the steep Santa Fe Trail toward the valley of the Kaw. As I watched from my seat on the wagon, I saw fresh-scrubbed faces, and some not so fresh, shadowed beneath bonnets and hats, turn westward; Stem and Captain Belshaw flew by us on their mounts with Quinn McGregor in the lead, all of them so full of vinegar that it made Pa laugh. Zach Koch reined in alongside of me, tipped his hat, and then spurred his horse on up the hill before he could be teased by the other men. I'm ashamed to admit I was glad when he was gone. There's a mean streak in the preacher's son, I feel, even though he tries to hide it beneath his mask of goodwill.

Our procession was slowed once, when one of the wagons being pulled by mules careened into some unsuspecting soul. Jack had quickly pulled away from our herd of cattle and went to aid the victim—a pretty blonde woman, from the look of it. He said something that made her laugh as he mounted up, then tipped his hat in her direction and rode off.

"Jack doesn't miss a trick, does he?" I called over the din of cattle and wagons to Pa, but I don't think he heard me. He had walked a ways out from our team, his eyes on the man still fighting his mules. His face softened a little when Jack headed in our direction.

"Mercer's likely to kill someone if he don't learn to handle that team," Pa called out, and Jack grinned, dismissing Pa with a wave of his hand.

"You worry too much," he hollered back, riding past us toward the herd. Pa shook his head, goading the team on.

As the train made its way out of the groves of timber, the uneasiness I felt was soon washed away by Rose's laughter. "Oh, Callie," she said to me, pointing ahead, "it looks like a little piece of heaven, doesn't it?"

In front of us, as far as the eye could see, were the rolling green hills of Missouri, quilted with wild indigo, larkspur, and the tiny purple flowers with yellow faces that we call rooster fights. The sky opened up around us, so wide and blue it took my breath away, and I felt cleansed. I saw that some of the others did, too, their worry lines relaxing a little as they gazed around. Maybe this is what it's for, I'd thought as I took it all in. Maybe we were all looking for a little piece of heaven we could call our own.

For miles, I watched the white canvas tops crawl across the prairie, gaps spreading between each of the teams as the train settled into the drive. I felt as if our dreams and hopes were a lot like those wagons— stretched to the limit, reaching out for what we couldn't see—and praying for the best.

Later—The pretty blonde woman's name is Grace Hollister. I found this out just after we settled into camp this evening.

I had been attempting to wave the billows of smoke away from my face long enough to get the cookall in the fire when I heard a husky chuckle come from somewhere behind me. I turned around to find the woman that Jack had helped earlier watching me with amusement. She looked to be of about thirty, I'd say, wearing a fine dove gray dress, lined and boned, with curlicue cording down the front. I felt plain in comparison, with my brown linsey dress and poke bonnet. Her smile put me at ease, though, that and her warm brown eyes.

"You know," she offered, "you shouldn't build your

fire so high. That smoke'll choke you out before you can cook anything."

I kept an eye on the fire and took the hand she offered.

"Grace Hollister," she said. "And you must be Callie Wade."

"How'd you know who I was?" I asked, and she told me that Jack had mentioned me to her earlier. I happened to glance down then, noticing her wedding ring.

"So, your husband, does he know Jack, too?" I asked.

"I had a husband," she said, "but he was long gone before I ever started this trip." She must've read my thoughts then, because her laugh was wry. "I said I *had* a husband. I ain't looking for another especially if he's anything like Jack Wade."

It was my turn to laugh then. It didn't take much to know what she'd meant by her remark. Jack wasn't exactly husband material and was likely to tell you so himself. He had too much of the wanderlust in him. Too much of the I-got-to-do-it-my-way to stay still long enough for marriage.

"Well, I best get. My youngest, Lizzie, she's a handful, and I can't let her out of my sight too long." Then she said real friendly, "If you need any help, just holler. I've been around the world a time or two, you might say."

Pa invited Quinn McGregor and the scout Stem to dinner this evening. I think Stem was as nervous as I was, the way he was fidgeting with his hat, standing off to one side like he wasn't sure what to do with himself. I can't say as though I blame him, after the bad treatment he got from some of the folks at the rendezvous, saying he wasn't "fit" to lead us—him being "part Negro" and all. But then I figure he'll find out sooner or later that Pa doesn't give a fig for what most people think, especially if they're in the wrong.

Dinner ended up being a tense affair, at least to me, that is. No one else seemed to notice. Rose sat in between Stem and Quinn McGregor, just like a tiny queen holding court, and Pa and Jack laughed and carried on as if they were entertaining in the parlor back home instead of beneath the wide, dark sky of the prairie.

Every so often, I'd look up to find Quinn McGregor studying me in that quiet way he had about him. As the night wore on I felt like we were both watching and waiting for something to happen, but I don't think either one of us knew what it was.

I did breathe easier after dinner though, when Jack and Pa took Quinn down to check on the cattle. Grateful for the reprieve, I took it on myself to ask Stem about Grace Hollister. There was something about the woman that appealed to me, a warm frankness that I liked, and I was curious to know more.

The "Widder Hollister," as he called her, had had a real hard time of it. It seems she traveled up from New Orleans with her four children and no husband to mention. Stem said he got it on good authority from the people she'd traveled with that her husband was dead. A gambler, they said, that was shot down during a card game.

"So, she came west, jes like the rest of us," he finished, as if it was as simple as that.

But it wasn't as simple as that, I knew that much. It took a lot more than hitching a wagon to some mules for a woman to brave the journey with four kids and no husband. It took courage.

As I sit here this evening, staring at the scattered campfires of the train, glowing and fading across the miles of Missouri hillside, my thoughts keep turning to Grace Hollister. I try to picture myself with four children, traveling alone across this prairie. I can only imagine how lonely she must be.

I wonder if she is asleep. Or like me, is she sitting next to her fire, waiting on tomorrow's food to cook up so she can go to bed? Is she listening to the night sounds, the whining howl of the coyotes beyond camp? Does she worry?

I wish I knew.

> *Along the Santa Fe Trail*
> *In transit to California*
> *May 2, 1859*

Mrs. Maggie Todd
Blue Mills, Missouri

Dear Maggie,

It's hard to believe, looking around me, that we're only two days out of Independence. As we near Kansas, the trail is already offering its sad stories of the folks that came before us. The ground on each side of our train is littered with pieces of their lives, hastily thrown from wagons to lighten their loads: rocking chairs, mirrors, washstands, trunks, and quilts and more food than you would imagine. It got me so down that when I saw a group of weary travelers who had turned back, I might have joined them if it weren't for Rose. "Ye jes felt yer first flick of the Elephant's tail," our old scout informed me, riding alongside of the wagon. The Elephant, Stem went on to tell, is kind of a symbol that stands for the price us emigrants pay for this journey. Little did I know only a few hours later I should have my first glimpse of the trouble this beast can cause. . . .

Our train had overcome another bound for California, and as we were ready to pass, I heard an awful commotion. I saw that some of our own company had stopped to lend a hand. Jack and "The Irishman" were scrambling for water, trying to douse flames that were eating away at one of the wagons. It was then I noticed a woman standing off to one side, her arms folded across her chest as she watched the fire. I saw two small children clutching her skirts, and I hopped down from my perch, quickly cutting the distance between us. "Is this your wagon?" I asked. "Was," she replied and looked back to the fire. "Wasn't much left in there," she said to herself. "He threw most of our things out . . . said we'd get more." Glancing at the ground around her, I saw fine shards of glass and a few strips of singed hemp, the kind you might find in an oil lamp. I felt an odd tingle crawl up my neck. I looked up once more and our eyes met and I knew then that she'd set fire to her own wagon. "I expect we will be going home now," she said with grim satisfaction.

When I climbed back up on my seat, I noticed that many of the faces of the women in our train were both horrified and sympathetic. In a way, I think we understood what drove her to do such a thing. After all, what little she had left of her life, her husband had thrown away—from the looks of it—some of their food as well. I think her setting fire to that wagon was her only way of fighting back. As much as I hate to admit it, Mag, I find myself wondering what the Elephant might have in store for me.

Such a sorrowful tale, I hope it will be the last for a while! I intend to mail this once we reach the Kaw River. I've heard there is a mail service at the ferry. I have to close for now, duty calls! All my love to you and yours. I will write whenever I can. I remain

> *Your faithful friend,*
> *Callie*

P.S. Store up all the news from home you can. I'll expect some long letters once we reach California!

Tuesday, May 3
Douglas County, Kansas

We have made only eight miles today; we were forced to camp early here, near the bluffs, because of the Pratts' wagon breaking down. I'm snatching a moment to write this while I wait on Pa and Jack to return from checking on our cattle. Rose is asleep, looking so peaceful that it's hard for me to believe she gave us all such a scare today.

I had been about to call her to dinner when I heard someone shout my name. I was already halfway through camp before I realized that it wasn't Pa's or Jack's voice that held such horror, but Quinn McGregor's. As long as I live, I don't think I'll ever forget seeing him coming toward me with Rose in his arms, her little body limp as a rag doll.

When I brushed her hair from her face to get a good look at her, I felt my legs nearly buckle, seeing how pale her face was. "What happened?" I asked.

"She was playing near my tent with the little Hollister girl when she just kind of wilted," he replied, and I saw his brow knit with worry. "I think we should get her to the wagon."

I almost reached for her then, but Quinn was hugging her against his chest, and when our eyes met, I saw a fear I didn't expect, him not being family. I followed close behind as he carried her across camp, a guarded weariness about him as he ignored the curious faces that peered up from their fires.

As soon as we got inside the wagon, I loosened her clothes and put my ear to her chest. She's fainted, I told myself over and over. She'd done it before. But Doc Hughes had warned me to listen for the rattle— that and the blood. My hands shook, just thinking about it, and Quinn shifted around, restless. "Callie," he said, but Rose coughed then. When I heard her heart beating like a caged bird in her chest, I laughed, but the sound came out more like a sob.

"Will she be all right?" Quinn asked, and when I told him she would, I saw his body relax. But there was blame in his eyes. "You shouldn't be taking her on the trail if she's sick," he said. "It'll only weaken her."

I looked at him hard, to silence him, and cocked my head to the bed, where Rose stirred slightly.

When we moved outside, he took me by the arm. "Take her home, Callie," he said, like he had known me for years. I nearly pulled away, but his voice, low and raw sounding, made me wonder if there wasn't something else that made him fret over Rose like he did. He seemed to want to say more but didn't, and I saw his face change, shadowed by something I couldn't place.

"Rose is why we're here," I told him. "The doctor thinks she'll at least have a chance out West." I think he must have heard the desperation in my voice, because his expression softened.

"Is she a lunger?" he asked, but I could see he already knew the answer. I ended up telling him the whole story: Rose's sickness, Pa selling the farm . . . pretty much everything that brought us out here.

As we sat together on the silent prairie, I found I liked the closeness, of feeling like someone else shared my fear and worries for Rose. "Might be that she will get well in California," he said finally. "It's happened before."

"That's what I told Rose," I said.

"Do you believe it?"

I told him I wanted to, and he nodded and said, "Sometimes that's all it takes."

Quinn stood then, and I suddenly felt the need to make amends for how I acted back home. When I told him I was sorry, he smiled. "Nothing wrong with being afraid, lass," he said. "Specially when your world's being pulled out from under you."

I wondered if he was making fun of me, but I saw

only warmth and understanding in his blue eyes. "Friends?" he said.

He held out his hand to me, and I took it, this time not caring how long we stood there.

Friends?

I keep thinking how lost I've felt without Maggie, without anyone to talk to or to share what I've been feeling inside. But, then, I hardly know Quinn McGregor, not really. There is *something* about him. The way he looked after Rose today showed me that. His fear was as real as mine. They say fear makes friends of strangers.

Truth is, I could really use a friend right now.

Later—Rose is sitting here by the fire, perched on Pa's lap, laughing, as if her fainting spell had never happened. "Just like a woman," Jack said, but I can see that he's relieved.

Wednesday, May 4

Up before dawn. We've made good time, having traveled over ten miles through some of the prettiest Kansas prairie I have seen so far. We have stopped to noon near a clear spring, which is where I am planted, writing this. I found an abundance of gooseberries here. Too bitter for me, but Rose liked them fine. She and Lizzie Hollister ate a good many even though Grace and I warned them about the bellyache. If there are any left,

I'll make a currant pie this evening, once we make camp. Jack and Quinn have gone off to hunt.

Later—Camped this evening here along Bull Creek. We're all tired, but in good spirits. I made a fine stew of meat shavings and beans, in spite of our empty-handed hunters. All had their fill of pie this evening as well—except Rose.

Jack just strolled by. He told me to save some room in this journal for his "daring exploits against the red devils of the plains."

I told him it made sense, him going after those *red devils*, since he was having such a hard time of it hunting down small game.

Quinn and Stem had a good laugh at that.

Thursday, May 5

Traveled due west today—still in Kansas. Made about eleven miles before we nooned opposite of Spring Creek.

I'd been lying in the grass on my elbows when Grace joined me. Her face was flushed, and strands of her blonde hair had worked themselves free of her bonnet. She looked young and pretty, sitting there with her arms hugging her knees as we both gazed across camp. We laughed as her little ones, their hair tousled from naps, burst out of the back canvas of her wagon, running with pent-up energy as soon as their wiry legs hit the ground. Their liveliness was something, considering the long morning. I'd said as much when Grace shifted in the grass, sliding me a grin as she rubbed her backside.

"I know I don't have any energy to spare," she said. "Lord, Callie, I imagine any extra flesh on our bodies will be jarred off by the time we reach California." We both chuckled.

When I saw Quinn rein in by our wagon to talk to Pa and Jack, I started to thinking about the day before and what he'd said, and so I asked her if she had ever been friends with a man. And as soon as the words came out of my mouth, I wanted to pull them back.

I got a skeptical glance as she pulled her bonnet off and fanned herself with it.

"Friends, huh? Who's the man?" she asked.

When I told her it was Quinn McGregor, she laughed. "What's so wrong with being friends with him?" I said.

"Nothing. But I swear, Callie, there ain't a man I've ever known that wants to be only friends. Even my husband, Grady. Oh, we became the best of friends— eventually. We just had to get past our general admiration of each other's finer points first, you might say."

That raised my brows some—but not much. Mama had taught me all about what went on between a man and a woman, Grandma Wade made sure of that. I saw Grace watching me with a pleased expression on her face, and I wondered if she hadn't been testing me in a way.

The captain sounded the call for us to get moving again, and we picked ourselves up and headed to the wagons together. I had started in the direction of my own wagon when Grace laid her hand on my arm.

"Being friends with a man ain't so bad. It's a start, at least," she said, a wide grin breaking over her face. "Besides, I think any woman around here'd agree that being friends with that Irishman is one of the nicer things that could happen to a person."

Tonight, sitting by the light of our fire, I can't help but laugh, remembering what Grace said to me this afternoon.

I think Grace is about the most interesting woman I've ever met. She looks like she was born to money, yet Jack tells me she can swear a blue streak, and he's seen her handle a pistol better than most men. The good ladies of this train don't know what to do with "the widow," who one day can be seen toting her well-worn Bible in hand and the next, taking part in a game of old sledge with the boys.

Some women might be embarrassed by Grace's forward nature, but I'm coming to like it. No frills or games, only the plain, simple truth. Every time we talk, I come away believing I could handle just about anything. And out here on the prairie, where all you have to call a home is the back of a wagon, that kind of feeling goes a long way.

Friday, May 6

Pretty tired. Decided to walk today. The sounds of the pull are still ringing in my ears: hooves hitting the hard ground, saddles squeaking, chains, teamsters calling, "Drive ahead!" "Gee haw!" "Move along!" and on and on. The wind was very high—if dirt was food, we'd all be fat.

Sunday, May 8

Not long after the preacher had his sermon, Zach Koch came by for Jack. He was real friendly and in a big way. I'm usually not one to judge so quick, but I think he's trouble.

Later—My hunch about Zach Koch being trouble has proved true.

It all happened shortly after Grace had gone to spell her son Dane from driving the team. I had been walking alone, far enough to the side to try to keep out of the dust when the wagons began to climb a long hill. The wind picked up over the rise, low and moaning and blowing hard. When I'd turned my face from a gust, I saw Jack ride out of the thick cloud of dust that surrounded the tail end of the train. I couldn't make out much more until he was right alongside of me. It was then that I saw that Zach Koch was with him.

Zach leaned against his pommel, smiling at me all the while Jack told me that Captain Belshaw had picked a place to stop just ahead.

No sooner had Jack rode away than Zach said, "I'll bet them little legs of yours could use a rest." There was something in his voice, something about the slow way he looked down at my skirts, that uneased me. I moved closer to our wagon and to Pa. After a minute or two I heard him ride off.

Only a short time had passed when I saw Della Koch, standing off to one side of the trail as the wagons rolled past, her mouth set in a hard, grim line as her eyes met mine.

Monday, May 9

I'm making a note to myself now to never make the mistake of walking with Mrs. Iverson and Della Koch *again*. Grace and I had been doing just fine until the two of them up and joined us out of the blue. We'd been talking when Grace suddenly said, "Well, look what the wind blew in." No sooner had she spoken, there was Della Koch, pinched-faced as ever as she followed behind Mrs. Iverson. Della was none too thrilled to see us, but I guess in weighing our company against being bounced around in the wagon, we won out. No sooner had we started talking than it went downhill from there.

"It's awful hot out here," exclaimed Mrs. Iverson, patting her cheeks with a handkerchief. "Been gettin' hard pains runnin' all down my arm, too . . . suppose I'm workin' on a stroke." Although she found more wrong than right with her body, Mrs. Iverson generally looked forward to getting better—or at least moving on to the next illness. Yesterday, she'd been contemplating blood poisoning in her leg after scraping it on

a rusted tongue. When I had smiled at her sympatheti-
cally, she beamed and patted my arm.

"But what would you know, pretty young thing that
you are?"

Della Koch looked up at us sharply then. "Did I
ever tell you about that nice girl I found for my
Zach?" she said. "She made the trip to California last
year with her family. I've been writing her ever since."

"Why ain't *you* married?" Mrs. Iverson peered at
me closely.

"You know, I had a cousin who had a stroke,"
Grace cut in. "They say it was because she crossed
her legs when she slept." Mrs. Iverson appraised
Grace with a keen interest, forgetting me for the time
being. I breathed a sigh of relief. Nothing short of
human sacrifice could've proved my gratitude at that
moment. I think Grace knew it, too, because she
caught my eye and winked as I quickly walked off
toward the wagon.

I'd already cooked dinner and served it and was
busy making some loaves of bread by the time Grace
found me this evening. As soon as I saw her face, I
knew that the conversation hadn't gone too well after
I'd left. When she told me she thought Della Koch
had it in for me, it didn't surprise me any. But when
she said, "She thinks you're after her son," I was
never so shocked in my life.

"Zach Koch would be the last person I'd set my
sights for!" I said. "Why would she even think a thing
like that?"

"Who knows?" Grace shrugged as if it didn't really
matter, anyway. "I thought I'd warn you; when I get
feelings about people I'm usually right. And I'll tell

you, Callie, I don't have a good feeling about none of that bunch."

I poured us both a cup of coffee and sat down next to Grace by the fire. I had a hunch she hadn't told me all that'd went on. Although the banter was light, there was something in her eyes that was different, a fleeting look of hurt I saw, that she'd tried to hide. If she'd been there long enough to learn what the preacher's wife felt about me, I just bet Della Koch had laid into her as well.

When I thanked her for helping me make my escape this afternoon, she smiled at me kind of shyly behind her cup of coffee. "What are friends for?" she said.

"Well, I feel awful, sticking you with them," I told her. "Those two would try a saint."

"Oh, honey, don't you worry about me none," she said. "I've handled worse than them." She stood, tossing the rest of the coffee into the grass. "And in prettier packages, too."

Tuesday, May 10

Jack says we've gone close to twelve miles today, heading toward the headwaters of the Wakarusa River. I can feel every mile of it in my bones, sitting here as I write this. It wouldn't have been so hard to manage if the preacher's wife hadn't made matters worse for me by doing what she did.

I got quite a tongue-lashing from that woman this evening, and all because I had dared to take my bonnet off in front of Zach. With my blood still boiling I tucked Rose into her bed and made her promise me that if I ever behaved in such a manner as Mrs. Koch, she would throttle me good until I came to my senses. A heavy silence followed in the darkened wagon as I moved to my bed. Rose's voice, solemn and sounding so old for a child of her age, broke the silence.

"A swift kick to the shins would do as well, mightn' it, Callie?"

Wednesday, May 11

Met up with Stem this evening when I went for a walk.

He was sitting in the middle of a tall thicket of prairie grass, his wooden leg sticking out at a jaunty angle as his dark eyes stayed trained to the sky. There's something about the old man that I've developed a fondness for. He's an interesting sort of character, with a kind of knowledge that people don't get from books, but from life. He's got mischief, too, for I've watched him rant like a crazy person when some of the women venture too near his wagon. Most think he's mad, but I think he just prefers his own company.

Bets had been placed around camp on how he lost the leg, and my curiosity must've been plain on my face when I sat down, because he grinned at me. "Guess yer wonderin' what happened ta my leg," he said simply, and then laughed at my obvious embarrassment. "Don't go lookin' like that—Curiosity ain't nothin' ta be ashamed of. That is, unless yer a thirty-year-old man that's got a hankerin' fer the wife of a Crow Indian."

"You lost your leg over a *woman?*" I asked him incredulously.

"Well, now . . . not jes any woman. She was a looker," he said, as if that explained it all. "Her husband must'a thought so too, because he shot me right through the leg. Probably would've done me in iffen I hadn't got back ta my own camp. Seein' there was no hope fer my leg, I tried ta saw it off m'self—but fainted dead away. Would've died, too, iffen my buddy hadn't known what ta do. I've traveled many a mile on this log since then."

"Don't you ever tire of traveling?" I said. Rumor had it Stem had journeyed all over the West, from trapping in northern Colorado to selling horses in California.

Stem reached into his pocket for a twist of tobacco and, after taking a mighty bite, chewed thoughtfully for a moment before answering, surprising me by breaking into a little ditty.

"I think I'll settle down, and I say, says I . . . I'll never wander further till the day I die. But the wind sorta chuckles: Why of course ya will! For once ya git the habit, ya jes' can't keep still."

"I never knew you were a poet, Stem."

"Raised on prunes and proverbs, I was!" We both laughed, and then his old face sobered some. "So, what's it that yer wantin' in life, Callie? It's gotta be more'n eatin' dust on this godforsaken trail."

"I don't know," I said. "I guess I get more questions

than answers out of life. I haven't thought of much else but hoping that Rose gets well."

"She's surely a delight. Little scamp's plucked more'n a few heartstrings in this camp, mine included!"

I wasn't sure, but I could of sworn that I saw tears in his eyes then, and it was all I could do not to lean over and plant a kiss on his weathered old cheek.

"What is it that you want out of life, Stem?"

"Oh, I reckon I've been chasin' the wind fer too long ta know, Callie. Don't have much family ta speak of, but I'll be tied if some nights I don't wish fer jes' that. I had a pa . . . once. Reckon I had a ma, too," Stem chuckled, "but she died when I was jes' a baby. 'Bout all I knew of her was that she was a slave."

I saw Stem's hesitation and remained quiet, deciding he'd say more when he saw fit. His warm, tea-colored face became thoughtful.

"My pa . . . well, now, I guess I'd have ta say he never played me false until he tried ta sell me."

He must have seen the horror in my eyes, because he said, "He were down on his luck. Person gets in a bad way sometimes . . . an' they don't always make the right choices."

Tears stung my eyes, and I wondered if anyone really knew Stem the way I saw him at that moment. Underneath all that toughness was a heart as wide and open as the prairie. It had to be a mighty big heart, indeed, to forgive a father who'd tried to sell you off as easy as last year's crop.

I'm not sure I could be as generous.

Once, on my way back to camp, I turned and saw Stem still sitting in the spot where we had been, staring off to the west, his silver head cocked to one side as if he were contemplating something. *Somewhere between fifty and forever,* I remembered thinking that first time I saw him.

I can't help but hope that forever is a long way from now.

Thursday, May 12

Nooned short of the Wakarusa River crossing. Pa says we're working north now. After I got everyone fed, I'd struck out for a walk and, by accident, came across the grave of a child. It seemed fitting, as I stood there thinking of what the poor mother must have suffered, that the storm clouds should roll in when they did, dark and foreboding. I'm not sure how long I'd stayed before Grace walked up. She took in the grave with a grim look on her face. I told her that I couldn't imagine the grief the family had to have gone through, leaving the little one behind—that I prayed we would never know it.

"Grief is grief, Callie," she said. "No frilly sickbed or fine coffin is going to change that. I agree sorrow must hurt worse out here . . . but it seems to heal quicker, too. Thing is, the world moves on in spite of what we feel—whether we're on this trail or back home." She put her arm around my shoulders then, and we walked back toward the wagons together.

I don't mind admitting that I envied her gumption. She seems to have learned so much about life. I told her as much when we were out there this afternoon.

She said to me, "Only by trial. As Mr. Hollister was dying, I ranted and raved, even tried to bargain with God. I took to praying, too, but He saw fit to take Grady anyways. Started thinking praying might be good, but it ain't going to feed the children. They say He helps those who help themselves, Callie. I'm thinking that maybe that ain't too far from the truth—"

I'd put my hand on Grace's arm, stopping her. "You know," I said, "if I had the strength you have in your little finger, I think I could probably walk all the way to California."

"You do, Callie," she said, and a wide grin stole across her face. "And you will—walk to California, that is." We both laughed, each heading in the direction of our own wagon.

Grace has the uncanny knack of making me laugh when I least feel like it.

Friday, May 13

Forded the Wakarusa River this morning. The water was something to be reckoned with; swift current rocking our wagons so hard I thought we'd tip for sure. Pa and Jack had a time of it on the horses; thigh deep in the murky depths as they cracked their whips over the stock. The poor things would swim halfway only to turn around and come out again. Mrs. Iverson's screaming was enough to try the patience of Job—Quinn said it rivaled the wail of the banshee.

Saturday, May 14

Trailed into camp tonight very tired. My only thought was to hurry with what chores I had, so that I could lay down and sleep. My head would have found comfort on a *rock,* for all I cared. Then Stem came riding up and said, "Spotted some Kaw Indians lurkin' outside camp. They was crawlin' along behind the herd, pullin' up grass, so's ta make out like they was a part of the stock." He must have read the horror on my face, because he chuckled. "Nothin' ta be afeard of, Callie," he said. "I'll be sleepin' with one eye cracked."

Little does he know that I intend to go one better and sleep with *both* of my eyes "cracked" just as wide as they'll go.

Sunday, May 15

We'd gone nearly fifteen miles today when we came across a dilapidated settlement of huts in the valley near the Kaw River. The old trapper who appeared to run the village came and met us amidst a tumble of dogs and children, inviting us to camp on his land and share dinner with him and his family.

By nightfall, the village and beyond was blanketed white by our wagons, and the smell of smoke and coffee drifted in the air as a few of us made our way to what we took to be the main house. A stunning Indian woman, the old man's wife no less, was waiting to greet us, and we quickly settled in for dinner.

"Ya have a fine woman there," Stem said after a while, plucking a dried peach from the bowl the woman offered to him.

"Bought her from her pa for near next to nothin'," the trapper boasted, and I looked up at the woman, startled. She gave no hint that she had even heard what was said—or maybe she didn't care. Her tawny face was composed, almost proud, her dark eyes staring past us as if fixed on some other place and time.

When she moved next to me, offering the bowl, I could not resist my need to comfort her. I reached out, brushing my hand over hers, and I saw her eyes widen in surprise. I smiled then, and maybe for a moment, I saw a kind of acknowledgment in her eyes.

" 'Twas a kind thing you did back there," Quinn said later; his deep lilting voice was soft as he watched me packing away our dinner wares. I turned around, and he smiled at me, a nice smile that almost took away the sadness in his eyes.

"I don't know what you're talking about," I sniffed, moving to the other side of the wagon, and I heard him chuckle.

There's a fresh honesty about Quinn McGregor that I like. A few times since we've been on the trail, I've noticed him watching me, not like Zach Koch—with his leering grin that makes me shudder—but with a warm protectiveness that's . . . different somehow.

* * *

Later—I witnessed humankind at its worst tonight, and I wonder if I'll ever feel safe again. It is with shaking hands that I write this down, but I fear that if I don't, my mind will not be able to rest.

We'd all settled in after dinner, and even though Rose was worn out from the hard day on the trail, her coughing was making it hard for her to sleep, so I decided to make her some syrup.

Mama had shown me more than once how to make a good cough syrup from the dried roots of the mullein. I carefully selected only one of the precious roots from the jar, knowing full well that my chances of getting more were slim. Rose coughed again, and I moved over to her bed, brushing her hair back from her forehead.

"Hurts, Callie," she whispered.

"I know, I know, honey," I told her. "I'm going to make something to fix you up real good."

Silently, I climbed out of the wagon, stoked the last of what was our campfire, and then reached for a dipper of water from our barrel. Nothing. I glanced around the camp, listening, but hearing only an occasional fire popping, the bawl of a calf; somewhere a man groaned wearily in his sleep. Grabbing the crockery jar from the wagon, I picked my way through the brush to the banks of the stream.

It was when I leaned forward for the water that I heard the soft cries of a woman.

"Stop—please." The cry came from the woods off to the right of me.

"Shut up." A gruff voice, filled with contempt, stung the air. "I've heard tell that you savages like it real well—want it all the time. Well, I'm gonna oblige you, sugar. Might even take you with me, if you please me."

The loud rip of cloth filled the hush of the night, and I held my breath, terrified, as I ducked behind the brush near the river. It was Zach Koch's voice. I remember thinking that there had to be something I could do. Instead, I sat there cowering, afraid of what might happen to me if I was spotted, and I hated myself for being weak.

"Don't—don't touch me," the woman screamed.

"I'll do more than touch you, squaw."

"I'll kill you."

At this Zach laughed, and it was all I could do to swallow the sickness that rose in my throat.

"I'll be right back, Pa!" I called out, hoping to fool Zach into thinking Pa was with me. There was a pause and then a sickening thud. The screams this time were Zach's.

I could see a figure running toward me, and I realized it was the trapper's wife. Even in the moonlight I could see the tears on her face, the torn clothes, the blood that trickled down from her nose and mouth. She hesitated beside my hiding place for only a split second.

"I'm so sorry," I whispered and watched as she ran on.

I was gasping by the time I returned to camp. As I bent over the fire, stirring the root into the boiling pan of water, a long shadow splashed across the ground at my feet. I looked up to see Zach Koch standing there, smiling. His hair was neatly combed, clothes straightened. It was almost as if what I'd heard and seen in the woods had never been, save for the long, bloody scratch that traveled down the length of his jaw.

He must've noticed I was staring at that scratch,

because he touched it briefly. The flickering flames lit across his features as the smile died from his lips. "You're up late, Callie," he said to me.

I nearly shouted for Pa or Jack then, but Rose hollered for me, her voice turning into a fit of coughs as I stood holding the pan of syrup in shaking hands.

"Best tend to your sister," Zach said, and then turned and walked away.

Monday, May 16

Confided in Grace this morning over what happened last night. I told her I wished I hadn't needed the water so bad, wished I hadn't gone down to that stream and seen it all.

Sad enough, her outlook was grim. "Indian woman?" she'd said. "Ain't much we can do for her, honey. Zach will just say she asked for it—and what's *her* word against his? Best thing for us to do is stick together, make sure he doesn't catch us alone. Strength in numbers I always say."

After packing our things away this morning, I found a beautiful pair of beaded moccasins, placed carefully next to Rose's bed.

I never saw the Indian woman again, even though I searched for her when we left.

Instead, the old trapper stood at the door of the dirty hovel he called home and waved a cheerful goodbye to us all.

* * *

It's been a hard haul on the trail today. Captain Belshaw has decided to call it quits for the day so that we can prepare to cross the Kaw River come morning. I wish I could shake this mood I'm in. Even the beauty of the Kansas countryside, with its thick grass and wildflowers, seems to have grown dim overnight. Pa and Jack, thinking I'm just weary, have tried to lighten my workload, but I've refused their help. Work has been the only thing that keeps me half sane. I've unloaded the wagon, built the fire, cooked, and mended Rose's dress, praying that it will be enough so I won't have the time to think.

But no matter how hard I try, the old trapper's place lives on in my mind. I can't erase the vision of that young Indian woman or her screams, or the terror when Zach Koch is near.

Later—Quinn was here. I wish I could take back everything that has just happened. It was more my fear talking than anything, my fear of Zach. I know that now. But Quinn doesn't.

I had been struggling to pull a barrel of flour out of the wagon and down a makeshift ramp when Quinn rode up.

"Whoa, there, lass," he called to me. "Let me help you with that." He dismounted and quickly cut the distance between us, reaching for the barrel as he climbed the back stair that led up to the wagon.

I yanked the barrel from his hands. "I can help myself, thank you," I snapped. He had caught me off guard, standing so close like he did. At that moment the barrel tipped. I would've fallen off the wagon had it not been for Quinn's quick reflexes; he caught me and righted the barrel with an ease that seemed earned by his large size.

" 'Tis not a weakness to ask for help, Callie," he said, a wounded look in his eyes.

"Well, I didn't *ask*." Frustrated, I stalked away, all the while feeling his eyes on me.

I hated seeing the hurt in Quinn's eyes. But how could he ever understand the fear that I feel? After all, men don't have to answer to anyone but themselves. There was no fear of being forced to submit to someone else's dreams, someone else's desires.

The memory of Maggie's fate is so vivid in my mind tonight. There are so many "Maggies" out here, so many women made to abide by the unwritten law of their husbands, most of the time with no thought to their own well-being.

I see Bess Mercer walking behind her wagon, carrying her baby boy in her arms, her belly already swelled with the promise of another. I see Grace Hollister working day and night, never resting as she fights for a new life for her and her children. And I see that beautiful, proud Indian woman, her fate sealed by the turn of a coin. And maybe I see a little of myself, of my fears for what may lie ahead—for my sister's life, and for my own.

Tuesday, May 17

This morning we came to the muddy banks of the Kaw River. Rose, spotting the Indians that ran the ferry, was so excited that I could hardly keep her in the wagon.

"I bet them bloodthirsty redskins have come to take our hair," she whispered with relish as Pa paid them before we were ferried across the river. It took everything in us not to laugh. Ever since our preacher from home had made mention of *heathen savages,* Rose had become obsessed with wanting to see one. I have to admit they were a bit more fierce-looking than the ones we'd seen come through Independence. Some were shirtless, with only a blanket draped over their shoulders, painted and beautifully adorned with feathers and beads, while others had what looked like brass rings around their necks and arms.

I suppose I should've known that the morning's excitement wouldn't be the last of Rose's curiosity. As our meal progressed this afternoon, I could see that Rose had taken a strange interest in Quinn. Between each bite of her corn cake I saw her stealing glances at him, her brow furrowed in concentration.

"McGregor," she said, mimicking Jack's drawl, "are you a redskin?" Rose's voice, although soft, sliced through the conversation, and an amused silence fell around the group as we glanced to Quinn McGregor. His fair skin *had* become red over the past several days, being exposed to the elements as we all were. To my surprise he laughed.

"No, fair Rose," he said. "I'm an Irishman—not a savage." He looked over at Pa and Jack and winked. "Although to some, they might very well be one and the same."

As everyone burst out laughing, Quinn's eyes met

mine across the fire, and I noticed that behind the good humor there was a sadness that had seeped back in, reminding me so much of that day I first saw him.

Tonight the memory of his pale blue eyes stays with me, eyes filled with neither hate nor bitterness, just endurance.

Wednesday, May 18

Progress was slow this morning. The mud and sloughs here along the Kaw River bottoms have made it nearly impossible for the wagons to go on for any length of time before getting bogged down again.

Around noon, we passed a grave in which a man had recently been buried. Standing near the pitiful site stood his grieving wife and children, apparently abandoned by their wagon train, which had moved on.

Stem and Quinn rode out and asked her to join us, but she declined, saying she would stay there with her husband awhile.

Later—Quinn's face looks haggard this evening. I wonder if he is thinking of his own family that he had to bury and leave behind.

How I wish I could have talked to him, but there is a distance between us now because of my pushing him away, and I'm not sure if either of us knows how to bridge it.

Thursday, May 19

Rose early. Had all the washing done by the time Pa, Jack, and Rose sat down for breakfast. Made nearly seventeen miles today. Glad at least to have the miry bottomlands behind us. We've just camped at Cross Creek. (Think we're somewhere west of St. Mary's, Kansas.) Tired tonight. Don't feel much like writing.

Friday, May 20
Kansas

Made ten miles today, trail taking us north for yet *another* crossing. Jack says "get used to it" since we have to stick close to the rivers.

The Little Vermillion was the most difficult crossing, with its steep banks and swift current. A few tense moments for Rose and me as our front wheels went down with a crash into the water, the torrent flooding the wagon bed, along with our skirts and shoes, until it was righted. At least the men had a better time of it handling the teams. Bess Mercer says the novelty of the trip is beginning to wear off. *Novelty?*

* * *

I looked for Quinn tonight all along the dusty rows of wagons—but to no avail. . . .

> *Waiting to cross the Big Blue*
> *Kansas Territory*
> *In transit to California*
> *May 21, 1859*

Mrs. Maggie Todd
Blue Mills, Missouri

Dear Maggie,
 We are now camped along the banks of the Big Blue River, waiting for our chance to cross. You wouldn't believe what a sight it is, the land around us covered by wagons—with more arriving all of the time. And the noise! Mules braying, lowing of oxen, women screaming at their children to keep away from the water. The cursing is the worst— shouted in every language you could imagine by madmen trying to get their teams across. As if that wouldn't be enough, we soon found we would have to camp some distance back from the river—as both banks have been taken over by emigrant graves.
 Mrs. Iverson, a fleshy, worrisome old soul, threw an all-out tantrum, seeing those graves. A "tantrum" is what her husband called it. I'm not exactly sure I have the words that would do it justice. Anyway, I think it sobered the rest of us right up, for we quickly went about unloading the wagons and generally pitched right in with the men. And the men seemed more than grateful.
 It's funny how circumstance can change the

way people think, Mag. Work that no man would ever believe a woman able enough to do back home, such as unloading heavy supplies for the ferry, yoking oxen, or driving a large team, are now done by most of us without much thought. There is no time to dicker about what is proper work for a lady, *either, for every hand is needed.*

In a way, I think it's a good thing, working hard. At least for me it is. There's a sense of being a part of it all, of having some power (little that it is) over what turns out of each day. And that's what I'm doing, Mag, taking it day by day. I've learned nothing beyond that is certain—the graves along the river are proof of that.

I have to close for now; it's getting late and we'll be crossing tomorrow. I'll be posting this letter in the morning, as they have a mail service here. I pray that you get it—it's a rough lot that runs the place.

> *Your harried friend,*
> *Callie*

P.S. I saw a colored woman this evening, tramping along the trail, all her worldly goods strapped in to a hand cart. She was alone, as far as I could see. Can you imagine? When I thought of what she had faced and would, I felt as if our journey wasn't anything more than a picnic.

Sunday, May 22

We had no more than got our supplies off the ferry and back into the wagons this evening when I heard Pa shouting and ran to see what was the matter. Evidently, Rose had snatched up a bright piece of ribbon off of one of the little graves near the river and promptly tied it in her hair. Pa got spooked seeing this and shouted at her to put it back, which scared her something awful. Pa has never laid a hand to Rose, let alone raised his voice in such a manner. Rose is too young to understand Pa's fear, but Jack and I understand—all too well.

I can't sleep tonight. There seems to be an awful presence of death I can't shake.

"I will both lay me down in peace, and sleep: for thou, Lord, only makest me dwell in safety": Psalms 4:8.

Tuesday, May 24

Rained today. Miserable weather. We plodded through the mud and drench until about noon, when Captain Belshaw decided we should stop. I'd been determined to get a fire going in spite of the downpour and had set about digging a hole in the miry ground when I heard riders approaching. Rain blocked my vision for a moment, and when it cleared, I saw Quinn and Stem easing their mounts near.

"What in the world are you doing, Callie?" Quinn said, startling me. "There isn't a fool alive that would be caught out in this."

"Then what are you doing out here?" I snapped. All the frustrations and worries from the past few days came washing over me—Zach, the graves, Rose. "Haven't I told you I can take care of myself?" I said.

I regretted the words as soon as I'd said them, but it was too late, because he said, "I guess you have." Then he gouged his heels into the horse's flanks and rode away.

How awful I felt at that moment. I thought about the days I'd watched for him down the dusty line of wagons and men, hoping to catch a glimpse of him. When I finally turned back to my digging, I was surprised to see Stem still there, leaning on his pommel, flicking the leather in his hands as he studied me.

"Don't take it so hard, Callie," he said. "It's been my learnin' that things mostly git worse before they git better."

I pray things *will* get better. I don't see how they can get much worse.

Wednesday, May 25

Weather better today, but travel has been slow through the mud from last night's storm. Shortly after Pa and Jack unyoked our team tonight, I set out to find the Hollister wagon. Tomorrow the train will be holding over so the men can make some repairs on the wagons, and the women have decided to get together to have a sewing social.

Grace was unloading her wagon when I found her.

"So, why won't you go?" I asked, watching her hand the boxes down to her daughter, Lizzie, from the back of the wagon.

Grace glanced up. "I don't take much to them segregated affairs—almost seems unnatural." When she saw I didn't exactly believe that excuse, she sighed. "If my memory serves me," she said, "these socials are a gathering of *friends*— I'd lay odds that that ain't the word they use when they mention me." I saw her hurt before she turned and reached for a sack in the wagon. "My husband, Grady, he used to read to me when I was sewing on my quilts."

Grace showed me a quilt shyly, and I marveled over the fine cloth, the intricate stitching. "He loved my quilts. 'Grace,' he'd say, 'those quilts will be your immortality.' Foolishness,'' she finished, but there had been tears in her eyes, and I touched her arm.

"You go ahead, Callie. I got too much work to do." She grinned at me. "Besides, if I got stuck between that Iverson woman and Della Koch, might be I'd have to smother them with one of their own quilts."

Later—Down a piece from our wagon some of the men are holding a card game. The raucous noise has been going on for hours now. But I have to admit I enjoy hearing their laughter and singing—even if it is off-key. I can't help but wonder, though, what the preacher and his wife must think of their son, Zach, whose voice carries loudest of all.

Thursday, May 26

Our little "get together" today went from good to bad without much time to spare in between. I'd curbed my tongue for the most part (only by biting it so hard it brought tears to my eyes). Della was in a mood, looking for sins the way others did Indians. Since Grace had refused the invitation to quilt, she naturally became the sinner of choice.

"Speakin' of unseemly behavior," Della Koch said. I looked up startled, for I had not heard anyone speaking at all. Bess Mercer cast me a grin, and I was hard-pressed not to giggle. "That Mrs. Hollister has taken to washin' and ironin' the captain's and his men's shirts *right* in plain sight," she sniffed. "I've heard they's payin' her three times what the work is worth, too."

"Lookin' for a new husband to take care of that lot of hers, no doubt," said Mrs. Iverson. "How many young'uns does she have—six, seven?"

"Lawks," exclaimed Mrs. Pratt. She did that often; it didn't mean anything, near as I can figure—except make her sound like a crow waiting for you to get out of the corn.

"I don't think she's got much religion, either. Ever watch her when we're singin' hymns? She don't know the words, just moves her lips."

I squirmed in my chair a little, wishing I had stayed back at the wagon. I myself had taken more than a liking to Grace. She was stronger than any woman I'd ever met, especially losing her husband and all. I remembered what she told me when we were walking one day. *"I took to praying, too,"* she'd said, *"but He saw fit to take Grady anyways. Started thinking praying might be good, but it ain't going to feed the children. They say He helps those who help themselves, Callie. I'm thinking that maybe that ain't too far from the truth."*

"I feel sorry for her," said Mrs. Mercer slowly, timidly. "Losin' her husband and all, her workin's the only way she can feed them kids of hers."

Most everyone ignored Bess Mercer, for she had the tendency to look at the good in everyone, much to the dismay of Mrs. Iverson and Mrs. Koch, who, it seems to me, take to gossiping like a flea takes to a doghouse.

"Well," snorted Mrs. Iverson, staring over the rim of her spectacles, "it ain't seemly, no matter how you look at it. Just like the widow Hays back home; oh, she started with laundry—but everyone knows what she turned to next. . . ."

"What?" Mrs. Koch finally asked, leaning forward in her chair.

"Lawks," Mrs. Pratt said, placing a hand to her breast.

"For heaven's sake, Amelia, will you stop that infernal croak?" Mrs. Iverson said, irritated. Then as one, all the ladies turned and focused on the figure of Grace Hollister, who was coming around the wagon with a pile of laundry in her arms. She nodded and stepped out of sight.

"Methodist," Mrs. Iverson continued. "She started goin' to hear a *woman* preacher. Went downhill from there. And she dared to call herself a Christian."

"Imagine that," I said, and Bess Mercer smiled.

"Talkin' of unseemly, I was up all night long with the racket the cap'n and his men were makin', playin' cards and laughin'. Liquored up, no doubt," sniffed Mrs. Pratt.

"And my Zachariah was made to keep watch," Della said, warming to the conversation. "Came to the wagon plumb tired, he did. I reckon it's for the best, that the boy's kept busy." She stared pointedly at me. "You know what they say about idle hands . . ."

I just smiled and jabbed at the quilt mercilessly.

A long shadow darkened Mrs. Koch's handiwork, and she jumped like a startled hare. Grace stood there with her hands perched on her hips, a wicked grin on her face.

"Idle hands, is it, Della?" she said. "Well, now, I'd appreciate it if you'd tell that boy of yours that he needs to pay up soon. Don't play the game if you can't take the pain, I told him." She laughed then. "Most of them men's faces looked just about the same as yours when I showed them a handful of fives all wearing the same complexion last night."

Somewhere beside me one of the women laughed but was quickly cut short by the fury on Della Koch's face.

"Gamblin'," Mrs. Iverson said, breaking the silence. "Grace Hollister, you've gone too far this time. The only riches are those in heaven."

"But it sure wouldn't hurt to have some pocket change before we get there, would it?" Grace tucked a wisp of blonde hair behind her ear. "Mr. Hollister always used to say that life ain't in holding a good hand, but playing a poor one well." She looked over at me and smiled. "That's all I'm doing, ladies."

"That's what marryin' a Yankee will do to you," Mrs. Iverson lamented, patting Della Koch's hand as we watched Grace Hollister make her way to her own wagon. "All that talk about Yankee husbands bein' so fair and gentle-like—it's nothin' but just that, talk. I'm thinkin' Mr. Iverson wasn't more right when he said a Yankee husband will make nothin' of his wife but a fool."

"My pa's always told us that a wise man can learn from a fool," I said, having had my fill of their nastiness. "That is, once you figure out which is which."

Bess Mercer actually laughed out loud.

I saw Della Koch stalk past the preacher this evening and haul off and punch Zach alongside of his head. I imagine it was because of his gambling, or maybe because she might have lost face in front of some of her friends. Zach didn't flinch or act surprised; he just stepped real close up to his mother and said, "Never again, you understand me, old woman?" I saw the bitterness and pent-up rage in his eyes as he pushed her hard. "If you ever touch me again, I'll kill you."

"The Lord ain't finished with you, boy!" Della

yelled after him, and I saw the preacher walk forward and try to grab Zach's arm.

"Son!"

Zach spun around with a look of contempt. "Son?" He laughed. "That's rich. No use trying to make up for lost time, *Pa*. Soon as I find a place with some action, ain't neither one of you'll ever see me again."

There was an old mongrel that slept down by our barn, I remember. She never let us get close to her. After a time, we found a litter of pups the dog had. I remember being surprised that she pretty much acted like those pups weren't even there. She never went to them, wouldn't nurse them, and finally they began to die. All except for one.

Pa said that puppy lived just for the spite of it. The darnedest thing was that dog would follow me all the way down to the barn, barking and nipping at my skirts, and after I'd set it out something to eat, it'd growl and carry on something fierce—like it didn't know any other way to get my attention, because hate was the first thing it'd come into this world to.

Saturday, May 28

Rode out with Stem and Jack early this morning.

We skirted along the Little Blue River for a while, shaded by the oak, willow, and cottonwoods. Then climbed the bank into the "uplands," as Stem called it. Jack eased Big Black in next to Patch and together, we watched Stem ride ahead to survey the trail. Everything had went along fine, until I saw his horse disappear over a slope. Then, for some reason, I started to feel uneasy.

"What do you think is out there?" I said to Jack, and he glanced over at me.

"See those trees," he said, pointing toward a line of thinned cottonwoods on the horizon, "they say past that it's nothin' but wide open space all the way to the Platte River."

I felt a queer shiver of fear ride over me, looking across that rolling countryside. If I could, I would have willed the land to stop. Jack must have sensed my mood, because the grin slid off his face, and he said, "Callie?"

"I need to get back," I told him then. I didn't wait, either. I turned Patch around, toward the train, and rode and rode, as if I could escape the emptiness.

Sunday, May 29

The sun's faded to a red ball in the evening sky tonight. Even though we'd only put about ten miles behind us, there wasn't one person who complained when the captain called for us to stop. It's been so hot.

With some light left, Rose and I set out to gather some firewood. Rose had decided to make a game of it, and she ran ahead of me, her soft laughter weaving through the rows of prairie grass. I smiled. She'd only had a few coughing fits lately, and I felt that was a good sign. Even though I knew there were a lot of hardships ahead, hearing her laughter made me feel like it was the best of times.

With our arms full, we headed back to camp and chanced upon Mrs. Koch. Rose, being the smarter, ducked around me and quickly made her way to our wagon. Recognizing the pinched expression on Della Koch's face, I realized too late she was on a mission.

As soon as she swiped the beads of sweat from her forehead, she began to chastise me for riding out front with Stem and Jack earlier in the day.

"You're a handsome girl, Callie Wade," she said to me. "It's not hard to see with them fine bones of yours you come from real good stock. But it's as plain as the nose on my face you haven't had a mama to steer you proper in a while. I'm surprised your pa allows you to keep company with those men like you do. And consorting with that Negro ain't proper either; it . . . well, it gives people ideas."

"That *Negro* has a name, ma'am," I told her, trying to keep my temper in check. "It's Stem. And I'm proud to call him my friend. As far as ideas . . . well, I don't think you can give somebody something they already have." I was glad that Rose wasn't there to hear Della Koch's words. We were raised not to judge a person by anything but character. Rose, being as young as she is, still hasn't figured there was a different way. How I wish everyone could see through her eyes.

I started to leave, when Della said to me, "I've seen you flaunt yourself in front of my boy, too."

That's when I knew that Grace had been right all along.

"You're wrong," I told her. Saying anything else would've been useless, and if I had said something, I couldn't promise what it would've been. And I wasn't so green as not to know that with a wag of the woman's tongue I might lack any female company except Grace's for the rest of the journey. But Della grabbed my arm and turned me around.

"Where there's no counsel, the people fall," she hissed. "And you will fall, Callie Wade, mark my words." With a mean swish of her wool skirt she was gone.

My eyes were burning from crying as I ventured through camp, and I was surprised to see Pa standing there with a worried expression on his face. I wondered if he'd seen anything, if maybe he was going to tell me I couldn't ride out in front anymore. Pa didn't say a word. Instead, he reached for the bundle of sticks in my arms and walked in silence with me back to our wagon. Just before we reached Rose and Jack, Pa turned to me.

"Quoting the Bible, she was," Pa said. He looked out across the prairie, and I stood very still, waiting to see what he'd do next. Pa has never been the kind to say much, so when he did, I felt inclined to listen. "Your mama used to say you can preach a better sermon with your life than your lips. 'Long about now, I can't help but think how right she was."

"I miss her, Pa."

Pa tipped his hat and gazed at the setting sun. "She'd be proud of you, Callie. I am," he said. "Let Della Koch throw stones; we'll show her how we Wades return them."

I watched Pa, his long, lean frame bowed by years of hard labor, and I don't think I ever loved him more than I did at that moment.

* * *

Candle is burning low here in the wagon this evening, but I can't sleep. Not yet. I've asked myself over and over again what it is that I've done to earn such hatred from the preacher's wife, but I've found no answer. Maybe that's the way it should be. There's no figuring what lies in another's heart, what it is that opens the door to the kind of hate that festers.

I don't have much in the way of forgiveness for someone like Zach Koch, but I sure can pity him.

Monday, May 30

Della Koch and *hers* have decided to shun me. I feel so wronged by these women, I would like to give them a good talking to, but instead I go on. Oh, if only Mama were here. . . .

Tuesday, May 31

The wagon is shaking with the force of the storm outside as I write. No worse than the one brewing between Quinn and me now, I guess.

Stem and me had been out riding when the first drops of rain began to fall. I hadn't worried, until Stem said, "Well, there'll be no rest fer the wicked today." I saw his face turn grim, and my gaze followed his to the dark thunderheads in the distance that were quickly rubbing out the blue.

"Best git ta the wagon; it's goin' ta git ugly."

I pulled my horse around quick, but had no sooner got her headed in the right direction when the rain began in earnest. Where it had only pecked at the ground minutes before, there were now gullies cut deep by the hard torrents that fell from the sky, hitting my face and shoulders. The packhorse stumbled in the thick mud then, and I heard a sickening crack of bone being twisted and broken. The mare screamed in pain, a horrible sound that I had never heard before and pray that I will never again. I jumped down and waved at the wagons that were coming close, then watched in shock as they passed me by—the Kochs, the Iversons, the Pratts. Not a one of them stopped to offer me help.

Jack and Quinn seemed to materialize out of the storm. Jack was the first to dismount. He took one look at my horse and pulled his rifle from the saddle.

"Determined to catch your death, you are!" Quinn shouted as he reined up alongside of me. He slid out of the saddle, his body shadowing me as he moved closer.

"I can take care of myself, I told you," I said between clenched teeth—chattering as they were.

Huge drops began to hit the both of us, striking hard, like hail, the wind whipping my hair across my face. Quinn grabbed me by the arms to steady me, and I heard the sharp crack of Jack's rifle.

"There's nothing you can do, Callie. You still have Patch, you know," he said, holding me to him as another swell of wind battered against us. I stood stock-still, unable to move.

He was so handsome, wildly so. I was close enough to see the change in his eyes, the way they darkened into a stormy blue when he looked down at me, close enough to feel his breathing, quick in my ear. I saw the hunger, too, but it no longer frightened me.

Quinn pulled off his rubber overcoat and covered my shoulders. Warmth flooded through me, and even though I told myself it was relief from the damp cold, I knew there was something more to it. Something that gave us both pause as we stood close to each other.

"Get up on my horse," he said.

"You're not my pa, Quinn McGregor," I said as I allowed him to help me up, my breath catching in my throat as his arms wrapped around my waist—and then he dumped me into the saddle, staring at me hard.

"Aye, I'm not your *pa*, Callie," Quinn said, his voice strangely gruff, "nor do I want to be. There's the trouble of it."

Later—Sitting outside, now that the rain has stopped. Thoughts of Quinn turn over in my mind. The way he looked at me, the way I felt when he held me in the rain . . .

Coyotes howling, entertaining me with their songs. These concerts are given free every night, I'm finding.

If only they were loud enough to drown out these restless thoughts.

Wednesday, June 1

Although the sun was beginning to set by the time we had picked a place to rest for the night, it was still blistering hot. I'd been walking down the rows of wagons when I spotted Zach Koch leaning against Quinn's wagon. I thought this was curious, as the two didn't seem to take to each other. The thought didn't go much further, because by the time I'd reached Stem's rig, they were arguing something fierce.

Stem, never one to miss a thing, peered at me as he continued to cook his pot of stew. "Damned idjits," he said. "They'll be comin' ta blows over ya before the trail's end, mark my words. That is, if ya don't do somethin' ta fix it."

Stem must have read the disbelief on my face, because he said, "Ain't nary a man in camp wouldn't fight fer a pretty gal like ya, Callie Wade." He pulled a plug of chew from his pocket and drew himself up a little taller. "I'd be in the thick of it if it weren't fer us bein' friends. That an' my age. Well, I always say, if yer too old ta hand out trouble, next best thing's advice."

"And what would you advise?" I asked.

"Oh, I'd advise ya ta take yer time, but not too long. Ya don't want ta end up old, takin' care of someone else's little ones an' wishin' ya had listened ta what yer heart tolt ya."

"Now you sound like Jack, calling me an old maid," I muttered. "As far as Zach Koch is concerned, I wouldn't consider him if he was the last man on earth. He's trouble, if you ask me."

Stem chuckled. "Before ya came along, I'd pretty much accepted any good conversation I'd be havin' would'a been with my horse, an' she ain't inclined ta listen most of the time.

"Yessir, ya beat all, Callie." Stem's face sobered. "But I wasn't talkin' of the preacher's son; I was talkin' 'bout McGregor."

The memories of the rainstorm came so thick I couldn't brush them away—the desire in Quinn's eyes, the slow warmth that crept through me when his hand rested on my waist.

"McGregor's been fallin' all over himself, tryin' ta help ya, and yer either too blind or too stubborn ta see it. Kind of remind me of my horse, now that I think of it."

I felt my heart skip when Stem peered at me, his eyes sharp but kindly. I had the funniest feeling he could read right through the jumble of emotions that I was trying to sort out inside of myself.

What he said next still weighs on my mind as I write this tonight: "A person's eyes will tell ya what they's afeard ta say aloud, Callie. Remember that."

Friday, June 3

Just a few short lines. My arm is still a bit sore from burning it.

Quinn had been sitting at our camp, talking to Jack

while I was cooking over the fire tonight. I'd let out a yelp when my arm grazed one of the logs, and he quickly rushed over. In a few short strides he was to the river and back, and before I had a chance to protest, he had covered the burn on my arm with a thick layer of mud. It cooled down some, but I was embarrassed at the way he fussed over me. "For heaven's sake," I said, "it's just a little burn, nothing to worry over."

"Never had much to worry about," he said wryly, "until I met you."

For a moment we simply stared at each other. But then a slow grin spread across his face, the promise of friendship long overdue—and maybe more. And I felt a shifting inside, like a part of me had been waiting for that smile.

Saturday, June 4

Warm weather today. Crossed Little and Big Sandy Creeks. Everyone is in a big way this evening, with the good weather and talk of the Platte River being so close—the river will be our guide all the way to Fort Laramie. Rose came and told me some of the folks are talking of holding a dance.

Later—I've just returned to our wagon. Had it not been for Rose's pleading, I wouldn't have even gone to the dance. I'd been embarrassed that the only clean dress I had to wear was a faded blue calico, and I'd heard many of the girls were wearing their best. Seems almost silly now.

By the time we got to the clearing, the bonfire had already been lit and the music was at full tilt. Red and yellow shadows from the fire glowed off the faces of the dancers. Single men with bandannas tied to their arms danced and sang, from time to time reaching out to steal an unsuspecting woman from her husband. Rose quickly scrambled over to where Lizzie Hollister was perched on a big rock, swinging her skinny legs to the time of the music.

If I hadn't been so busy watching Jack and Grace moving together through the crowd of dancers, I might have noticed Zach Koch coming toward me.

"Want to dance?" he said, and bowed clumsily. Even before I saw the flush on his face, I knew he'd been drinking; the stench of whiskey was strong in the air. Zach being so close scared me, and I found myself searching the crowd for some way out.

Zach might have been drunk, but he wasn't stupid. "Oh, no, you ain't leavin'," he said. "Not yet, anyway." His smile chilled me to the bone. I'd seen that leer before, and I knew what festered beneath it. To my relief, Stem appeared, stepping in front of Zach as he tipped his hat to me.

There was a tense moment when I took his hand. I saw Zach's brows drag together as if he didn't fancy the idea of Stem touching me.

"Age before beauty, I always say," Stem said over his shoulder, and then quickly ushered me into the crowd. "Thought I'd rescue ya," he chuckled.

"Had a lot of experience rescuing damsels in distress, have you, Stem?" I asked.

"Don't know nothin' about *damsels,* but I've rescued more'n one smart-aleck redhead in my time," he sniffed, and I laughed.

Stem whirled me through the crowd, light on his feet in spite of his wooden leg, and when I complimented him, he studied me with a glint in his eye and said, "A lot ye'd be surprised about, missy." Then, with a smoothness that I would never have expected, he somehow managed to maneuver me face-to-face with Quinn.

"Hey, son!" Stem called to the fiddler, stalking away with purpose. "Give me that derned fiddle. Yer playin' them strings like they's still in the cat!"

As we stood there, Quinn and I were both surprised by the sweet slow melody that sprung from Stem's fingers when he began to play.

"He couldn't have *planned* it better," I said, and Quinn laughed.

"Maybe we shouldn't deny the old man this one pleasure," he said, and then his face sobered some. "Will you dance with me, Callie?"

I answered by stepping into his arms, and we began to move around the fire, dancing like we were born to it.

When I told him how sorry I was for everything that had happened between us, and for the way I'd spoken so rudely to him, his eyes softened. In that moment, I realized that I was falling for him. "It doesn't matter now, does it?" he said.

"No," I said, and suddenly I no longer worried about the faded dress or my old mud-spattered boots.

Round and round we waltzed with the other bedraggled men and women of the wagon train, sun-bleached skirts fanning the dust kicked up by booted feet as people closed their eyes, remembering the barn dances and socials back home. It struck me then why everyone had been so thrilled with the prospect of a dance.

It was moments like these, the good times and the laughter, that you learned to hold on to tight, moments that would erect a wall against a tomorrow where nothing was certain.

After the dance was over, Quinn walked me to our wagon, and as I was getting ready to climb the back step, he stopped me.

He smiled, tucking a wild strand of my hair behind my ear. "Sometimes I forget how beautiful you look," he told me, "because I've come to know how beautiful you *are.*"

His hand lingered on my face for a bit, and then he was gone.

> *Along the Big Sandy Creek*
> *Nearing Nebraska Territory*
> *In transit to California*
> *June 5, 1859*

Mrs. Maggie Todd
Blue Mills, Missouri

Dear Maggie,
 It's nearly dawn, but I had to stay up and write you a little of what your wayward friend has been up to. We had a dance last evening. Can you imagine it? We dust-coated travelers, with no homes yet to speak of, gathered together for a dance? Nothing fancy, mind you. Just a floor of hard-packed dirt and a bonfire to guide our feet. Some of the music was played by our scout, Stem—simple and sweet, his fiddling's first-rate, if

you ask me. And the laughter, it never sounded so good! The feeling that went along with this night is one that I don't think I'll ever forget, Mag.

Do you remember when we were kids and we would play all day, never stopping long enough to get a bite to eat or a drink—but when we did sit down at Mama's table—do you remember that feeling? Like the food had never tasted better in your life and the water was never so cold? In a way, that's how I felt last night. It was as if I was experiencing something new—or feeling something that I hadn't felt in a long time. And I wasn't alone. Oh, Mag, if you could have seen their faces; so drawn at first, but then, ever so slowly, the weariness began to fade. And as we all began to twirl around that bonfire, there was a hope that bloomed—like a burden had been lifted and for a while, we didn't have to think about what lay ahead.

You would have laughed to see everyone, as tired as they all were, fighting like kids to stay awake just a bit longer. Ah, well, tomorrow this time, our little dance will be a memory, one to tuck in with all of those from home that we hold so dear.

Mama used to tell me that memories were gifts, given to us to get us through the toughest of times. I can't help thinking, Mag, that last night was one of those gifts.

Until I write again—with more love than this letter can carry,

Your friend,
Callie

Sunday, June 5

I had been leaning over the stream, filling some crocks with water, when I heard Quinn's and Rose's voices late this afternoon. I didn't take much notice of it at first, as Rose had become as common as his shadow lately, but when I heard her talking about Mama, I sat back on my heels and watched the two.

"I don't remember much about her," Rose was saying. "I shut my eyes hard and try to see her, but I can't. Callie says I look a lot like her, though."

"She must've been a beauty, then," Quinn said, and Rose beamed at him, taking his hand.

"Do you remember your mama?" she asked then.

"I do," he told her, and he bent down, bringing his face close to hers. "She was a lot like you, come to think of it. She loved to laugh and sing. And she used to tell me stories of the land. She used to say you could hear its song, if you were to listen close enough."

I watched as Quinn stood and led Rose up to the crest of the hill. "Hold your hands out, Rose," he told her. "Now, close your eyes and listen."

I saw Rose close her eyes; her small face filled with wonder as the breeze stirred across the plains. There was no fear as a crack of thunder rolled in the distance, just contentment. "I hear it," she whispered.

"Bend down here and feel the earth. That's it. Do

you feel the hum of the ground? 'Tis said that every blade of grass, every flower, every tree, all have their own song to God."

"It's wonderful, isn't it?"

"It is," he said, his voice soft.

"I sure wish I'd known her," Rose said after they stood there awhile, and I knew she was talking about Mama. I saw Quinn reach for her hand, and together, they slowly made their way to camp.

There's something I enjoy about watching the two together. Quinn is such a large man, he looks like he'd be better suited to the field instead of weaving tales of fancy to a small girl. Maybe that is what impresses me so about him.

After dinner I walked out past the wagons to the crest of the hill where Quinn and Rose had stood. Holding my hands out to my sides, I closed my eyes and listened, hoping I could hear and feel what Rose had. Instead, I heard only the howl of the wind and smelled the rain that threatened in the air. I shivered. Quinn suddenly appeared out of nowhere and walked slowly up the hill.

He smiled, and for once there was no need for words as we stood there, the both of us, staring off across the stormy plains. The land had opened up, wide and never-ending, and for some reason I longed for the stout oaks and hickories that had rolled along the prairie only days ago, longed for their shelter and safety. "It looks so horrible," I said finally, hugging myself. When Quinn sat down on the ground, I took my seat next to him, as if it were the most natural thing in the world to do.

"Aye, 'tis frightening," he said, "but beautiful if you look at it the right way. Understand it, that is."

"What is it you see?" I asked.

"I see promise. The way the land rolls on and on. Like it will carry your dreams past what your eyes would see." He plucked a blade of grass from the ground, staring at it earnestly. "Sometimes I think the shame of it is that most people never learn that. They never touch the clouds, you see, because they fear the rain."

"I never pictured you the dreamer," I said, and when he smiled, I understood all too well how Rose could be so taken with him. How at odds he appears to be with himself, I thought, this big Irishman with callused hands and the build of a man that was no stranger to hard work, and yet, he had the heart of a poet.

The smile on Quinn's face seemed to say he was laughing a little at himself. "My ma used to say to me, 'Tis all right to hitch your wagon to that star, Quinn McGregor, just be sure it's your feet you keep to the ground.'"

"And I'm so rooted to the ground it's a wonder I didn't make Pa and Jack carry the house with us when we left Independence," I said, and we both laughed. I was thinking how handsome he was when he smiled when he moved closer to me.

"You're too hard on yourself, Callie. There's more of the dreamer in you than you think." When I smiled, he surprised me by reaching out to brush the hair back from my face. His hand rested underneath my chin, and he looked deep into my eyes as his thumb caressed my jaw. "Ah, she smiles."

So many times I had dreamed of that very moment

in the safe place of my mind, where I could imagine a life with no fears of sickness or death, no fear of not knowing what tomorrow might bring, a life filled with love and laughter.

"You know, the first time I saw you, I felt as if I were gazing upon something so special I might never feel that way again. And then, when you looked back at me," Quinn whispered, "With those green eyes— and those lips, so full as a man could only dream of knowing. My God, lass. You don't know how many nights I've dreamed . . ."

Quinn must've seen the same needs in my own eyes. He gently pushed me down into the grass as he leaned over me, propping his arms on either side of my face as his mouth sought my own, and for a while I allowed myself to get lost in the feeling, wishing for things I shouldn't, until I finally pulled away.

"I can't . . . I'm sorry," I whispered, touching my fingers to my lips. I so needed him to understand my reluctance.

"You need never fear me, Callie," he said gently, and then rose and walked away.

I stayed out there on the prairie long after Quinn had gone. I watched the storm take hold of the sky, its thick black clouds hanging low over the land, the wind picking up as it brushed through the grass and churned the waters. For the first time in my life I felt the wild freedom of the land take hold . . . and I was awed by it.

Part Three

To the Platte River,
Nebraska Territory

"Love is like age—it doesn't stay hidden long."
                    —Amanda Wade

Monday, June 6

The wind is rocking the wagon so that I can hardly write this evening. But then, who do I have to worry about reading this scratch anyway? The Kansas prairie is behind us now, and we are camped along this forlorn-looking ridge between the Little Blue and the Platte River in Nebraska. Not much to see besides sage and cactus.

Quinn just rode up. He brought me a pretty bunch of flowers, little yellow-hearted daisies that sprout from the stony crags of rock along the trail. "Tiny but tough," he said, smiling. "Just like you."

I think I'll press them here in this page to keep.

Tuesday, June 7

For a reason I still can't figure, Pa stayed behind in camp instead of going off with Jack and Quinn to check on the cattle this evening.

At first, I thought I might be in some kind of trouble, the way his eyes seemed to stay on me all the while I cleaned up after dinner and fussed over Rose getting off to bed. But when I'd headed back to the

fire, my arms heavy with a kettle of dough, I saw that
he was staring way off into the night and didn't even
so much as stir as I set the pan of bread over the fire.

When I sat down next to him, he looked at me for
a long moment, like he was trying to remember where
he was, then he smiled.

"I was just sittin' here thinkin' how much you've
had put on you since your mama died," he said in a
low voice, "and I can't recall ever hearin' you
complain."

I watched him close, and when he peered down into
his cup of coffee, I started to feel uneasy that he spoke
of such things.

"Not even a cross word," he finished.

"Oh, I imagine I've said a word or two, Pa," I admitted, trying to sound light, and was relieved when
he laughed.

"You've grown up fine, Callie. Real fine. I imagine
one day soon you're goin' to make some man proud
to call you his wife."

"Well, I'm not going to worry about *that* anytime
soon," I said firmly. My cheeks had started to burn,
so I stood and checked on the bread, opening the lid
enough to peek, then shutting it down tight so the
mosquitoes wouldn't have so much of a chance. "Besides," I said, "Jack says I'm too stubborn to marry
off now. He says you should've made me take Frank
Keller's offer when you had the chance."

" 'Jack *says*,' " Pa repeated, like he thought it was
funny. "That brother of yours would just as soon be
tied to a rock and dumped in the river as get married."
He reached forward and ran a rough finger down my
nose, like he'd done when I was little. "You remind
me so much of your mama. She was about the same

age you are now when I met her." He looked away for a moment, and then said, "You just listen to your old pa. The man that falls for you will count himself lucky all his days."

I could feel my eyes well up, and I turned away. Pa talking that way was so unlike him that it took me by surprise. So, instead of letting him see that, I made myself busy, checking on the light bread again over the fire.

"Rose appears to be gettin' along real well out here, Callie," he commented while I kept my back to him. He sounded determined to make it so, but I think he was still a little unsure, because then he said, " 'Course, we ain't there, yet."

"But we're almost to the Platte," I told him, trying to push my worry back. "Stem says it's a sight to see, Pa. He says there'll be buffalo."

"I'd thought you'd be tired of hearin' about buffalo, the way Jack and Rose have been carryin' on," Pa chuckled. "Jack actin' like he's preparin' for war and your sister stickin' her ear to the ground enough that I'm surprised her head don't sift when she shakes it."

"Anyplace would be better than here," I said, thinking how much the land had changed so sudden, from the rolling prairie of the Little Blue to this small belt of desert, where only wind, cactus, and sage lived. Turning around, I saw that Pa's face had gone all somber again.

Pa stood and stretched his legs. "Well, I can't argue you that. I know I'll rest easier once we're through these hills," he said, almost like he was talking to himself. I watched him dump the rest of his coffee and look past the fire into the dark, where only the tall gray hills of sand stood outlined in the moonlight.

It was the first time since we left Independence that I saw something like doubt cross Pa's face, and I realized how weighted down with worry he was. Questions with no answers worked at him—I saw it clearly when he glanced in the direction of the wagon where Rose slept.

"Can't imagine anything living out here, can you, Callie?" he asked, trying to smile. He pulled his old hat on then, looking at me once before he walked tiredly toward his tent.

As I sit here, putting these words to paper, I can't help but think the sooner we pull out of this place, the better we will all be.

Wednesday, June 8

The worst day of my life . . . it's all happened so fast.

We had been moving slowly along the hills of Nebraska Territory all morning, the sandy soil tugging at the wheels of our wagons. Twice our teams had paused to pull around a wagon whose wheels had got caught. Just as we started again, I heard a shout come from the front.

I looked up, spotting Jack as he spurred Big Black hard down the hill toward the lead teams, and saw Stem and Quinn follow close behind. Before the second shout went up, I had already started searching for Pa, who had ridden out earlier.

Wagons began to jangle to a stop, and still no Pa. Trying to remain calm, I halted the oxen behind the other wagons and left Rose to watch over them as I quickly made my way toward the crowd of men standing around the Mercer rig, their faces stiff with shock.

"It's all my fault, Callie," Bess Mercer was crying. "I told Henry to whip them mules . . ." I didn't want to hear her. I pushed my way through the crowd and felt my legs begin to shake when I saw Jack kneeling next to the Mercer's upturned wagon, where Pa lay on the ground.

"The team got spooked comin' down the hill. Your pa pulled Bess and her boy out of the way just in time . . ." I heard one of the men say, and I saw the blood that trickled from Pa's mouth. ". . . wagon ran plumb over his chest, Jack."

Pa tried to raise up, but when he did he started to choke up more blood. He looked over at Jack and me like he was sorry.

"No!" Jack rasped hoarsely, and I felt the horror and rage the same as if it had been me that had yelled. I sank to my knees then and gently laid Pa's head on my lap.

"Mary, Mother of God," Quinn groaned, kneeling next to me.

"Fight, Pa . . . please," I whispered.

Pa's eyes met mine, as if to tell me it was going to be all right. But I knew by the expression on his face that nothing would ever be all right again.

"You're leaving me," I said, choking back a sob. "You said you'd never leave us." Pa looked up, and I knew he remembered the promise he'd made to us when Mama died. I saw regret shine in his eyes for a moment only to be replaced by something else.

"Somebody go get my sister," I begged. "Hurry!"

"Callie?" Pa looked at me like he was far away. "You remember those daffodils your mama used to plant back home? I just bet they're in full bloom about now. . . ."

All the pain seemed to leave him then. The worry lines and weatherworn creases from years under the sun seemed to disappear, as if someone's hand gently smoothed them away.

"Amanda." Pa whispered Mama's name, and he was gone.

I heard Rose's voice then, scared, coming from the edges of the crowd. "Callie, what is it?"

It was Jack's idea to bury Pa next to a large boulder that flanked the side of the trail. It was his only way of making sure Pa's grave could be found again if we ever had the chance.

With no wood for a coffin, Grace gave us one of the extra canvas cloths she had. When she saw how my hands shook, she took it on herself to sew it for Pa. I sobbed, thinking how unfair it was, us not even able to give Pa a proper burial. Stem and Quinn helped Jack dig the grave as people started gathering around us to pay their respects.

The preacher's face was sorrowful as he began his sermon, his voice rising and falling with the wind that whipped the sand and dirt all around us. He talked a lot of "being carried up into the hands of the Lord," which made me feel better, but when he started talking about Pa in *wases* and *hads*, saying that Pa *had* been a God-fearing man, that Pa *was* a good husband and father, I started crying. If Rose hadn't been holding on to my hand so tight, I think I would have gone crazy with grief.

"I sure wish I'd of knowed him, Jack," I heard one of the men say as they helped lower Pa into the ground. "They say he wasn't much of a talker, but folks tell he was a good man."

"A lot of things I've heard people say ain't ever worth repeatin'," Stem replied quietly. "I imagine it was what he *did,* not what he said, that impressed us all."

Simple as it was, I couldn't help thinking as I stood there that Stem's eulogy was more fitting than that of the preacher's. I looked up then and saw Quinn watching me from across the grave. He started for me, then stopped as Jack scooped Rose up into his arms and pulled me close to him. When I glanced up again, Quinn was walking slowly across the trail, back to the wagons.

A long while after everyone else had drifted off to camp to tend to their own families, Rose and I sat out by Pa's grave. Around dusk Jack came along and fetched us. "Come on, now," he said to us, "we're going to have to get some sleep so we can be up in time to pull out."

Jack's voice was gruff, and the way he looked didn't set much better. Rose and I stood and, without a word of argument, walked on to our wagon.

When I tucked Rose in her bed, she peered up at me, her eyes wide, her little face, like mine, still streaked with tears and dust. "Do you think Pa's with Mama, now, Callie?" she asked.

"I *know* he is," I whispered.

"Callie, will you lay by me until I fall asleep?"

I pulled the covers back and snuggled in next to

Rose. I held her close and stayed with her long after the sobs that shook her little body quieted to sleep, welcoming the dark, where no one could see the tears spilling down my own cheeks. After I was cried out, I got up and went to find Jack.

I checked the area where they kept the cattle and was surprised there was no sign of Jack. Not knowing where else to search, I started back for the wagon, when I heard a strange noise carry in the wind, like the steady hammering of metal against metal off in the distance. I started to follow the sound, and soon enough I realized it was coming from the direction of where we'd buried Pa.

In the dim light of the moon I spotted Jack leaning against a tree not far from Pa's grave. He was so intent on watching whatever it was, he didn't see me until I was right in front of him.

"That noise," I said, shivering. Jack nodded.

"It's McGregor," he supplied. "He's markin' the boulder with Pa's name."

Once my eyes adjusted to the dark, I saw Jack was right. I saw the silhouette of Quinn. He had a chisel in one hand, a hammer in the other, and with hard, determined strokes, was cutting away at the rock.

When he'd paused for a moment to wipe the sweat from his brow, I started for him, but Jack held me back with his hand on my arm.

"He doesn't know we're here, Callie," Jack said. "I imagine that's why he waited until now. Don't you see? This is somethin' he wanted to do just for Pa."

"Can't we stay, Jack?" I begged, turning to him. "Just for another day?"

"The captain says we're pullin' out at first light, Callie. We don't have any choice but to go."

"Then let's go back. Let's go home."

Jack's smile was sad.

"Pa sold the farm, Callie," he said quietly. "There ain't no home for us to go back to."

I think I'd rather live in the streets of Independence than go on and told Jack as much when we got to the wagon. He reminded me that we're making this journey for Rose. He told me he thought Pa would have wanted us to go on, for Rose's sake. He told me, too, that Pa would have wanted us to have courage.

Courage?

Oh, Pa, of all the things you taught me in life, why is it that you left me with the most important lesson to learn on my own?

Thursday, June 9

Captain Belshaw left a note on the tree near where Pa was buried, telling the folks that would come behind us that he'd named the spot "Wade's Point" in honor of a man that had died a hero.

We were led off not long after that, all the wagons rolling into a line. The herders behind shouted and whistled, riding among the animals. I heard a woman's laughter and a baby's cry, and as our wagon lurched on, I turned and looked back at Pa's grave one last time. I saw the note on the tree tear loose from the nail that held it. Over and over it tumbled until another gust of wind carried it far out of sight.

Near the Platte River
In transit to California
June 10, 1859

Mrs. Maggie Todd
Blue Mills, Missouri

Dear Maggie,

How do you begin a letter that bears the burden of grief?

Pa's gone, Mag, we buried him day before yesterday. If there's a more desolate-looking gravesite than the sand hills of Nebraska Territory, I can't imagine one. It took so much out of us, leaving him behind like that. But then, we weren't given much of a choice.

It seems the trail doesn't give much thought to our grief, or anyone else's, for that matter. Another day dawns and it's move ahead, gain every inch, every mile you can, and don't look back. But the nights are even worse. No matter how tired I am, the sorrow I've carried tucked away inside of me creeps out in the dark to keep me awake. I worry about Jack most of all, even though he doesn't say much; the haunted look in his eyes is enough. I worry about Rose, too, although she seems to have found comfort believing Pa has joined Mama in heaven. "They're together, now," she reminds us, with such strong certainty in her eyes that I yearn for that same feeling.

Seeing Pa, his chest crushed, lying beneath the Mercers' wagon after saving Bess and her son, I prayed like anything that he might live, but the

*good Lord didn't seem to hear me. I'm ashamed
to admit when we buried Pa I wanted nothing
more than to stomp my foot like a child and
shake my fist at Providence. But then, who am I
to question Him? Oh, Mag, how He must hang
his head at my stubbornness.*

*How I wish you were here! I am so lonely to-
night. I feel like I'm holding my hand out in the
dark and there's no one there to take it. Pray for
me, will you, Mag?*

> *Your grieving friend,*
> *Callie*

Saturday, June 11

Made ten miles today, walking most of the way behind our wagon over the rough, sandy terrain.

So tired. But I can't sleep. How can I? If I try to
lay down in the wagon, I find myself waiting for Pa
to peek in through the back curtain to check on us
like he used to, with that half-smile of his hiding up
under the brushy old mustache that hadn't been
trimmed since we left home. And the way he'd look
to Rose and me that spoke more than words. Maybe
if I could see him just one more time, just long enough
to say the things I never got a chance to, it might help
me let go of this horrible ache caught deep in me that
chokes my will. I . . .

* * *

Quinn was just here. He said Jack told him I wasn't sleeping, wasn't eating, either. When I didn't say anything, he sat down next to me and watched me with a worried look as I poked at the fire. After a while, I got up to leave.

"I was getting ready to turn in," I told him, hating the lie, but hating even more that he saw my pain, so fresh and raw that I felt bared by it.

"Don't." Quinn stood and reached for my arm.

I tried to jerk away, but he held on, and I felt all of the pain and bitterness that I kept inside boil up in me. "It should have been someone else!" I shouted, "not him. He had a *family,* people that needed him. Why was he taken? Why not—"

"Someone like me?" he cut in, and there was a horrible silence that followed, filled with the ugly truth of what I had been about to say. But when I looked, his eyes told me he understood, maybe more than anyone else ever would.

He pulled me close and hugged me tight then, so tight I could smell the scent of the trail fresh on his clothes. The tender way he held me started to unravel what I had knotted inside of me, and I felt first one tear then another slip down my face.

"Let it go, Callie," he told me, and everything that I'd kept in, so scared to let go of for fear of losing something of Pa, began to break free. I began to cry, a horrible wrenching sound that seemed to come from someone else. Quinn held me for a long while until the night sounds came back, shaking me out of it: the wind mingling with the restlessness of the herd, the high-pitched bark of a prairie dog somewhere off aways.

"I'm sorry," I said as his hands touched my face.

"Don't ever be sorry for feeling, lass," he said to

me. "It's when you don't feel anything, that's when you should be sorry."

"Do you ever miss them, your parents?"

"Every day."

He took me by the hand, led me to the fire, and sat next to me. Looking down at his hands, he told me of how he had shut himself off from everything and everybody when he lost his family—of how he would work and work until he was so tired he'd fall into his bedroll and know nothing but blackness until morning came.

His eyes met mine. "And then I saw you at the rendezvous, with those green eyes that hid nothing," he said, "and something inside of me started to feel again. I started remembering how hard my da and ma worked for us back home in Pittsburgh. How my da dreamed of us having a better go of life. And my ma washing other people's clothes, her hands blistered from the lye, so we boys would never have to know the coal dust beneath our nails . . . or in our lungs."

Quinn did something that surprised me then. He threaded my hand in his own and held it against my heart, and we both sat there feeling the strong beat beneath our fingers. "Life," he said, "it's what your pa gave to you, and a good one at that. Mourn your loss, Callie, but don't profane his memory by shutting yourself off from everyone that cares."

He left me then, to think on all that he had said. And as I sit here writing this, I know he is right.

Sadly enough, it doesn't make it any easier.

I just found Pa's hat caught between my mattress and the sideboards. I remember taking it off Pa's head the day he . . . Anyway, I hope Jack doesn't want it. I'd like to keep it for myself.

Sunday, June 12

Early this morning Jack and I rode out to join Quinn, Stem, and two other outriders that were scouting the trail that lay ahead to the Platte River.

Jack had surprised me after breakfast with Patch, saddled and ready for me and a look that brooked no argument as he mounted Big Black. The pain of losing Pa was still fresh between us both, but I could see a new resolve in Jack's eyes that hadn't been there yesterday. I climbed up on the horse and waved to Rose, sitting next to Grace's eldest son, Dane, who had offered to take over driving our team for a while, and steered my mount toward the open range.

As it turned out, it was what Jack and I needed. We had all heard about the Platte; talk around camp had been of nothing else. But actually seeing it was something altogether different.

The Platte River was like no other river I had ever seen, wider than the Mississippi, I think, with no banks or trees, nothing to hold it back save for the rough line of towering sand hills that lay in the far distance. The valley surrounding it, so vast and wide that it appeared to go on forever, was blanketed by an ocean of blue sky that made me dizzy to look at it. Limitless . . . that's how it felt. And it gave me hope, like just about anything could come to me, and for once I didn't think about good or bad. It just *was*.

"Somethin' else, ain't it?" Stem said. His long, silver hair, now well past his shoulders, blew around him in the wind as he headed his horse down over the crest of the hill. Jack and I held back, partly to wait for Quinn and partly to just look.

"I'd wondered if it would feel like this," Jack said softly as we gazed across the valley. I nodded, not trusting myself to speak, and I felt something forge between us then—a thankfulness to be alive and to-gether—and I saw that Jack felt it, too. For the first time since Pa's death we both smiled.

Hearing Quinn's horse coming up from the rear, I turned in my saddle. When he saw Jack and me smil-ing, there was a sudden gentling of the lines around his face—a face I'd seen watching me, dogged with worry, over the past few days.

"Have you ever seen anything like it?" I asked him, motioning toward the valley.

"I don't believe I have," he said. But he wasn't looking at the valley. I felt my face flush as I recalled his same expression that evening out on the prairie. And when I looked up again, his smile was soft on me. The smile seemed to say he knew what I was thinking, and for some reason I couldn't help staring at his mouth—remembering before and how he'd kissed me.

"You boys goin' ta jes' sit up there lookin' pretty or are ya goin' ta help me git these flags set?" Stem called from below, breaking my thoughts.

Quinn grinned, nudging his horse, and Jack and I trailed behind him, down the rough slope, following the tattered flags that led us around the deep breaks cut into the soil as we headed for the river.

Later—We've found prime camping ground along the bottoms of the Platte this evening. Problem is, so have a small herd of buffalo.

Stem spotted them just over the next rise as the wagons were drawing in and came to warn us all to keep our animals close. The herd of buffalo had split, he told us, moving along either side of the train. The eerie thing was, we couldn't see them. Dark had settled in, and anything the fires around camp couldn't reach was soaked up by the night.

When I went to help Jack hobble Patch, Big Black, and our pack mules, I heard them, the lows and grunts of the beasts sounding so loud when the wind died down that my hands shook, and I'd hurried to finish working the rope around Patch's front legs.

Jack, being Jack, winked at me and hurried to fetch his rifle once we got back to camp, leaving me to worry. And that's just what I did.

I sat outside and worried and watched. I saw some of the men cutting sage and stacking the bushes around our wagons and others sitting off a piece, with their rifles in tow to shy the herd away with a shot.

By that time the buffalo had moved close, so close I could feel the heat of their bodies envelop the camp. I'd pulled Pa's hat off and was fanning myself with it when I saw Quinn riding through the cloud of dust that hung in the air. "By God, Callie," he said to me as he dismounted, "it's something out there. Couldn't see a foot in front of me, but I'll be damned if one of them buffalo didn't nearly unseat me when it barreled past."

"You could've gotten hurt out there, you know," I said to him as he slipped down next to me. When he smiled at me like he did, I saw a part of him I'd never seen before, a boyish mischief staring out from his rugged face. A glimpse, I think, of what he'd been like before he lost his family.

I was on the verge of telling him he was beginning to remind me of Jack when he reached out to touch my hair. He bent over and kissed me lightly, and I heard the humor in his voice. "I've been wanting to do that all day," he said.

I had wanted it, too. But I wasn't sure if it was right for me to admit it, so I didn't say anything. His smile deepened, he seemed to understand.

"Your hair looks fine, down like that," he said, and when he trailed his fingers through my hair, I leaned back and he kissed me again, harder, for I don't know how long. It was the sound of riders approaching that caused me to finally pull away. I know I wouldn't have done it otherwise—to be honest about it. The truth is, I don't remember hearing much of anything until that moment, then suddenly it was like a loud blast of sound and we were in the thick of it again; our own cattle bawling, the heavy pound of the buffalo hooves, men shouting and whistling. Quinn helped me to my feet and turned and grabbed his saddle horn, swinging himself up.

"You know, if the only good thing to come of this journey is our meeting each other, it will be worth it," he said, smiling softly. Not waiting for an answer, he gigged his horse toward the slope beyond camp and headed in the direction of the herd.

* * *

Later—A swarthy crew of fur traders rode in to camp alongside Zach Koch a while ago. They're on their way home, having unloaded their wares at Westport Landing, although you wouldn't guess it from the smell. Captain Belshaw instructed them to camp some distance away from the train.

Monday, June 13

Traveled over eight miles of rough road pocked by buffalo hooves before we reached Fort Kearney this afternoon. After over a month of nothing but wilderness, wagons, and dirt, it was a sight for my sore eyes to come upon those ramshackle buildings that bloomed up from the middle of nowhere.

"Most pitiful thing I ever saw," I'd heard Mrs. Iverson mutter to her husband when they moved by. But she'd hurried like the rest of us, through the sutler's and across the parade grounds, to post our letters.

When we finally rode out, I'd felt a pang of envy, seeing the soldiers stepping out of their sod houses, seeing the little vegetable and flower gardens. Quinn, who had been riding quietly alongside of the wagon, spoke up then. "One day, Callie," he said, "you'll have your home."

"Maybe," I said, and I'd smiled at him, thinking the way he talked of things made me almost believe they could come true.

Tuesday, June 14

Weather very warm today. Rose and Lizzie played near the banks of the river while Grace and I walked along gathering buffalo chips in our aprons, as there isn't much in the way of wood around here. The preacher told us this morning that they're the work of Providence; he said that no one would survive this leg of the trail without them. I told Grace it was easy for him to say, since he didn't have to pick them up.

She grinned at me.

"If Della has anything to do with it, he will," she said.

It couldn't have been over an hour later when we caught sight of the preacher, trudging along—collecting chips. He really isn't a bad soul. I think he deserves a medal for putting up with his wife. With his son, too—I can't imagine what he must think of Zach taking up with that rough lot of fur traders.

Later—Grace and I, no longer able to stand the dirt, slipped down to the river to bathe, in spite of Jack warning us against it because of the mosquitoes. We no more than got our faces and arms washed when we were hit with a horrid swarm of the nasty things. Jack and Quinn, having caught sight of the two of us as we hightailed it back to the wagons, had a good laugh at our expense. I would have liked to throttle them both, but it was so good to hear Jack laugh again.

Confound those mosquitoes!

Wednesday, June 15

Rode horseback nearly all day with Quinn, following along the winding Platte. We made nearly eighteen miles today before we stopped to camp after crossing Plum Creek. I'm so sore all over that I can scarcely move, but at least there's no sign of mosquitoes. Stem just came to tell us he spotted a buffalo herd over the next ridge. "By God, it'll be good to taste fresh meat," Jack said, and Stem smiled.

"Jes' what we can eat and take with us, boys," he said then. "Where there's buffler, there's Indians. Don't want ta ruffle no feathers."

The men are in a big way this evening. They've become the hunters instead of the *hunted*.

Thursday, June 16

Before the sleep was out of their eyes this morning, the men had begun to talk of hunting buffalo.

Quinn and Stem joined us around the fire for biscuits and coffee, but had no more than a mouthful and a drink before they were picking up their rifles and following Jack to their horses. As I watched them ride off, grinning like boys, I heard Grace chuckle behind me, and I turned around.

"I was just thinking about men," she said. "Most of them ain't got the sense God gave a chicken, but they sure look fine riding off on a hunt, don't they?"

I laughed. "Well, if we can't join them, what do you say we watch?"

Grace and I took the girls and climbed the hill that overlooked the massive herd. I was awed by the sight, my heart thudding in my chest as the valley came alive under the vast, rolling ocean of black. Stem had talked of the herds getting smaller, but I found it hard to believe, seeing the dark smudges that filled the horizon, looking like they would go on forever. There was a beauty about them, too, even in their heavy loping— and for a moment I had almost wished the men would call off the hunt.

Their sounds came to us then, in the clear air of the Platte: yellow calves bawling as they ran on new legs, bellows and grunts from the old. Dust swirled around us, stinging our eyes and noses, as the ground beneath us rumbled like thunder. And the herd pushed along slowly, as one, unaware of the band of men and boys that followed some distance back.

As they moved forward, I saw Stem motion to Jack and another man at opposite ends of the line, and the hunters spread out and began to form a U shape at the tail end of the herd. The fur traders narrowed in on each side.

What happened next, I'm still not sure. The men were just a hair away from closing off a small portion of the herd when a rifle discharged. I saw a large cow go down, her huge body lurching forward. A bellowing came from several in the herd, and all at once, the buffalo began to stampede. It was hard at first to see anything, because of the huge clouds of dirt, but then I spotted Jack, and I screamed as a bull, its muzzle foamy-white from running, turned and rammed into Big Black, sending Jack tumbling over the mount's head. A mist of fine dust raised up once more beneath the pounding hooves.

I was sure, so sure, that I'd lost Jack that my mind traveled forward, seeing my life without him. Quinn would be there, I knew that. Stem, too. But it wasn't enough.

When the mist cleared, I saw the bull charging at Jack, who was running across the field on foot. I screamed Quinn's name over and over, knowing he would never hear me, but screaming just the same. Then Quinn looked back suddenly. Without pause, he dug his heels into his own horse and rode through the mass of rolling humps to Jack, slowing only long enough to lower his rifle and fire at the bull. I didn't hear the shot, but I saw the bull go down. I let go of my breath, shaking as I watched Quinn grab Jack by the scruff of the shirt and pull him with a mighty heave up onto his horse. It was no small feat, Jack weighing nearly two hundred pounds himself. The rest of the hunters and hunted rumbled on, leaving behind the huge shaggy humps of black that would run no more.

We stood there for a moment longer, listening to the drag of the herd dwindle down, becoming farther and farther off.

"Come on, Callie," Grace said then. "Let's see if we can help put that rascal back together."

By the time I delivered the girls to Bess Mercer and got to Jack, his tent was crowded with men, the air inside hot and close, sweat mingling with the pungent odor of leather, dust, and buffalo. I saw Grace leaning over Jack's cot, wrapping the gash he'd earned from Big Black's hoof with cotton strips soaked in what smelled like whiskey.

"As soon as we topped the rise," Stem was saying, "I saw Jack were in trouble. If it weren't fer McGregor here . . . Well, I'd like ta find the jackass that fired that shot."

I saw Quinn standing with Stem, his large frame seeming to dwarf everything else in the tent. When he looked at me, I felt my chest swell with something akin to pride. " 'Tis a charmed life he leads, your brother," he said, then grinned when he saw me roll my eyes heavenward.

"Reckless is more like it," I said, glad that he was alive but mad at his carelessness.

"Well, now, Callie, a man can't reform in just one day." Jack smiled at me and then turned his attention to Grace. "You did a fine job, Mrs. Hollister," he said, peering at the bandage that ran from his shoulder to his wrist. "I'd marry you myself . . . if I was the marryin' kind."

"Well, ain't you the sweet talker, Jack Wade," Grace laughed, hands on hips. "But who said I'd marry *you?*"

Hearty male laughter filled the tent as Grace and I stepped outside. "That brother of yours is a charmer," Grace said, and I noticed that her face was flushed, her eyes distant. "Reminds me a little of Mr. Hollister when he was young." She grinned then. "Lord, I do pray for the girl that finally wins him."

I'd stood outside that tent for a while after Grace had gone off back to her own wagon, thinking about Jack and the way he'd rode blindly into that herd of buffalo, about his thirst for adventure. I'd long given up on hoping he might settle down. There's a lot of mischief in him, a lot of stubbornness, too—but no meanness. It's just that Jack was cut from a different cloth than the rest of us.

From where I sit this evening I can hear the men laughing inside of his tent. Between the folds of the doorway, I see Jack propped up, downing another cup of whiskey to kill the pain. Jack's smile is warm and friendly, but his eyes, as always, are focused on that nameless place that he dreams of.

I wonder where it will be that those dreams finally take him.

Later—Stem gutted the buffalo Quinn gave to us and then proceeded to build a tiny scaffold to support the strips of meat that he smoked over a slow fire. What meat was left after that, he hung outside on the wagon covers, the same as the rest of the train. By the time we were finished, there were red strips of meat hanging everywhere. The entire camp looked like it was decorated with coarse red fringe. Even though I worried over too much dirt or sand getting in the meat and tainting it, Rose was delighted.

"It's almost like Christmas," she said, pleased with the "decorations."

"Any day'd feel like Christmas with ya around, honey," Stem said, his callused hand patting her on the head. I was surprised to see the wistful expression that crossed his craggy features.

When I looked at Quinn, I saw that he'd been watching the exchange, too. It seemed like we were both wondering what kinds of Christmases Stem had ever had.

Just woke up. Sounds of gunshots off in the distance. I heard the drum of horses' hooves and peered through the back curtain of our wagon in time to see Quinn, Stem, and Captain Belshaw riding out of camp. Wonder where they're off to.

Friday, June 17

Another warm day. We made only eight miles along the Platte, being that we were held back in camp this morning by Henry Mercer. Bess had been feeling poorly all night and he wanted to lay over. I was as surprised as any at Captain Belshaw's decision to move on. But then, he and Stem had been acting out of sorts all morning.

"Can't stay here," Stem was saying to the folks when Grace and I walked up. People started to protest, but he raised his hand. "It ain't a discussion." There was something in Stem's voice that made me feel uneasy. I tried to catch his eye, but he was staring off toward the trail ahead, as if he wished we were there already.

"Bess might get bad off if we move her," Henry Mercer called out from the crowd, and I'd heard the fear in his voice, just under the frustration. "If any of you was sick, I think you'd want the train to wait. . . ."

"Try ta make her as comfortable as ya can, Mercer," Stem said over his shoulder. "We're movin' out shortly."

After he walked away, Grace and I quickly went to gather up whatever we could find to get Bess situated and hurried on to her wagon.

Bess's face looked peaked, but she put on her best smile while Grace and I fussed over her, tucking an extra mattress tick and some quilts under her to buffer against the jar of the wagon.

"I'll be fine," she told us. "But Henry worries so. Ben here, he took near two days to come."

Bess was still on my mind when Stem rode up, following beside me as the wagons pulled out. "Bad place fer a woman ta give birth," he said.

"Well, I imagine she's more put out than you, having this baby in the middle of nowhere," I told him, hawing the team on. I felt Stem's eyes on me for a moment longer, then I heard him ride off.

We were only two or three miles out when we came across a small herd of buffalo, or what was left of them. The bloodied carcasses that lay scattered along the Platte Valley bore no likeness to the animals that had filled me with such awe. A few of the new yellow calves I'd seen only yesterday, frolicking on the outskirts of the herd, were poking their confused noses into the skinless bodies of their mothers, and I saw the wolves hunker around, drawing their circle tighter, their yellow eyes greedy. My gaze moved to the rickety rigs of the fur traders, and I saw the canvas tops pulled down snug, but not so snug that I couldn't see the bulky hump underneath—buffalo skins.

* * *

Later—Camped late tonight along the Platte. We would've kept going, but Bess is all but played out. Fear has been high ever since Stem spotted some Pawnee Indians only a few miles off.

Making matters worse, Zach Koch showed up at our campfire this evening. He was in a foul mood, I learned later, because of the captain and Stem forcing the fur traders to move on. The longer he stood there, raving about the Pawnee, and no one paying him much mind, the angrier he became.

"Why run the fur company out? What are you tryin' to do, protect the Pawnee?" he ranted, pacing in front of the fire.

"We're tryin' ta protect the train," Stem said evenly. "There ain't no doubt in my mind they seen them buffler. An' it's them *friends* of yours we got ta thank fer that."

"Hell," Zach said, "Pawnee ain't nothing but pesky animals."

"Been around here a sight longer than us. The way they look at it, might jes' be we're the nuisance."

"Indian lover," Zach sneered. "But I guess one color is the same as the other when you think about it. What color are *you* anyway?"

"I ain't yeller, that's fer sure," Stem said easily.

Zach moved toward Stem, and I saw Quinn start to rise from the fire. He was held back by Stem's hand on his shoulder.

"Ya kind of remind me of a *squaw*-killer I knew up north," Stem said then, eyeing Zach. "He came ta no good end though."

"Oh, yeah, what happened to him?" Zach had tried to remain casual, but I saw his eyes flick over to me,

trying to judge if I'd said anything to Stem or Quinn
about the trapper's wife.

"Why, his head got so swelled from killin' all them
women, he thought he should try shootin' a brave. He
missed." Stem smiled. "The brave didn't."

Zach shouted after Stem as he turned to go. "I
could shoot you for talking to me like that, nigger!"
he yelled, and I saw Stem stop dead in his tracks.
He looked off to one side of camp, as if he were
contemplating something.

"You could try," he said in a voice I'd never heard
before. A patient but hard voice, reminding me of a
hawk that circles slowly before diving for its prey.

Zach heard it, too. I saw the undisguised look of
relief on his face when Stem finally walked away.

Oh, how I wish this journey were over. These hardships are changing us all—and not for the better, I fear.

Later—Quinn was just here. He told me it was his
turn to help stand guard, but that he had to see me
first. I didn't realize how much I needed him to hold
me until he did.

Saturday, June 18

Rose and I were riding in Grace's wagon this morning when we came face-to-face with the Pawnee.

Lizzie, the little scamp that she is, had leaned too
far out of the back of the wagon and had fallen, scaring us near half to death. We had no more than got

her settled in next to Rose when I noticed that we'd dropped quite a distance behind the rest of the train. I had turned to mention this, and that's when I saw Grace's attention focus to the right of us.

"What is it?" I asked.

"Not *it*, them," she replied, and I felt my heart stop as I followed her gaze.

The Indians seemed to have sprung up from out of nowhere, as if the ground had retched them up, horses and all. I held my breath and watched as the column of Pawnee rode toward us, their half-naked bodies gleaming under the glare of the sun. A young brave who looked of some importance broke from the group and rode quickly toward the wagon as the rest of the party cut a line in front of us so we couldn't pass. "How de do! Damn you!" he yelled, greeting us.

"Well, that's a relief," Grace said wryly. "He speaks English."

What appeared to be their leader then rode forward, urging his pony in front of the younger one's as he studied us with something like contempt or disdain. He had a matted hank of hair that curved back like a horn and eyes that were hard.

"Food," he said simply, and then waited as if he thought we were going to serve him.

"I imagine a strong fella like you is able to get your own," Grace said politely, and I stared at her, wondering if she'd gone crazy. I don't think they understood a word that she'd said. Some of the Indians even laughed, poking at each other. But all eyes took notice when she pulled the gun from the folds of her skirt.

A tense silence fell around us, and I felt a chill run through me—until I heard Rose and Lizzie whimpering in the back of the wagon, then anger took over. I think Grace felt it, too, because she fired off her gun near one of their horses, causing it to skitter to one side. The leader sneered at her, like he figured she didn't have it in her to do much more. Grace then fired the gun once more, hitting close to the hoof of his horse. "My rifle," she whispered, "it's in the wagon." Not knowing the first thing about guns, I hesitated. When I finally moved, I heard the wagons up ahead of us suddenly jangle to a stop. The Pawnee seemed to notice as well, because the leader said something and they all quickly rode off. I turned back to Grace and was surprised to see trails of sweat on her forehead.

"For Godsake, next time pick up a gun, Callie," she said. "Two'll scare them off quicker than one."

"I don't know how to shoot," I said, feeling frustrated at my own helplessness.

Grace seemed to understand. She studied me thoughtfully, like she was weighing a decision, and then said, "It ain't going to be the last of them. Might be just the time for you to learn."

Later—Camped near a clear stream this evening that runs close to the river; good water and grass.

Stem came by to tell us to stick close to the wagons. He told us that the Pawnee were just playing with us today, kind of testing the waters. He said he figured they'd be back.

Jack remained quiet as we sat next to the fire, but the frustration in his eyes mirrored my own. *"Just what we can eat and take with us, boys,"* Stem had said. *"Don't want to ruffle no feathers."* The warning had come back to haunt us. It was maddening to think that those fur traders had been so greedy, knowing we might be the ones to pay for it.

Not long after Stem walked off, Rose climbed up in Jack's lap, rubbing the short stubble along his face like she'd done with Pa when she was scared. When Jack's eyes met mine over the fire, I felt the strength of Jack's and my love for Rose come together, and it made me feel bigger somehow, less selfish.

"We're going to be okay, aren't we Jack?" Rose said then, looking between the two of us.

"Better than okay, honey," Jack said, and I saw a bit of Pa in the way he wrapped his arms around her and held her tight.

There's a wolf howling somewhere over the river, dismal-sounding, as I write this. But I'm not exactly alone. Quinn is sitting just a short distance away atop of his wagon, a rifle across his knees.

Sunday, June 19

Early morning—Cloudy today, but no letup from the heat. We woke to find three of our cattle missing, and there's no doubt in any of our minds that it was the Pawnee. Still, we remain in camp. Bess Mercer's condition is worse, and her husband believes she will have the babe anytime soon. Mama always said that babies come in their own good time—not ours. This little one is proof of that.

* * *

Later—I had been mending one of my dresses, trying to make use of idle time as I kept an eye on the Mercer wagon, when Grace appeared. She'd eyed me for a moment, then said, "I've decided to teach you how to use a gun, Callie."

I was more than a little wary as I followed her down to the river. I watched her walk forward and tack on a low-hung branch a block of cloth thats center had been rubbed with tar. Returning to where I stood, she slipped the gun belt off her shoulder, where it had rested, and deftly buckled it low to her waist. I felt some of my wariness fade, watching the easy way she carried it like wearing a gun was second nature.

"A gun in your hand can either kill you or save you, Callie," she said. She turned the fancy-looking pistol over in her hand, thoughtful. "You know, after Grady died I didn't think I'd ever pick one of these up again," she said. "After a while, though, I realized that it wasn't the gun but the man that did him in." Grace straightened her shoulders, as if to shake the memory off, then laid one of the guns in my hand.

She raised her pistol and leveled it at the target.

"Protection is what I'm aiming to teach you," she gritted out, pulling the trigger, and I saw the cloth billow from the impact. She looked pleased, and I felt a pang of envy at how easily she handled the gun— how easily she handled life, for that matter.

"Don't you ever get scared?" I asked. I saw her face sober, and she slipped her gun in its holster. She hesitated, then sighed, like she'd made up her mind.

"Scared?" she said. "Callie, I can't think of the last time I wasn't." She reached forward and showed me how to hold the gun, and then said, "I guess I'm scared for my kids mostly. Lizzie more than the others, she's her daddy all over."

"Well, I'm tired of being scared," I said, and Grace laughed.

"An annoying thing, fear," she said, "but it keeps us on our toes, doesn't it?"

I tried to mimic Grace's stance then, turned, and pulled the trigger.

The spatter of applause surprised us both, and we looked behind us to find Quinn and Jack lounging in the grass. Quinn's long legs were stretched out. He smiled a slow, easy smile.

It took me close to ten tries after that before I actually hit anything but dirt.

"I'm thinking the Indians will be in grave danger, should they attack us, Jack," Quinn said, chuckling.

I was, I admit, becoming quite the "expert" at missing the mark. But I did manage to hit the tree three times after Quinn made that comment. Stem, who had joined the audience by that time, noticed the improvement—and what provoked it. He chuckled, slapping Quinn on the back. "That red hair don't lie, does it, McGregor?" he asked.

Later—The loud, lusty wails of a baby broke the stillness of camp this evening. Word has quickly spread that Bess Mercer has given birth to another boy. The proud father is beaming ear to ear, taking his congratulatory whacks on the back with a good nature induced by the "nerve tonic" Stem is passing man to man.

Monday, June 20

On the move once again. Starting out this morning, we were met by about a hundred Pawnee—a few I recognized from the other day. They were returning from their own hunting trip, from the looks of it, their ponies burdened with furs and dried meat. I breathed a sigh of relief as they passed by us with no more than a civil "Howdy."

I learned later, however, that as soon as they reached the tail end of our train, they relieved a few of the men of most of their clothing, knives, and tobacco and stampeded a team with Mrs. Iverson in the wagon.

Later—Everyone is so tickled about Bess Mercer's baby. Even the harshest men ambled over to the wagon to get a glimpse this evening. It was as if they were hungry to celebrate life, to see a new beginning in the midst of the hardships. I think I welcomed the distraction most of all.

When Henry handed me the little boy, he let out a wail in my arms, and Lizzie said, "Mama, I think Miss Bess needs to send him back; he don't have any teeth!" We all laughed, and when I looked up, I caught Quinn staring at me so intently that it jarred me a bit. It was as if a question had been raised between us, holding me still where I stood.

Sleep is elusive tonight. I've been sitting here by the fire for a long while now—entertaining thoughts I suppose I shouldn't. The look of longing I saw in Quinn's eyes remains with me. So deep—as deep as my own feelings, if I'm going to be honest about it. Love would be so much easier if we weren't on this trail, if life wasn't so uncertain.

Sometimes I try to imagine what *could* be instead of what is . . . Quinn and I together in a nice house with a big porch for Mama's rocker, a tumble of kids at our feet.

Then the wind moans and I'm reminded of where I am.

Tuesday, June 21

Rode out with Quinn today, along the river. Wind was high all morning, forcing us to tuck our chins into our chests so that the sand wouldn't sting our eyes. Quinn said, "Imagine it's the California seashore." I laughed at that, and he moved his horse close to mine, so close that our legs brushed, then he kissed me.

Feeling much better today.

Wednesday, June 22

When our wagons trailed in this evening, I saw Stem turn his horse toward the open plain once more. It was then I caught sight of a colored woman—the very same woman I saw a while ago—pushing her handcart just as easy as you please. Her clothes were worn, but clean, her back straight, as she marched stoutly on. I saw her stop as Stem reined in next to her. She shielded her eyes against the setting sun and looked up at him as he spoke.

Her hands went to her hips, and she put her head back and began to laugh.

Stem steered his horse toward camp then, a foul look on his face. When he finally reached us and we were able to ask what had happened, he said he had invited her to travel with our train. "I told her it was safer than goin' it alone," he said.

"What did she say?" I asked innocently enough.

"Why, hell," Stem replied grudgingly, "she looked me up and down and said, 'I'll take my chances.' Then she laughed."

The whole crowd of us began to laugh, much to Stem's annoyance. He spurred his horse on, calling us "damned idjits," which made Jack and Quinn laugh harder.

Later—Rose and I have just returned from visiting the lone fire beyond our camp. The woman that Stem talked with earlier is set up out there. She was bending over a simmering pot beneath a sturdy little lean-to when we found her. When she stood, I was shocked to see how tall she was, being at least a head taller than Jack. She was wary at first, but when she saw Rose standing behind my skirts, her face kind of changed.

"Come on over here, sugar," she coaxed. "I don't bite." When Rose walked forward, the woman smiled, and I thought I'd never seen a more handsome face. "My name is Jessie, Jessie Bell. A'course, that ain't to be confused with *Jezebel*."

Rose tried her best to hide the smile but couldn't.

The woman didn't seem to mind. As a matter of fact, I think she took to Rose right then.

"Well, ain't that somethin'," she said, shaking Rose's hand. "Child has a sense of humor after all." She laughed, a smoky kind of laugh that made you feel good, and invited us to sit awhile. All the questions I wanted to ask, Rose did, and the woman told us about losing her "man" and deciding to "start new while she had the strength." California was her destination and, like us, where she hoped for a better life. When she told us about her children, her face shined with pride. She said once she got settled, she was going to send for them and they would have a fine reunion. For a moment, she looked wistful.

When I asked her why she was alone, she said, "People figure I'm a runaway. I ain't, but there's some that'd soon make me one." Such a brave woman! I felt bad when we finally had to go, but she seemed to take it all in stride.

"Maybe we'll run into each other in Californy," she called out to us as we walked away; then she laughed like it was a fine joke.

Thursday, June 23

Walking with Grace alongside the wagons today, I'd happened to mention meeting Jessie. When I told her I'd overheard Mrs. Iverson saying Jessie was probably a runaway, being that she was traveling alone like she was, Grace smiled sadly.

"What are any of us doing out here?" she said. "Did you ever think she might be running *to* something instead of running away?" She studied me then and said, "Things ain't always what they seem, Callie." She appeared to want to say something more but just shook her head and walked off.

Later—It wasn't until late this evening that I understood what Grace had told me earlier. I had been packing our dinner things away when she walked up and took the bull by the horns, so to speak. She said, "Got something to show you, Callie," then turned around and headed for her own wagon.

Curious, I had followed on. By the time I pulled myself into the back of her wagon, Grace was already sitting on a mattress, rifling through a large trunk.

"Here it is," she announced triumphantly. As I sat down beside her, she handed to me a beautifully framed photograph. On closer inspection, I realized that it was Grace, maybe ten years younger. She was dressed in the finest clothes I'd ever seen, her hands resting on the shoulders of an older gentleman, her face confident and smiling.

"That's my pa, Callie," she said, grinning. "You seem surprised."

"Well, you look kind of *starched,*" I said, for the lack of a better word, and Grace laughed outright.

"If you would've asked my mama back then, she'd of told you, 'My Grace, she's going to be a lady . . . whether she likes it or not.' My mama was determined, all right. But then, so was I. I wasn't but seventeen when they sent me off to practice poise and social grace with all the other young ladies in town that summer. Bored me to tears." Grace nodded, as if remembering. "So, instead I found my 'passion' in the back room of the only saloon in town. Lost my first game of cards there . . . and my heart."

"Grady Hollister?" I asked.

"The one and only, honey," she said, her eyes soft.

"Did you ever regret being with him?"

"No. Grady didn't have much money, Callie. But I knew that when I married him. But he gave me something I'd never had—my freedom. You see, I'd spent my whole life being taught to be a lady, about *propriety*." Grace grinned. "I was so miserable, so restricted. Grady made me happy, he made me laugh and I loved him for that. So you see, I wasn't running away, like most people thought," she said finally. "I was running to something . . . something better than money could buy."

Friday, June 24

Made an early start. Sandy soil was deep, making it hard for the oxen to pull, so Grace and I decided to walk. We had a good time watching Rose and Lizzie scamper through the honeycombed prairie dog villages. They would shriek with laughter when one of the pups would pop out of its hole and bark. Lizzie had us in stitches with her determination to capture one. She'd take off, her dark curls flying. "I'm gonna get one, Mama, you just wait and see!" she'd call over her shoulder.

At one point Grace wiped her eyes from laughing. "I swear, she's going to gray my hair before it's time." She said it wryly, but I saw the love—the same kind of love I held for Rose. When our eyes met, I felt something deeper than the friendship we shared take hold, silent understanding that spoke of little fears and a whole lot of endurance.

Later—Saw Jessie Bell heading down the trail past our camp tonight, tramping along through the dust with a blanket and some provisions tied to her back while she bravely pushed her little handcart onward.

Sunday, June 26
Nebraska Territory

Passed many new graves today; most were nothing but mounds rising up from the sun-baked earth, maybe a pile of rocks, a piece of wood, or a shred of cloth to mark a loved one's final home. Stem told me that it's been his experience that the graves average about one a mile along this never-ending river trail.

There was one grave that quite struck me, for it was so tiny. At the head of the grave was a crude marker, made from what appeared to be the sideboard of a wagon. On the marker it simply read: "He sleeps in Jesus, gone but not forgotten." The mound was covered with prickly pear, I noticed. As if this harsh, uncompromising land had relented for a moment and paid respects in its own way to the tiny babe.

Grace had noticed it, too. I saw the stricken expression on her face and the way she pulled Lizzie close to her side as she hurried her oxen on past.

Monday, June 27

I would give all that I own to be able to wipe out the memory of what has happened today.

Grace's daughter Lizzie has been taken from us. It seems she got ahold of one of Grace's guns and somehow the gun accidentally discharged.

It was just about noon when we heard the crack of the gun go off. My first thought was that the Pawnee had crossed our trail again. Rose stood on the seat of our wagon. "That came from Miss Grace's wagon," she said.

I pulled the oxen to a stop, and Rose and I rushed down through the crowd that was already forming at the front of the train. I felt a horrible sense of doom, the scene reminding me so much of the day Pa had died. The crowd parted, and suddenly there was Grace, sitting on the ground in her fine dress, swirls of dust and sand surrounding her as the rest of the wagons jarred to a stop. I felt the cry from deep in my soul as I spotted Lizzie cradled in Grace's arms, a telltale red stain soaking the front of her dress, an ivory-handled pistol at her side. As Grace rocked her small, lifeless body to and fro, I saw her brush her hand over Lizzie's little freckled face with an expression that seemed to be hoping against hope that Lizzie would wake up. After a while, her hands paused, and a shudder went through her body. When she looked up, her face was washed with a grief beyond tears, and I felt her pain so deeply it became my own. "She's gone," she said dully, gazing around. "Dane, you go fetch my best quilt, a needle, and some thread."

I dropped down in the dust next to Grace, hugging her and Lizzie to me. We sat like that for a long time, through the gawkers and the grief-stricken, through the hour that she painstakingly stitched together the prize quilt that would be her daughter's coffin.

It was Quinn and Jack who dug the grave. Stem pulled a sideboard off his own wagon and fashioned a cross of sorts to mark Lizzie's final resting place. When I offered to help her prepare Lizzie's body for burial, Grace shook her head.

"I have to do this myself," she said softly. Then she looked me straight in the eye. "I can't help her in this world anymore . . . but I can help her through death."

Later, Grace and I stood together by Lizzie's grave, her children surrounding us like a great fortress, as the men rolled their wagons over and over the pitiful mound. Grace had refused to move from the spot until they did so, saying she didn't want the grave to be dug up by the wolves.

Bess Mercer came through the crowd along about that time, holding her new baby tight to her as she began to sing "Nearer My God to Thee." And when her voice faded off, all sound had died away except for the soft cries of Lizzie's brothers. Bess's and Grace's eyes met, filled with pain and understanding. "Precious Lord," Bess Mercer whispered, turning away, "take this child's hand. . . ."

"I'm her mother," Grace said, staring off. "Where was I when she needed me? She didn't want to come. 'Mama,' she'd say, 'I'm so tired, let's go back.' " Grace looked to where her boys were standing. "Over and over I told her, just a little longer, Lizzie, just a little longer. Worse thing is, she believed me."

Rose let go of my hand then and ran to Grace. I'd feared for Rose, her and Lizzie being nearly inseparable from the beginning. Rose, however, stood staunch as a pillar next to Grace, holding her hand.

"Miss Grace, I prayed awful hard for Lizzie," she said. "I'm figurin' that I'll miss her somethin' awful, but Callie says that Lizzie's in heaven, so I'm thinkin' Lizzie won't be so lonely," she said, smiling. "My ma and pa'll take care of her."

Grace touched Rose's cheek. With her shoulders back, I watched her gather her strength and walk away from the grave, the boys following solemnly behind.

"Did you see that? Not even a tear," I heard Della Koch whisper to one of her cronies, and I felt my body go rigid with rage. When I turned around, Mrs. Iverson at least had the decency to look shamed.

If they saw so much, how had they missed the tortured look that was etched in Grace's face as she stared off across the plains, the look that begged for a reason, knowing there would never be one good enough? If they saw so much, how had they missed the handful of dirt from Lizzie's grave that Grace had gingerly tucked into her handkerchief, as if it were a precious gift?

I sat with Grace a long while after the funeral. Together, we silently watched the sun sink behind the horizon.

"You know, some would say that it's easier for me to go on, having as many kids as I do," Grace said after a while, and then she glanced down at her hands.

"My mama lost a little boy before she had Rose,"

I said. "And you know what she once told me? If I lost a finger, and some fool told me that I still had nine fingers left, it wouldn't mean that I didn't miss that lost one any less."

Grace wiped the single tear that traveled down her cheek and rose from the fire. "I don't think I'll ever forget the look in her eyes, Callie," she said, "so frightened, so full of helplessness. . . ."

I watched her gather herself together and head for her wagon. "Grace. . . ." I wasn't sure what to say, so I stood there feeling empty. She turned to me, her smile sad.

"All the miles . . ." she whispered, her face bitter with the maddening irony of it all. She didn't say any more after that, but her eyes spoke volumes. *Why?* they asked.

She never waited for the answer, but instead climbed silently into her wagon.

I sometimes wish I could be free of all of this grief. Free from depending on anyone and anyone depending on me. I suppose it's awful to think this way, but it scares me some to know Rose depends on me so. Tonight was the first time I've felt grief that was not my own.

Staring into Grace's face, I saw the bitter sorrow of a mother who was helpless in saving her own child from the grave, and it has chilled me to the bone.

What if I can't save Rose from the pain or sickness on this Godless journey we're forced to take? I no longer know what to expect from life.

"Blessed are those who expect nothing . . . for they shall not be disappointed"—Alexander Pope wrote that. It's fitting, I think.

Tuesday, June 28

On the trail once again, heading toward the ford of the South Platte. It was with a heavy heart that I watched Grace pull away from camp this morning. Wagons creaked through the grainy soil as the lead teamsters called out loudly to move on. For the briefest moment I saw Grace glance up to the perch where Lizzie had sat. She then goaded her team on, and I saw her face, so determined, turn westward.

Not once did she ever look back.

Later—Camped late on a high table above the river this evening. Jack told me at dinner that Grace had given him her husband's pistols to dispose of. He said that she didn't want them around anymore, because of Lizzie, that she said she was wrong about the guns after all.

"She thinks they're cursed," Jack said, glancing at Quinn and me over the rim of his tin cup. "I'm figurin' on keepin' them."

When he brought the guns out, I felt a stirring of fear come over me. Flashy was what they were. Gamblers' guns. The kind that hunted for men, not for game. Just by looking at Quinn, I knew he was thinking the same way I was—Jack needed those pistols like he needed a hole in his head.

"Grace wanted you to get rid of them, Jack," I said, and he stared at me like he'd heard wrong.

"Get rid of them?" he said. "Do you know how much a set like this'd cost?" He frowned and then said, "Listen, I won't even wear them, not until we get where we're goin'."

"I don't want them in the wagon—not near Rose," I said.

"Good God, Callie," he said, "do you think I'd let harm come to Rose?"

I felt uneasy as I watched him walk away with Quinn. It's not that Jack's bad; it's just a feeling I have. Like there's something wild and untamed waiting to bust out of him.

"Life has a funny way of taking the decisions right out of our hands." I remember Mama telling me this once, and I don't know why, but I wish Jack would've thrown those guns away instead of keeping them.

Wednesday, June 29

Stem sat up next to me in our wagon for a while this morning to keep me company. I could tell he was in a mood, wanting to talk. He likes to say that talking to a person is the best way to take the sting out of any trouble that came their way—that you could either bore a person, so that it makes them feel their troubles aren't anything at all, or you could get lucky, if you go on long enough, and figure out how to make it better.

He had his work cut out for him with me, though. Seeing Lizzie buried so soon after Pa has caused me to become more than a little fey about life in general. As we pulled on and on past the endless stretch of river, past the high, ragged bluffs, I felt my spirits sink lower. If the truth be known, the only way I could figure out not to cry was to bite the inside of my cheek. It hurt just enough to keep the tears back. I had about everybody fooled . . . everyone, that is, except for Stem.

"Ya ain't ever goin' ta find a reason fer that child dying, if that's what yer after," he said after watching me awhile. "Not from the Almighty or otherwise."

"Why?" I said.

"Because we're not supposed ta, that's why. I guess our nature is ta see things the way ya would through a spyglass, kind of narrow and room fer only one thing at a time. Near as I can figure, the Old Man up there's got the big picture, and I reckon He'll keep it that way, knowin' us fools like He does."

Stem's voice trailed off as we both caught sight of Grace's wagon pulling out of the line in front of us. Before I could slow the team down, I felt a hand on my arm.

"It'll take her a while, but she'll be all right, Callie," Stem said, cutting his eyes toward Quinn as he rode up. "After a spell, you'll see, most folks get used ta it, death happenin', like it does out here."

"*I'll* never get used to it," I said hotly.

Out of the corner of my eye I saw Quinn move toward me as I pulled the wagon to a halt and we stepped down. Stem held him back.

"Sadly enough, honey," he replied, "you will."

Later—Found Grace by the fire, baking ginger cakes to celebrate Dane's birthday. When the makeshift table was covered with all that she had made, we gathered around it and sang. Somewhere in the song I felt Grace's hand find my own, and she held on, squeezing it tight. She was smiling, a thin, wavery smile that trembled on her lips.

Life, it seems, goes on.

Thursday, June 30

No rest this afternoon. We've traveled nearly twelve miles without stopping, not being able to find any good grass or water for the animals—the only water along this stretch being tainted. I've climbed into the wagon for a moment to write this—and to escape the wind. It's awful, blowing clouds of sand, so that I have to fight to walk. Dead cattle and oxen are hardly ever out of sight now—as well as the lame. It broke my heart to see Rose's forlorn face, staring after the poor animals that were left behind, too weary to go on.

I saw quite a few wagons that had turned back for one reason or another: no supplies, death, or just loss of hope. One man had painted "Pike's Peak and Busted" across his wagon. The suffering on his wife's face was heart-wrenching.

Later—Came eight more miles before we camped near the bluffs this evening. Captain Belshaw told us all to toss out anything that will lighten our loads before we cross this treacherous part of the river. He says it's better to lose a little now than a lot later. As hard as it was, the sorrow was shared with the trains ahead of us, their castoffs scattered far and near: clothes, baking ovens, tools. The most unsettling was a baby's cradle that was rocked to and fro by the wind. I almost imagined it was by a mother's hand.

Friday, July 1

Camped this evening near the junction of the north and south forks of the Platte River. There was a terrible thunderstorm that struck early and kept up with such fury that we were finally forced to pull over and camp. As night set in the storm finally cleared. I was attempting to make a fire to boil some coffee as I waited for Quinn and Jack to return from corralling the herd when I was surprised by Zach Koch. He was standing in the shadows near our wagon with another man, a foul-looking fellow I didn't recognize, who grinned at me before he took a long swallow from the flask that Zach had passed to him.

"She's purty, all right," the man said after he took a breath. "A piece of tail like that could take a man a long way. I kind of wish I'd seen her first."

The man guffawed at that, and Zach laughed, too, but it sounded weak, like he wasn't sure why he was laughing. "Well, you didn't," he said, his voice slurred with whiskey. "Ain't that right, Callie?"

Anger burned into my cheeks. If anyone back home had talked so filthy to me like they had, I wouldn't have thought twice about slapping their mouths. But the whiskey scared me. Maggie had told me more than once how purely evil her pa became after drinking, and I had never forgotten it. When Zach took a step toward me, I backed up.

"I was just going to help you with the kettle," he said, trying to sound hurt.

I think he would have done more if Quinn and Jack hadn't walked up at that moment.

"Zach," Quinn said. When he stepped into the light of the fire, I was surprised at the hard look on his face. "Is there something you were looking for?"

"Nothing personal, McGregor," he said. "I was just talking to Callie, here."

"Well, now," Quinn said softly. "That makes it *personal,* then."

"No harm intended," Zach said with forced cheer, but the bitter look he shot Quinn when he turned to walk away uneased me.

"It was just the liquor talking," I said, trying to convince myself as much as Quinn or Jack—but I don't think they believed it any more than I did. The look that had passed between them told me that much.

"I don't trust him," Jack said finally. "If he comes near you again, I want you to tell one of us, Callie."

I told him I would.

Saturday, July 2

Forded the South Platte today.

The crossing had gone better than expected, only a few things in the rear of the wagon getting wet. I'd happened to look back across the river to see how Jack was faring getting our cattle and pack animals across, when I spotted Zach Koch on the bank opposite of us. At first, I thought he was waiting for the rest of the cattle to clear out of the river before crossing, but a considerable amount of time had passed and he was still staring down into the rough, turbid water, his horse pawing at the bank. That's when I got to thinking maybe he feared the river.

Quinn had seen Zach, too. He glanced over at me with a question on his face, and we both turned to see if he would cross. Zach seemed uneasy—as if he had recognized something in that water.

To our amazement, he suddenly kicked his horse hard in the flanks, as if to force his own hand in the matter. The horse didn't disappoint him and charged through the rough current as if it were no more than a stream, pulling them both up on the other side, no worse for wear.

*　　*　　*

Camp is quiet tonight. Most everyone is exhausted. I say most, because I happened to walk past Jack's tent only a short while ago and saw quite a few of the men taking a turn at the jug. "Just for spiritual consolation," Jack informed me.

Sunday, July 3

How, in the space of one day, can everything change so abruptly?

Here between the South and the North Platte the soil is so sandy, the dry air so full of grit and alkali that Grace and I were forced to wear kerchiefs across our faces all afternoon so as not to breathe the foul stuff as we pushed the teams on. When Rose gave out to a fit of coughing, I quickly put her down in the wagon, giving her a piece of linen to hold over her nose and mouth. Oh, the trust in her eyes when she looked up at me! It took all I had not to cry. Grace must have seen the fear on my face when I stepped down from the wagon. "She'll be okay," she said, touching my arm. "Your sister's tougher than you think." When our eyes met, I saw a fierce hope on Grace's face—almost a challenge against me to say any different. I realized how important Rose making the journey had become to Grace, and I hugged her hard, so she couldn't see my tears.

Quinn and I sat together for a long while around the fire this evening. We didn't say much to each other at all, as worn down as we were. But then, just knowing he was with me was more than enough.

Monday, July 4

A sorry way to celebrate the Glorious Fourth. The heat has made everyone's tempers short. All day, through cracked lips parched from sun and sand, the men yelled at the oxen, prodding them away from the pools of alkali. Some had even taken to beating them to keep them from drinking the water that can kill them. A more pitiful sight, I can't imagine, than to see those poor faithful creatures look so hurt, so defeated as their weary bodies were goaded along—I was glad Rose had been in the wagon and didn't see it. Hardly anyone spoke as we trudged through the drifts of sand until at one point, Mrs. Iverson called out that she'd spotted a stream, and we all went running over, scooping the water with our hands, but our joy faded with the telltale stench of alkali.

"By God," Stem said, breaking the silence, "if ya weren't inclined ta believe in hell before, ya will now."

I think it was the only time that none of us women chastised him for his language.

Later—Found Bess Mercer out past camp this evening. She was sitting, rocking the baby. When she glanced up, I noticed for the first time the gauntness in her wind-burned face. "He ain't doin' so good, Callie," she whispered, looking down at her son. "My milk's all dried up." And then she started to cry. I took her back to her wagon and helped her the best

I could with warm compresses and made a sugar tit, adding what little milk I could eke out of our cow. Sadly enough, it didn't seem to matter; defeat in her eyes said that she was headed past hoping.

When she layed back against the mattress tick, I saw how dirty and ragged her clothes had become. Her son Ben crouched next to her, his face streaked with dust, his eyes hungry. She was giving up, I figured, and for some reason, something in me hardened. "We're all scared, Bess," I said. "But these little ones need you. How are you going to help them if you can't help yourself?"

Bess was quiet for a long time, then she said, "I shoulda fought this journey." She sat up, weary, but her eyes had become sharp, as if strength had come back to her.

I left her not long after that, glad at least that her baby had taken to the sugar tit, weak but steady. I said a silent prayer that we would *all* find the strength to make it through this journey west.

Oh, what I wouldn't give to be ignorant of this sorrow. I wish there were some way I could scrub away the memory of the pain I've seen and felt, as easily as I can the dirt from this trail.

Tuesday, July 5

It has rained!

I was packing our things away this morning when I heard the patter of water hit the canvas top, first a few drops, then more and more. Rose and I looked at each other and grinned, scrambling out of the wagon to join the rest of our wearied group. We laughed and hugged each other like we were all one big family. Quinn picked me up, twirling me round and round, his breath warm on my ear.

I ignored the glares that came: Della Koch and Mrs. Iverson, their lips pressed together hard. I didn't care who saw us, feeling alive and bold.

"Crazy as loons," Stem declared.

But he stood out there with us anyway, smiling as the thick drops of rain splashed down over the brim of his hat.

> *Approaching Court House Rock,*
> *Nebraska Territory*
> *In transit to California*
> *July 6, 1859*

Mrs. Maggie Todd
Blue Mills, Missouri

Dear Maggie,

Do you remember how we used to sit in the back of Mrs. Harper's classroom and dream of traveling to some far-off country? I'm beginning to think that dreams like that don't really die; they just get changed to fit where life takes you.

Well, the Platte isn't exactly Europe, but I'll tell you, it's breathtaking in its own fearful way. When we came in sight of the "Court House Rock" today, I thought of you and wished with all my heart you were here to see it. The huge group of grayish white rocks standing tall to meet the sky looked like they should've been placed somewhere more exotic, like Egypt or Rome. I'd said as much when one of the women of our train (the preacher's wife, no less) said it looked like the Tower of Babel to her. Jack winked at her and asked if she'd like a boost up. "Same ol' Jack," I can hear you laugh.

Rose is holding up, although the loss of her little friend, Lizzie, who accidentally shot herself by her father's own gun the other day, has cast a shadow over us all. Funny thing is, I think Rose accepts death a lot easier than I do. She acts as if going to heaven is as simple as moving to the next town. Why is it that children seem to be so much closer to God than the rest of us, Mag? I think it must be easier for them, maybe because they're not yet as jaded by this world as those of us who have been around longer. But you know Rose, another day holds a world of chance and she's right out there to reach for it. She's changed from the pale little girl we used to worry so over, and Jack and I are beginning to breathe a little easier.

I've changed, too, I guess. Oh, I suppose I look the same, save for a few more freckles across my nose and so much sand in my hair I wonder if I'll ever get it out. But I feel different, Maggie. I was real scared when we first started out. Homesick, too, I don't mind saying. But then that part of me I'd kept hidden since Mama died, it started to come alive again. It's almost like I've woken up from a long sleep and I can't help but look around me and wonder. There's a beauty to this rugged land that's hard to explain—it's like gaz-

ing at the vivid colors of a snake's back and having to remind yourself that there's danger lurking beneath that beauty. And believe me, if you don't keep mind of the danger along this trail, you're sure to get bit.

I've seen some bad things happen . . . but then, I've seen good, too. I've seen a strength in these women that would put a general to shame, and I've witnessed people risk their own skin for perfect strangers. I've made friends, too. Good friends. "Ah, and what of the Irishman?" Maggie asks. Well, he's a friend, too. Maybe more. But that's something I'll save for another time. . . .

> *Your wandering friend,*
> *Callie*

Thursday, July 7

Camped near a spring tonight. Everyone glad for the fresh water. Have a good view of the notorious Chimney Rock—eerie and beckoning at the same time with its long spindly arm of stone that rises high from the naked plains. Hard to imagine, but Stem says in his day it stood one hundred feet higher. I wish I could see it up close.

Later—Sometimes I wonder if Quinn knows my mind better than I do.

He came to me late this evening as I was packing

up the supplies. I didn't see him at first, as dark as it was, but I *felt* him. Even before he drew out of the night, stepping into the light from the campfire, I had known. He took the box I had been carrying and set it to one side. "Come with me," he said, holding out his hand. "There's something I want you to see."

We walked and walked until all noise faded from my ears: the contented snorts of the animals over the fresh stream, their bellies washed clean from the brackish water; thuds of chips being tossed into dwindling fires; even the horrible hum of the mosquitoes had been driven out, until all that remained was the wind.

The silence out there was different from the night-quiet of home, deeper, as if it could soak up your restless thoughts without much effort. I reveled in it, feeling like Quinn and I had become a part of the plains as we stood together on a ragged outcropping of rocks. "Look there," he said all of a sudden, his voice hushed but pleased. A shooting star stretched across the black sky, and I stared in wonder as its path arched over Chimney Rock, painting the stone with yellow and crimson, then deep blues and purples until it faded and dipped to the ground. Quinn's hand tightened over mine, and I felt let down in a way, wishing it had lasted just a little longer.

"Saw them fall while I was out guarding the cattle," Quinn said. "That's why I came for you."

"Why does it always seem that the things that take our breath away are only here for a moment?" I asked. "Why not longer?"

He didn't answer me right off, his face thoughtful. Then he said, "Maybe if these things were around all of the time, they wouldn't hold the same magic. It's a fickle breed we are, Callie."

I'd opened my mouth to deny it, but I found I couldn't. What he said had the ring of truth, and it sobered me. Quinn must have sensed the change in my mood, because he sat down, pulling me with him to the sandy ground, and when he wrapped his arms around me, it took all that I had not to sigh. More and more I had begun to yearn for those arms—and the feeling of safety within them.

"There are two rules that I live by, Callie. The first," he whispered in my ear, "is to grab each moment when it comes."

He pulled me close, and I held on to him, never before feeling so alive as he slipped his hand through my hair and pulled it loose from the pins. The breeze off of the stream was cool, crisp, and felt good against my parched skin.

Then he kissed me, and I felt something inside of me break loose and open up to him, and I kissed him back, meeting him with the same urgency that hinged on desperation. *Our* moment, I'd thought, one that could fade away into nothing . . . or it could mean everything. With all that I had in me I wanted it to go on, to never stop, but after a while Quinn sat back, telling me we had to return before anyone missed us.

I'd felt cheated, and the sound of his voice made me think he felt the same, so I reached for him again, and it didn't feel shameful or bad, just natural, us being like that. When he kissed me again, it was hard, and the force of it stayed on my lips even after he pulled away.

"What was the second rule?" I asked when he helped me to my feet. He rubbed his thumb across my lips then, a smile tugging at the corner of his mouth. "The second rule," he said, "is to never forget."

Friday, July 8

Stem galloped into camp this morning as we were packing up. He came to tell us that several of the people in the party traveling ahead of us had taken sick with the cholera. He said that one woman had died already and her husband is very near death himself. He said that they are planning to leave him, that the men of the company have commenced digging the poor fellow's grave right in front of him so as not to lose time.

"How far ahead of us?" Captain Belshaw asked then, wiping the sweat from his face.

"By wagon, a half day at the most," Stem replied. "But, they'll be pullin' out soon, anyhow. Grave's almost dug."

"Single-minded bastards," Quinn said suddenly, and I watched him stalk over to his horse and mount up. "Have one of the men see to my wagon," he called to Stem. When he looked my way, I saw my own feelings of horror and disbelief mirrored in his eyes. He didn't say a word to me as he turned his horse toward the trail ahead. He didn't have to.

I knew. I knew that he was going after that sick man just as sure as I knew the sun would shine again on another day. As I stood there watching him ride off, I suddenly felt as if everything had gone still, becoming sharp and vivid: the blue canopy of the sky cut up by the tall, jagged bluffs, the caw of the crow overhead, even the sounds in camp, laughter, a woman softly crying—was it Bess Mercer? Quinn glanced back at me once, and I recognized the look in his eyes, a look that wanted to make promises but knew better than to.

When he finally faded out of sight, I couldn't help remembering the night before and the way he kissed me, and the sound of his voice when he told me to never forget. Rose had slipped up beside me then and placed her hand in mine, and when I looked down at her, her smile was warm and comforting, reminding me of Mama. At that moment I wanted nothing more than to lay my head down on her shoulder and cry. Instead, we headed to our wagon to pack away what was left from breakfast. I saw Jack standing near the wagon, one oxen yoked while he pinned the bow and spoke to its teammate. He looked worn out, his smile more like a grimace when Rose walked over to him.

How much will this trail take from us?—Quinn, always trying to make up for the past that haunts him; Jack, with dreams broken by Pa's death; me with my fears. How much more?

Later—Quinn never showed up for dinner this evening. I waited until I couldn't bear it any longer, then I went out to the edge of camp and stared hard into the dark, as if the effort could make him appear. Jack strolled up not long after and stood by me, not saying anything for a while as he looked off across to the bluffs, whose shadows loomed tall against the night sky. "I'm goin' to find him, Callie," he told me finally. "I don't guess either of us will sleep much until I do."

Saturday, July 9

Morning—Still no word from Quinn or Jack. Waiting. Why does it seem like I'm always waiting? Every time I hear the sound of a rider, I find myself watching and hoping. And when it's not them, the ugly voice inside of me starts in. *They should have been back by now,* it whispers. *Maybe he's dead. . . .*

I just looked up from penning this to find Zach Koch watching me closely, like he was figuring out what I was thinking. Then he smiled real big at me, like he hoped the worst was true. Why . . .

The captain has called for us to move out. There's an uneasiness amongst the train knowing we'll be coming upon the campsite of that poor man. I'm praying we'll find Jack and Quinn well. More later.

Spotted the red flag warning us all against the cholera. Camped a good distance away. Waiting.

Later—I had been sitting in the wagon when I heard the pound of horses' hooves coming near this evening. Not wanting to take hope too soon, I stayed where I was until I heard someone yell, "Jack!" then scrambled out just in time to see Jack ride up. When his eyes met mine I saw the stark fear in their depths; I'd felt like running.

Without dismounting, Jack said that the man Quinn was tending was as near death as he'd ever seen. The picture he painted was grim. He said the man had been left with nothing but a bedroll; the party he'd been traveling with had burned everything he owned, trying to stamp out the plague. "If you could've seen the old guy . . ." Jack rubbed his hand over his face, paler than I'd ever seen him. "I didn't go near him. McGregor wouldn't allow it. He had the man wrapped in his saddle blanket tryin' to force some water down him, workin' on him somethin' fierce. He looked up only long enough to tell me to leave him there."

I felt as if someone had taken the air from me. When I looked around, I was surprised to see that a crowd had gathered around us. I saw the preacher move forward then, Della following close behind. "As much as it pains me to say," he began, "I think it's for the best that we leave him where he is. There's lives at risk here. Priceless lives of women and children. . . ."

"Priceless ain't free," Stem cut in. "Reckon I'd favor McGregor's God ta yers, Preacher, if ever I was in trouble."

Captain Belshaw was just here. He came with a few other men to tell Jack that the wagons would be moving out in the morning regardless. When he took his hat off, I noticed what little hair he had was salted around the edges, and it made me think how much the trail had aged us all. He told Jack then that it was important that he saw their way of thinking. Jack said, "Well, there's two ways of lookin' at important . . . yours and mine. I believe I'll wait a spell." When the men faded off, Jack turned to me and said, "I want you and Rose to go on with them."

I'd felt an awful tightness in my chest. I would be

waiting again . . . as always. "Let me stay," I told Jack, surprising even myself.

Jack studied me for a moment, like he was seeing me for the first time. "See if Grace can manage Rose; tell her we'll meet at Fort Laramie," he said. "I'll talk to Dane about seein' to our stock. Though we best keep one of the cows. I'll get McGregor's rig."

"You won't regret it," I said.

"I probably will," he said, and frowned at me before he turned to walk away. "You're as fool-headed as McGregor. It's no wonder the two of you belong together."

He can call me a fool all he wants. All I know is that this is the first time in a long while I feel like I've made the right decision.

Sunday, July 10

I was so sure last night, but a flicker of doubt has run through me, seeing Rose ride off in Grace's wagon. Such a brave little soul. Her only thought, as I was packing some of her things early this morning, had been for Quinn. "McGregor, he'll lick that cholery, won't he?" she'd asked, her sweet face so earnest. When I told her I thought so, she'd smiled, satisfied, and walked on to Grace's wagon without so much as a whimper. I tried to take heart in that and forced myself to smile and wave as the wagons rolled out.

When I'd glanced back, I saw Jack's long, lean

frame, looking so much like Pa's, hunched over, cleaning sand out of our steer's hoof. I saw him smile and wave to Rose then. But then he turned away and reached for a bucket of tar and slowly began to fill the cracks in the worn hoof.

Later—Jack told me tonight that he thinks he'd be better fit to tend to Quinn should he show up sick. "The cholera is ugly, Callie," he said, like he'd thought the whole thing over. "Ain't somethin' you can put a splint on and be done with. Flux, muscle cramps . . . Some get cold and sweat all at once. Gotta work to keep the water down, keep them warm. Sometimes all the work ain't enough . . ." His voice trailed off, and he looked down at the hat in his hands, worrying the brim of it. He didn't say anything for a while, but I knew he was thinking of us losing Pa not so long ago and maybe wondering if one of us would be next.

Monday, July 11

Later—Have only a moment to write. Quinn is back—but so sick.

It was the dun's nicker that drew me out of bed just before dawn. When I peered out of the wagon and saw Quinn's body draped limply over his horse, my first thought was that he was dead. Not thinking, I had run to him. I was so relieved to find him alive that it wasn't until I'd turned and saw Jack standing by our wagon that it dawned on me what I had done. I can still see Jack's face—so grim, so filled with worry. "Try to get him to his wagon, Callie," he said quietly, but I hadn't missed the terror his voice held.

Desperation seemed to take over, blotting out my fears for my own well-being, and I somehow managed to get him to his wagon and into bed.

I've been nursing him the best I can, trying to coax liquid into him, but he hasn't been able to hold it down long. The cramps grip him so hard that I fear he'll soon be drained of whatever strength he has left. When he opens his eyes, he stares but doesn't really see me.

I have tried to tell myself that a man of his strength, of his size couldn't be taken so easily. Yet when I look at him, he seems just a shell of the man that rode away from me only three days ago.

This sickness is so cruel. What if . . . No, I won't even think it.

When I stepped out of Quinn's wagon earlier, I saw a pile of supplies Jack must have left for me and went to gather them. Even in the dim light I could see Jack sitting by the fire a short distance off. He'd stood when he saw me and walked as close to me as safety would allow. "Callie," he said, then stood there looking uncomfortable, "you take care of yourself, you hear?"

I saw the frustration on his face as he tried to find the words he wanted to say, and it touched my heart. "I love you, too, Jack," I said.

Tuesday, July 12

Quinn isn't much better this morning, most of the time talking out of his head—can't make sense of what he's trying to say. I tried to get some tea into him, but his stomach heaved, and he started retching again so hard it scared me. Cramps and muscle spasms came again—worse. Massaged his legs and arms, talking to him, hoping that he can hear me somehow.

The mustard plaster seems to be helping his stomach cramps. Jack made some broth and left it at the edge of the clearing for me. Quinn has kept it down, and I feel it's a good sign.

Later—I may have spoken too soon. Just now got Quinn back to sleep. He woke up about an hour ago, thrashing around. He rose up at one point and startled me when he spoke. ". . . not the banshee, Patrick," he whispered with force, " 'tis the wind. We'll be riding again soon, I promise you." His sad eyes stared past me for a moment before he collapsed against the mattress tick, his face drawn by memories that seemed to stalk him as sure as the cholera. As the night wore on, his skin became cold, covered in sweat. When I took his shirt off again to sponge him with warm water, I noticed a small gold cross that lay on his chest. I had barely touched it when Quinn suddenly sat up and looked at me, his pale blue eyes strangely alert and filled with pain. "No!" he rasped and grabbed the chain in his hands. He doubled over in pain as the spasms in his stomach and legs came again, and I quickly set about working his rigid muscles, rubbing and rubbing until my hands and arms ached. I talked to him, soothing him until some of the tension left his face and he collapsed once more.

He seems to be resting easier. But seeing the tight hold he still has on his cross unnerves me—almost like a death grip.

Doubts creeping in. Jack's words haunt me tonight: *"Sometimes all the work ain't enough."*

Oh, please, dear Lord, spare him.

Wednesday, July 13

Early—I was surprised to find Quinn half awake this morning. His bleary eyes tried to focus when I leaned over him to check the plaster, and I saw his brows drag together, as if he was trying to figure out who I was. "Callie?" he said after a while, and I started to cry. When I moved closer, his arm snaked out and pulled me to him and he pressed my head to his chest, and I heard him sigh with relief. "I wasn't sure if you were real," he said, then passed out.

Later—I was standing outside the wagon, gathering up the berries and fresh water Jack had brought, when I heard the awfulest commotion, then Quinn's thick accent. "Glory be to God!" he roared all of a sudden, and I jumped near out of my skin. "Whoever 'tis stuck this bandage to my body take it away. It stinks to heaven and back!"

Jack and I grinned like fools at each other across the way. "I think he's on the mend," Jack said, and I laughed. Quinn's bellows shook the silence.

Have just now got the old bear off to sleep—only *after* I was forced to remove the plaster.

The worst of the sickness seems to be over and I'm not showing any of the symptoms. Quinn was able to take some broth and a few of the berries. Though I couldn't prove it, he appeared to *enjoy* me waiting on him. He still looks haggard, his face thinner and darkened by stubble, but the familiar light in those pale eyes is back. He told me I was "foolish" for risking my own health and mumbled something about "as stubborn as a mule" before he dozed off—but he held on to my hand nearly the whole time he slept.

Thursday, July 14

Quinn and I had dinner out by the fire this evening, as he was feeling well enough to sit up. We were having a good time of it until I asked Quinn about Patrick. Here, all along I'd thought it was the man he nursed with the cholera. How was I supposed to know Patrick was his *brother*?

At first, I thought he just didn't feel well, the way he closed his eyes and leaned his head back. But then he sighed and said, "He was my brother, Callie—a fine one at that."

The pain on his face was so real that I had to look away. Mama had always said that the hardships in life could either kill a body or make them stronger. But why did it seem that for some the hardships never ended? I wanted Quinn to tell me everything. Yet, I didn't know if I could endure it. Losing Mama and Pa and my fears for Rose welled up in me.

"What was he like?" I asked finally and saw his expression turn bittersweet.

"Patrick was full of mischief at times," he said, "a bit like Jack, I'm thinking. He took our folks' death as hard as I did, just showed it different. We stayed in Pittsburgh for a while, but then we got word our uncle Tommy had died before working his claim in Rich Bar. Patrick, he was the first to saddle up for California. He was convinced we could make a go of it. He was so full of dreams. Those dreams are now mine."

When Quinn grew silent, I'd reached out for his hand, hoping to comfort him somehow. His eyes met mine and when he finally did speak, his voice was husky with emotion.

"Just before we reached Independence, Patrick was bitten by a cottonmouth," he said. "I dosed him with hartshorn, and he seemed to be taking to it. I only turned away for a moment, just to see to the horses. When I got to Patrick, I saw him sitting up just where I'd left him . . . but as I got closer I noticed he was holding his body funny. 'Patrick,' I said, nearly shouting, but he didn't answer . . . and then I saw his face.

I heard myself screaming then, and I remember thinking, it couldn't be me screaming, because I couldn't *breathe.*

"I cursed God, Callie, and anyone else that would hear me. Patrick had beat the sickness. He was supposed to have a second chance. I ran like the devil knew my name after I buried him. I guess sometimes I wished I had died, too."

Quinn reached under the bandanna on his neck then and produced the gold cross and chain that he'd been so protective of. "It was our ma's," he said. "After she'd died, Patrick and I would share it between us; the one who was in trouble or sick or making a journey alone would wear it. The night he died, Patrick had taken it off of his neck. I found it in his outstretched hand. It was as if he was saying, 'It's your journey now.'" Quinn looked across the fire at me. "Who was it that said, 'The tragedy of life is what dies inside of a man while he lives'? Something had died inside of me after that, Callie . . . until I met you."

A silence fell between us then, an easy silence, from the comfort of knowing that we were together—both of us had been alone with our fears for so long.

"None of us know what road fate will take us down," Quinn whispered, leaning forward to brush my hair back from my forehead, his large callused hands so tender it brought tears to my eyes. "I just pray that you'll be with me."

The fire is all but gone now, not much light to write by. But still, I remain out here listening to the wind . . . and to my own heart. Where has this man come from, so strong, so filled with goodness? I'm not so sure what life has in store for me anymore—maybe I've never been sure. But one thing I do know is that come what may, I'll count myself lucky to have known Quinn McGregor.

Friday, July 15

I burned the wagon and all of Quinn's clothing and bedding.

Still a little weak, Quinn leaned on me while we watched the fire grow tall, and I felt a grim sort of satisfaction seeing the last reminders of his brush with death turn to ash. Ah, and the emotion when we looked at each other; something deeper and stronger forged between us at that moment—triumph. How sweet it felt for once to have the upper hand in the midst of all of this uncertainty!

When the flames died down, we headed in the direction of Jack's camp. Tired as we were, there was an eagerness to get back to normal.

Jack, who looked a little haggard himself, saw us and rose slowly from his fire. He stared at our fresh-scrubbed faces and clean clothes, as if he couldn't exactly believe we were really there. For a moment we'd all stood, staring at each other, as if one was as surprised as the next that it was finally over.

"Well, I would've dressed better if I knew I was goin' to have company," Jack said finally, a grin breaking over his face, and we all laughed.

Saturday, July 16

On the move again, headed for Fort Laramie.

Came to a beautiful valley surrounded by tall ragged bluffs, where we camped early, as Quinn wasn't yet up to a full day of travel—although a person would be hard-pressed to get him to admit it.

It wasn't long after we'd settled in that a group of Sioux appeared—so different from their Pawnee brothers—being handsome and not inclined to beg or steal. They do, however, like to trade and are good at driving a hard bargain. Jack lost no time haggling over a fine beaded knife sheath one of the braves was wearing, trading his old watch for it while I traded for some moccasins for Rose and me.

One very large fellow sat with Jack and Quinn for quite a while, trying to teach them the language. He seemed pleased that they tried so hard. Then he offered to trade them three of his ponies for *me*. Jack grinned and told him he wouldn't feel right, being that the fellow had never done anything to him. Quinn laughed so hard I was sure he was going to get sick, and I tried my best to look fierce. I doubt the Indians understood, but those Sioux braves laughed and carried on anyway, slapping Jack on the back before they mounted their ponies again.

They rode away not long after, a blur of feathers and copper skin and sleek horseflesh that blended and moved together as one over hills dotted with cedar and pine—not reckless, just easy, like they were born to it.

Later—Quinn and I stayed out by the fire for a while after Jack turned in. In the distance we could hear the low chant of a brave begin in song. A sound that seemed to rise and fall with the wind, so beautiful and haunting that I became caught up in it, forgetting where I was for a little while. When I turned to say something to Quinn, he appeared to be asleep, but when I leaned forward to shake him, he pulled me into his arms, catching me by surprise. I laughed, a startled kind of laugh, and Quinn brushed a loose strand of hair back from my face and said, "If I could make you laugh more often, I might die a happy man." I told him not to think of dying, and he smiled and said, " 'Tis the furthest thing from my mind." Then he kissed me, a slow lingering kiss that promised more. I'm almost ashamed to admit it was Quinn who finally pulled away, even if it was reluctantly. I . . . It's so hard to put into words what I feel tonight— but maybe that's for the best.

Sunday, July 17

The Sioux were waiting by the side of the trail as we rolled out of camp this morning. At first we worried that they, like the Pawnee, had come back to rob us, but we soon found out through a new addition in their group (who spoke a little English) that they had come to bid us good-bye. He told us that the braves were sorry to see us go—that they had parted ways with other "whites they did not regret so much."

There was an old Sioux man I noticed, however, that chose to remain atop his horse up on the bluffs above us. His dark hair, streaked with white, hung loose past his shoulders, and the way he held himself was almost dignified in spite of his scrawniness. He watched us for a while, his expression unreadable. Then I saw him look behind us to the distance, and when I followed his gaze I recognized the faint glimmer of white canvas weaving slowly toward us—quite a large wagon company, from the look of it. When I glanced back at the old man, I saw him turn away from the sight. He seemed sad.

Distance is deceiving. It has taken us nearly all day to get through the valley. We drove over the last hill into another valley, where we are now camped near a spring. Jack shot two sage hens, and I made a stew with them. Jack says we are only a short day's drive from Fort Laramie. I've been worried that the train has moved on without us, but Jack says that the Sioux told him of wagons being held up at the fort because of the river being too high. I pray it's true.

I can't wait to see Rose. I've missed her something awful.

Later—They talked me into playing cards with the two of them this evening—something I never thought I would do. Probably shouldn't again—I was *good* at it. I can see now why Jack is so taken with it. Quinn was genuinely impressed with the speed at which I picked up the game. "Chancy thing, playing with you Wades," he said, and Jack and I laughed.

Such a good night tonight. With the laughter so fresh on my mind, I can't help but wish that we could be like this always—free with our laughter and our feelings—not hampered by worries about what some might deem unladylike.

Monday, July 18

It was the closest thing to a homecoming, seeing Rose, Grace, and Stem standing at the edge of camp as we pulled into the wagon-gathering spot at Laramie's Fork this evening. When Rose saw me, she came running. I knelt down and opened my arms to her, and we hugged each other hard. I couldn't help touching her hair and face, just to make sure she was real. And the look in her eyes when Quinn walked up! She smiled big and said, "You licked that cholery just like I said you would, didn't you, McGregor?" and then laughed with delight when he scooped her up into his arms. I can't describe how wonderful it was to hear that laugh!

Everyone embraced each other like long-lost kin— even Stem, who generally kept to himself at such times. He shook Quinn's and Jack's hands so hard I thought for sure he'd lose his balance. He struck up a tune with his fiddle not long after we got settled around a fire, and Grace sang along. We had a good time of it . . . even in spite of Della Koch commenting loud enough for us all to hear that "decent folks" couldn't get a good night's rest with all the noise.

Part Four

Fort Laramie,
Wyoming Territory,
To the South Pass,
Rocky Mountains

*"The heart is happiest when it beats
for others."*
                                    —Amanda Wade

Tuesday, July 19
Fort Laramie

Forded the Laramie River this morning to visit the fort—more Indians than any of us witnessed before in one place—enough to keep Mrs. Iverson quiet as we were floated across in Sioux skiffs. Grace made me laugh when I shouldn't have. Inclining her head Mrs. Iverson's way she said, "Last time I saw knuckles that white was on a two-bit cardsharp whose faith didn't quite match his hand."

Mrs. Iverson's back went all stiff, and Della Koch looked ready to say something—probably would have if we hadn't come to the other bank.

With the fort before us, all talk stopped. There was the oddest combination of wildness and civilization any of us had ever seen spread behind those adobe walls: fine frame buildings that looked odd standing in the middle of nowhere; soldiers lounging, eager emigrants, gaunt in their brown homespun; a few scraggly trappers in front of the post sutler haggling with a brave who sat, regal as could be, on what looked like an old nail keg next to the door. They looked up quick when I walked past them and into the sutler—the brave especially—which is why I didn't see Zach Koch until I'd nearly run full into him in the store.

"Well, lookie here," he said, pleased, grabbing and holding on to my arms even though I tried to pull away. "And I didn't even have to wait in line." I heard a few of the men in the room snicker at that, and once my eyes had adjusted to the light, I saw the trader behind the counter was giving me a rotted grin. I'd no more than turned back to see where Grace was when Quinn came through the door.

"I guess you don't have anything better to do than be a nuisance," he said, and even though his face was still a little drawn from the sickness, the look in his eyes was enough to put Zach back on his heels some.

"At least I don't have to get sick to find my way into a lady's heart," Zach said, but he inched back just the same.

"Aye, you'd just bully your way in."

"Stop it," I said, mad, but not really at Quinn. Mad more at the fact that the rest of the men in the store were like Zach, dirtying things with a word or a look. I'd stepped outside then, walking fast once I spotted Grace standing outside of the post office. But then Quinn was there beside me, matching my stride.

"I was only trying to help," he said.

"You should be resting," I said, lowering my voice when I noticed Della Koch and Mrs. Iverson watching us with keen interest. I saw Grace grin, and Quinn whispered back to me: "Did you think I'd leave you in there alone?"—which sounded more like: "Did ya think I'd lave ye in there awlone?"

It was then that I'd nearly smiled. It was easy to tell when Quinn got riled, for his accent got hard as the head of a nail. But I knew better than to let him see me laugh, lest he got it in his head he could boss me.

"What are you trying to do?" I snapped. "Get sick

again?" The way he stared into my eyes gave me a start, deep and searching.

Then he smiled. "A means to an end," he said. "I could use some more nursing."

As usual, he didn't wait for an answer but walked off toward the bank of the river, leaving me behind blanketed in Grace's laughter and a good dose of my own imagination.

Later—Captain Belshaw says the North Platte has dropped enough to ford in the morning. I put Rose down early this evening, she's a little worn. Quinn, Jack, and I sat together and listened to the evening roll call at the fort. Heard the sound of a bugle. I think it made us all homesick in a way I can't quite explain.

Wednesday, July 20
Black Hills

Started early, weather very hot. Traveled close to twelve miles before we nooned near Warm Springs. Hard travel after leaving the springs, winding among rocks and cliffs. Crossed Bitter Cotton Wood Creek more than a few times before we finally camped near it. Quinn and I had a chance to view Laramie Peak in the distance as the sun set. I gathered a handful of large white flowers that looked like tulips for Rose, but she was already asleep by the time we got back to camp.

Thursday, July 21

Rode horseback ahead of the train with Quinn this morning for the first time since he took sick, traveling over steep hills and winding trail, passing more cast-offs: furniture, tools, broken-down crates and trunks that'd been thrown from the wagons as they climbed into the mountains. And graves . . . two of which some thoughtless trail doctor had marked with his name and fee. It all made me feel miserable. I told Stem, who had been ranging ahead, as much when he passed us on the way to see Captain Belshaw. He smiled and said, "Ya'll be changin' yer tune soon enough."

It was only an hour later that we pulled into the valley to rest, and the view nearly took my breath away: wide open and cupped with ridges of yellow pine that seemed to climb the sky, and a clear stream that ran through it, begging you to drink from it. When we turned the horses loose to feed, I looked at Quinn and saw that he felt it, too, felt the raw beauty of it, the wildness, and I couldn't help thinking how well he fit the land. Rose came running over then, and I watched him scoop her up onto his shoulders, heard their laughter, and for a moment, I closed my eyes and named it California, and there were no more miles or sickness or uncertainty. For a moment we were home.

I noticed, as we pulled out onto the trail once more,

I wasn't the only one who looked back to the valley with longing.

I'm worried about Rose. When we came into camp, I asked Jack where she was and he told me she had decided to take a nap, that she had walked a good part of the morning and was feeling a little peaked.

When I checked on her I felt uneasy; she looked more than tired. The circles under her eyes were darker than I'd ever seen. Why haven't I noticed it before?

I tried to talk to Jack about Rose, but he wouldn't hear any of it. "She's just tired is all," he said, the look in his eyes almost daring me to say any different. He left without another word to go check the cattle.

Later—The doctor that Stem found was from the company in front of us. Dr. Tilly, the very name, if I'm not mistaken, that was on those grave markers. A true whiskey-soak if I ever saw one, with a paunch and wide girth that made it difficult to move inside of the wagon as he checked Rose over. The only good thing about him I noticed was that his hands weren't as dirty as the rest of him.

Rose, of course, was indignant about the whole thing, saying she was fine. But the doctor had a different opinion.

"Consumptive," he'd declared when he left the wagon and looked down his nose at me as if I was foolish, as if I didn't know my own sister was sick. "It's the alkali in the air, it irritates the lungs," he said. "She should start to feel better as the altitude rises. Besides that, she has about a half a chance of surviving it." Watching him leave, I felt as if all of the blood had rushed out of me. No one had ever spoke of the chance she *wouldn't* survive before.

I checked on Rose again after he left. When I saw her eyes flutter open, I put on my best face and asked how she was feeling. She smiled sweetly.

"Just tired is all," she said.

"Don't you worry, Rose, we'll beat this together," I said, but she had already drifted off to sleep.

I'd never felt so horribly alone before as I did watching her then, her pain-spent body so frail. I scrambled out of the wagon, sick with fear, and ran past where Quinn waited for me, past Jack and Stem. I didn't stop until I was far from camp. Finally, coming over a rise, I sank down in the tall grass, alone—or so I thought until I saw Quinn brushing through the grass toward me. When he sat down next to me and put his arms around my shoulders, I started to cry.

"I'm so afraid for Rose," I told him. "I'm so scared she's going to die. I've tried so hard, and now I'm not sure it's been enough."

"You've done more than your share, Callie," he told me. "You'll see, she's going to be just fine." He sounded so sure of everything, so confident that I clung to him. When he kissed me softly, I felt a little of the hurt fade and I found myself wanting more, willing everything else away but Quinn and me. His strength was what I longed for. What I *needed*, and for once I didn't want to think about right or wrong.

It was when I reached for him that he told me he loved me. He said it so simply, so easily . . . and then he pulled me against him as his mouth pressed harder into mine. Even in my inexperience I felt a fire building between us and the assurance, after all these months, of knowing that he wanted me. And I wanted him. More than anything, I wanted the moment to store away, free of guilt or regret.

When we fell back against the grass, I saw a rawness about him that I hadn't ever seen before, a pure look of need and want, but there was hesitation, too. I pulled him to me and every muscle in his body seemed to tense. "We shouldn't," he said, and I saw the war that raged within him.

"I need you," I told him.

"And what of the consequences?" he said softly.

In answer, I wrapped my arms around his neck, pulling him closer still. God forgive me, but I didn't want to think of consequences, of what had happened or what would. His eyes met mine, and I felt as if he were searching for the answers in me. Whatever he saw seemed to sway him, and he began to slowly unbutton my dress. As long as I live I will always remember the feeling of abandon that swept over me when he looked into my eyes—wild and powerful, like a force of nature. Then his body settled over mine and the grass rustled around us. And when the pain came, I welcomed it. I welcomed it all: the heat, the freedom, the pull of being brought to the brink of another's soul until everything else faded away.

When it was over, I layed in the cover of the grass, watching the breeze sway the tall stalks around us. Off in the distance the faint sound of camp life barged in, and I felt myself being torn between staying and going to Rose.

Rose needed me, and in my heart I knew it would be that way until she was well again. Until we had a home again. Quinn had been staring into the dimming blue of the sky, his gaze focused on nothing in particular, when he turned to me and our eyes met. His expression was so pure, so full of love that I couldn't have fought my heart had I wanted to. "Where have you been all my life?" I asked.

He didn't say anything at first, just raised up on one arm, his pale eyes boring into mine once more. A single tear stung my skin, and he reached out and brushed it from my cheek. Sun creases at his eyes crinkled and a faint smile stole across his mouth.

"Looking for you," he answered.

Even though we made sure to return to camp separately, I still felt as if all eyes were upon me as I started dinner. Quinn watched me between spoonfuls of food, sitting across the fire, and I'm not sure if I imagined it, but I felt like Stem was watching us both real close. Later I caught Jack staring at me like he'd never seen me before, and when his eyes met mine, he quickly turned back to his meal, a sheepish look on his face. Flustered, I finally took to our wagon and sat with Rose until she fell back asleep.

I pray that no one ever finds this journal—but I can't bear *not* to write. How circumstances change a person. Had I been back in Independence, none of this would've ever happened, but I won't say I regret what we did, because I don't.

"What of the consequences?" Quinn's words came back to haunt me this evening, and in some ways I'm definitely glad that I brushed my fears aside. In other ways I wonder if I'm a fool . . . or worse, mad.

It wasn't madness that spurred me to do what I did, though. It was the hunger to feel alive again, to know, at least, if there's no guarantees for the future, that we will have a past.

" 'Tis only the beginning," Quinn had said to me when we parted.

I didn't have the strength to tell him any different.

Friday, July 22

Noon—stopped to rest along Big Timber Creek. I drove the team all morning while Rose rode in the wagon—she says I'm "coddling" her, making her rest all the time. I'm *determined* she's going to get well is what I am. Quinn and Jack just headed out to tend the stock, thank goodness. I need time to think.

Camped in a pretty place this evening, mountains off to the left, the North Platte to the right stretching as far as the eye can see. Shortly after dinner Quinn walked with me down to the stream when I went to fetch some water. I wanted to tell him then how torn I felt between him and Rose, how I felt spread thin, worrying over giving too little to each of them, but then he kissed me and those reasons didn't seem to matter. Just one more time I told myself, and fool that I am, allowed him to pull me down into the soft mossy bank next to him.

Saturday, July 23

Quinn has just left, angry. Why does it have to be all or nothing with him?

"Let's get married, Callie," he'd said, just like that,

and I'd stood, stock-still, feeling the heat of the camp-fire lick at my shoes but unable to move all the same. It wasn't that I hadn't expected it—I guess I had. I just wasn't sure what to say or how to tell him I needed time.

"Let's wait," I told him finally.

"For Godsake, why?" he said. "I thought you felt the same as I do. You can't tell me you don't."

"I do . . ." I said, but when I saw the hurt on his face, it seemed everything else I'd wanted to say left me. I'd wanted to tell him I was afraid to hope for too much out here, that marriage meant a future, meant that you had faith in tomorrow. I wanted to tell him I was afraid that anything I tried to hold on to would be taken away. "Wait," was all I knew to say.

"For what?" Quinn thundered then, baffled. "Good God, Callie, none of us knows what the future holds."

"That's what I'm trying to say!" I shouted back. "Don't you see? There's Rose—"

"Don't," Quinn warned, and I could see the anger in his eyes. "Don't bring Rose into this. This is between us, you and me."

"But it's not just you and me, though," I said.

"What are you saying?" Quinn said. "That we will never marry? And what good will that be for Rose when you've bittered yourself to life and she begins to see the blame of it in your eyes?"

"I'd never blame Rose!" I shouted.

"Maybe you're right, maybe you won't blame her," Quinn said, looking sad. "I hope to hell you won't. But there will come a time when she'll blame herself. Your sister may be sick, Callie, but it's you that's to be pitied. You're so afraid of death you refuse to take a chance on life."

I saw the pain in his eyes, heard the hollowness in his voice before he walked away, reminding me of that first day we met. And I knew that he had gone back somewhere within himself, and I hated myself, knowing I was the cause of it.

For a moment, I stood there and listened for his footsteps in the dark, almost hoping he'd turn back around. But it was only the wind that greeted me. I thought of running after him, but I didn't. Instead, I forced my feet in the direction of the wagon and slowly climbed inside. I'm laying on my bed making this entry. Sleep doesn't come easy tonight. Does *anything?*

Woke up tonight hearing the ragged sobs of a woman. It wasn't until I touched my own face, streaked with tears, that I realized the cries were my own.

Sunday, July 24

This morning came overcast. The clouds that hung low over the ridges seemed to fit my mood. Very steep going most of the day, climbing higher into the mountains. Nooned at Red Bank Creek, then camped early, after going on only ten miles more—one of the wheels on the Pratts' wagon splintered while traveling over a jagged outcropping of rock. Oh, why am I writing this anyway?

Monday, July 25

Made Rose as comfortable as possible in the back of the wagon before we started off again, as I heard the road was rough ahead. After traveling ten miles over nothing but a trail of broken rock, broken knobs, and ravines, I can vouch for it. Finally camped near a warm spring, and although my body rebelled a bit, I set about washing our clothes, thankful for the distraction—thankful for anything that will take these restless thoughts from me, even if it's only for a while.

Tuesday, July 26

We stopped late this evening. Men are still up; talk being on crossing the North Platte once again. Rumor is that the water is too deep for fording, and we will all have to improvise at ferrying. Once we get a little closer, the men will build rafts. At least there's still plenty of wood to be had.

Later—Rose asked me why Quinn hasn't been around. How in the world can I explain my actions to her when I don't understand them myself?

Wednesday, July 27

Zach suddenly appeared while I was alone at the river this evening filling our water casks. I thought at first he was up to no good, but he walked on past where I stood, quickly dipped his canteen in the water, and left with only a casual smile my way.

Later—Camped early. No travel tomorrow, no rest either. The men have set about gathering wood to build the rafts, the unpacking goes to us women. So weary, and there seems no end in sight to our struggles.

Thursday, July 28

Mama always used to say that a crooked tree'd never straighten its branches. I guess I had to find out the truth of it the hard way. Zach Koch is being held under guard this evening—because of what he did to me.

I'd gone to the river to make use of the idle time by washing some of the bedding and had no more bent over to commence scrubbing when I felt someone near. Zach was standing off to one side, a strange expression on his face, and I'd wondered if he'd been drinking.

"I've been watching you, Callie Wade," he said slowly as he moved toward me. "It pains me to tell you that I don't much like what I've been seeing."

"I don't know what you're talking about," I said. "Why don't—"

"I guess you feel real good about helping McGregor back to health," he interrupted me, and I saw the rage on his face. "I'm not the fool most are. I think something else went on in that wagon."

"You're mad," I spat out, but he pretended he didn't hear me, so I gave up talking and started to walk away.

"You know, my mama doesn't much like you. She says that you've got wanton ways about you," he said, grabbing me and yanking me down to the ground. "Trouble is you're *wantin'* the wrong man, Callie." Zach laughed at his own joke. His smile disappeared as I tried to rise, and his grip tightened on my arm. "I've come to show you the error of your ways."

The rank smell of whiskey and dirty skin smothered my senses as he pressed me into the grass, his body covering my own. Ragged fingernails raked my skin as he tried to hitch my skirt up. Then I felt the cold, hard jab of steel press into my belly, and I realized that in his haste he'd forgotten to take his gun belt off.

"A gun in your hand can either kill you or save you." Grace's words came back to me, and I felt stronger suddenly. I reached down and grabbed for the butt of the pistol, tearing it from the holster, praying that it wouldn't discharge.

"Get off me," I choked out, pressing the gun into Zach's stomach.

Zach quickly rolled away and stood, watching the gun in my shaking hands warily.

"You're gonna be sorry for taking that dirty Irishman over me," he said slowly. "Real sorry."

Jack was standing in the clearing before either of us could blink, his rifle aimed at Zach as well. "I think you're the one that's going to be sorry, you bastard!" Jack came closer to me and pulled the pistol out of my hands. "Move," he growled, following Zach up the embankment. "I'll get Grace, Callie," he called over his shoulder, and I felt my legs buckle beneath me as I dropped to the ground, hot tears of anger and shame spilling over my cheeks.

But it wasn't Grace who came, it was Quinn. I wouldn't look at him for a long time, but he sat with me anyway through the awful silence.

"Your brother's with the preacher," Quinn said, taking off his coat and wrapping it around my shoulders. "He'll watch over Zach in case he tries to run." He sat down next to me in the grass, and rocked me back and forth in his arms.

"It's his shame, not yours, Callie," Quinn said finally. He then picked me up and carried me to my wagon and told me he'd go fetch Grace. As soon as he said he was leaving, I began to shake, and Quinn kneeled down next to me.

"Look at me," Quinn said, turning my face toward his. "I'll never leave you again, I promise you. I'm not sure where we go from here, lass, but I am sure that I won't ever let harm come to you again."

Tonight—The men are riled up, heated talk going round and round the big bonfire outside. They're talking of hanging Zach Koch. If they do, it will be on account of me, and as much as I want to see him punished, I'm not sure I can live with *that*.

I've just climbed back in the wagon after confronting those men by the bonfire. I'd been listening to them for what seemed like an eternity when I decided I had to do something.

I admit I don't think I've ever been so nervous as I was talking to that crowd of angry men.

I'd stood for a while, hidden to the side of the Mercers' wagon, listening to the discussion. There were eight or ten of the men from our company, huddled beneath a good-size tree with its large branches jutting over their heads. I saw Stem holding Zach, his hands tied behind him. The preacher stood on one side and Quinn on the other, his rifle pointed at Zach's belly. Jack faced them, a long, thick rope dangling in his hand.

"It's a sin before the Almighty, Jack Wade," the preacher was saying. "Vengeance is *Mine,* sayeth the Lord." He stood there, not really condemning the men, as I could see, but pleading with them for his son the only way he knew how.

"When it comes time to meet my Maker, I imagine the only thing he might object to is that I didn't send this bastard to hell sooner," Jack said. "An eye for an eye, Preacher."

"Look, your sister, she's not harmed," the preacher said. "Not really. How can you all justify a hanging for what he done?"

"And if it were your sister, or better your wife?" Quinn asked, the heat of his anger thickening his accent. "Would it be justified then, Preacher? And who's to say he won't try to force himself on another woman?"

When an angry murmur went through the crowd, the preacher held his hand up. "I'll give you my word he won't," he said. "I'm a man of the cloth; that's got to mean something!"

Unmoved, Jack dropped the rope over Zach's head and set the knot tight. The look on his face was hard, but it slipped a little when he spotted me standing behind the wagon. He swore under his breath. "Get back to the wagon, Callie," he ordered. "This ain't no place for you."

Some of the men glanced away, embarrassed to see me there. The preacher pulled his hat off, and Zach stood quiet, his eyes moving between Jack and me.

"I can't let you all do this," I said then, and Jack stared at me like I was crazy. "Don't you see? Right or wrong, it will be because of *me*. I'm not sure I can live with that. Dear God, Jack, hasn't there been enough death?"

Jack stood there for a long moment, studying me. I was as surprised as the rest when he pulled the noose over Zach's head and let the rope fall to the ground. He was face-to-face with Zach. At a casual glance he might have even seemed calm, but his eyes chilled me; there was a dull glitter to them, as if his soul had been squeezed out of his body to be replaced by just one thought—to kill. He didn't say anything—he didn't have to.

When he walked away, it was Quinn that spoke up, his voice hard.

"You'll not hang today, Koch," he said. "But if you ever go near her again, I'll kill you myself."

Friday, July 29

I'd set out today to gather some wood for the fire, when I was surprised by a male voice and turned to see Zach Koch sitting on the bank of the river. "I wonder how many more crossin's we got," he said, as if talking to himself. "I'd just as soon know so I could at least get them over with in my head."

He'd stood and walked a little closer then, and I noticed that his face had the pale yellow tinge of a man that was recovering from too much alcohol and too little sleep. My first thought was that he'd come back to get his revenge. "You best get out of here," I told him, "before Quinn or my brother see you talking to me."

Zach sighed and said, "I don't care if they do. I reckon anythin' they give me, I got comin. I came to say I was wrong, Callie . . . and that I never meant to hurt you."

I looked up in surprise, then tried to read what lay behind those eyes. I saw the signs of a man that had suddenly awakened to what he was—and hating himself for it. But I couldn't bring myself to forgive him.

"Do you believe me?" he asked, watching me carefully.

"I don't know," I answered honestly. "And even if I did, I'm not sure it would matter."

Zach stood still for a long moment. Then he smiled sadly and walked away.

Saturday, July 30

The view of the North Platte River didn't set well with any of the men this morning; dark and churned-up as it was, the current fast. They had no more than set about building some rafts when Zach got loud and mouthy, saying that it was a waste of time and that he could prove it. Most ignored his remarks until we began to ferry out.

Before any of us realized what was happening, Zach charged into the river, horse and rider wading into the current. Faster than anyone could stop him he pushed ahead, and when his horse reached midway, he looked over to me on our raft with a grin on his face that said, *"I made it anyway, by God!"*

"Git out o' there, ya damned fool!" Stem called from the raft behind us; then everything seemed to go wrong at once.

Zach's horse lost its balance, throwing Zack into the river, then turned around and made its way back to the far bank. At first, Zach cursed, dragging his hat out of the water as he swam toward the ferry I was on. He grabbed our raft, but then, without warning, was pulled under. I screamed, realizing that he was caught in the current. Zach resurfaced then and, in his desperation, grabbed the hem of my skirts, and I felt myself slipping over the edge of the raft, doomed I was sure, to be pulled in.

"My God, man, let go of her!" Quinn shouted over the din of hysteria. "You're going to drown her!"

Zach caught Quinn's eyes at that moment and then looked at me. It seemed as if there was a great battle raging within him. If he let go of my skirt to grab on to something else, chances were he wouldn't make it. Yet, if he had held on . . .

"Callie," he rasped and then let go of me, his body yanked down into the vicious swirl of water.

In that brief instant before he died, I saw a part of Zach Koch that probably no one else ever had. Gone was the cold, calculating look, the smugness. I saw Zach's face change with a kind of painful understanding. In that one, last selfless act, I saw the man that he could have been.

Later—In spite of Grace's urging me to stay in the wagon with Rose, I stood at the riverbank and watched as Quinn, the preacher, and some of the other men formed a chain across the river to search for the body. It was nearly dark when I heard one of the men shout, and I saw Quinn lift Zach, lifeless, from the watery grave. The preacher climbed up the bank behind Quinn and stood and cried over his son. When I looked to the far bank, I saw Zach's horse, still saddled, grazing nearby. I remember putting my hand over my mouth so I wouldn't scream, and when I felt Stem's arms go around me, I turned and sobbed into his shirt.

Stem patted my hair like Pa used to and held me tight.

"Rest his soul," he said, his voice heavy. "Rest his soul."

Sunday, July 31

I stood with Quinn at the edge of the crowd early this morning as the men slowly lowered Zach's body into the newly dug grave. Like everyone else, I went to pay my respects. I soon found out, though, that I wasn't just another face at the grave when Della spotted me, her eyes bright with hysteria.

"It's all her fault," she shouted, pointing to me. "My boy died on account of her! Whore! Murderer!"

I was shocked and unable to move until Quinn grabbed my hand and quickly led me back to the wagon. "Crazy is what that woman is," he said. "She'd blame anybody but who she should. I'm here if you need me." He turned and walked away then, and I knew that the peace between us was still fragile, old wounds not yet healed. For a moment I almost shouted for him to come back and hold me so I could feel safe again.

Instead, I climbed up onto the seat and goaded the oxen on, pulling into line as the train moved out once again.

I had no memory of falling asleep after we made camp this evening, but I must've, because the next thing I knew Jack was shaking me awake, telling me that the preacher had come to talk to me.

I sat up in my bed, smoothing over my skirts.

"Haven't the Kochs said enough, Jack?" I said, feeling miserable and wishing he could fix my hurts as easily as he'd done when I was a child. "I can't do anything to change what's happened. If I could give them back their son, I would. I can't bear to hear any more."

"I don't think it's like that, Callie," he said. "He says he came here to thank you."

"Thank me?" Jack looked as doubtful as I felt, but I climbed on out of the wagon anyway.

The preacher's face was haggard, but relief was clear on his face when he spotted me. He walked toward me slowly, as if he were afraid I would run off.

"I'm glad you agreed to see me, Callie," he said. "I admit, I wasn't sure you would after the horrible things Della said to you."

"I'm sorry about Zach," I said, and the preacher looked away.

"I am, too," he said after a while. "I loved him . . . more'n he knew, I think. But I knew his ways, too. I knew what he'd done to you was his doing, no one else's. Della's got it in her head to blame you. But I think maybe that's cause she couldn't bear to blame herself. I guess what I'm trying to say is thank you, Callie," he said, staring at the hat in his hands.

"For what?" I asked.

"Well, now, I prayed like anything that my son would change," he said, "that somehow he would be the man I always dreamed he'd be when I held him as a baby. You helped my prayer to be answered."

He must have seen that I was confused, because then he said, "Prayers are funny things, Callie. Sometimes they're answered in the oddest ways. Zach was going downhill fast, we all could see it. But there was something about you that had given him a little hope.

I think he was starting to believe there was good in people. That maybe he didn't have to hide behind that bottle like he did.

"Maybe it was because you never lied to him. All I know is when he had to make that choice out there in the river, to let go or pull you in, it was because of you that he made the right one. So, I thank you for that. You gave me back the little boy I'd always believed in . . . even if it was only for that moment." The preacher left me then, the weight of his sorrow bowing his narrow shoulders down.

I couldn't help thinking how sad it is that by the time we get to know a person, most of the time it's too late.

I wish I could talk to Quinn tonight, feel his arms wrap around me, but my loneliness is my own doing. *Go to him*, the little voice in me urges. Instead, I sit next to this fire . . . writing.

Coward.

Wednesday, August 3
Wyoming Territory

Traveled through a valley and passed near several alkali lakes. The dust is strong, stinging eyes and noses so much that I kept Rose in the wagon. A few miles further we came to the Sweetwater River and then to Independence Rock, named on account of most of the emigrants reaching it around the Fourth of July. Grace, Rose, and I took a walk out to the rock. It's covered with names of emigrants that came before us. We had only just decided to carve our names when Mrs. Iverson happened by. Grace, being in a mischievous mood, invited her along, at which point she snorted and said, " 'Bout the only thing I want to be *independent* of is this dust." But she stayed and watched us carve anyway.

Later—it's nearly dawn and I've just come back to the wagon, more confused than ever. Grace and I sat by the fire for a long while this evening and talked. Well, I guess I did most of the talking. I told her everything that had been going on between Quinn and me (not *everything*). But I did tell her about him wanting to marry me and that I told him no. She nodded and listened most of the time, and I thought for a moment she agreed with my decision. But then she gave me a look that was pure Grace and said, "So, if it's for the best, how come you two are so damned miserable?"

Thursday, August 4

Six miles brought us to Devil's Gate this morning, where the Sweetwater has hollowed a path through the mountains of rock. Nooned along a mountain stream, where Jack caught some trout. Went several miles more before we camped near the river.

Bad feelings remain strong since Zach's death. Even though I know the truth of it, the look of blame in some of the folks' eyes hurts.

Later—Jack told me there's talk of the train splitting. Some planning to go on along the California Trail, and others, like ourselves, will stop over in Salt Lake. Jack didn't say it in so many words, but I have a feeling the Kochs have something to do with the split, being that they're held in such regard by most folks.

Friday, August 5

Rode all day through a river road that cuts through the Rocky Mountains. Met up with a Bear River Indian who traded Jack some things for his old coat, which the man quickly shrugged on once the bargain had been struck. Rose got the giggles, seeing his bare legs sticking out from underneath it. Air is cool and free from sand for once. Can see Wind River Mountains standing smoky in the distance.

Later—Jack and I talked long into the night about splitting off from the train and going on to Salt Lake. He told me that Stem has already agreed to collect his wages from Captain Belshaw and join us—as well as Grace and her boys. He didn't mention anything about Quinn.

Saturday, August 6
South Pass

Here we are obliged to part ways with the rest of the train. Aside from Grace, Stem, and Quinn, no one else elected to go on with us to Salt Lake this morning. Jack and Quinn cut our stock from the herd as I watched the remaining wagons gather behind Captain Belshaw, only a few looking our way. Then the Mercers' wagon pulled last into the line and I saw Bess hesitate by the wagon and then suddenly turn and come to me.

"I want to thank you," she said, and I saw her lips tremble a little, but she didn't cry this time. In spite of her ragged appearance, she seemed stronger, and I couldn't help thinking Bess had changed for the better and that she just might make it to California after all. "I wish I was going with you all," Bess said, after Grace and I hugged her. "I kind of hoped we'd be neighbors. . . ." Bess's husband called her away then.

When they rolled out, I saw Captain Belshaw glance back where Stem was with a look that reminded me of a child that wasn't sure where to go with his newfound freedom. "I do hope they fare well," Stem said, his browned face screwed up with worry. "They's a little bit like children." When I looked around our little ragtag group, I got the idea that we were pretty much feeling the same, like wayward children with no home to call our own.

Sunday, August 7

Passed over good roads all afternoon—hard to imagine we're traveling through the great range of the Rocky Mountains, the road being as smooth and wide as any in the states. The beauty of this land, the high peaks, the sharp clean air, seems to put us all in a better mood. Jack says God himself can't be more than a holler away from here. Even Rose seems more animated. She spotted a strata of rock standing out edgeways and laughed, saying it reminded her of an old porcupine's back.

I found Quinn watching me play with Rose this evening. He stood off from us for a while, taking it in, a half-smile on his face. Then Jack called him to help with the stock, and he set off toward the herd, but not before he looked back one last time and not before I saw the longing in his eyes.

Later—Rose found me crying as I was cooking over the fire. "Smoke is all," I told her, and when she frowned at me, I didn't know whether to laugh or cry harder, seeing her little waiflike face, solemn as a barn owl.

Monday, August 8

Following main road to Salt Lake. Camped on a level plain surrounded by high tablelands. Beautiful scenery, with the Wind River chain of the Rockies to the east of us, capped in snow. I find myself yearning to share it with Quinn. . . .

Later—With the boys keeping an eye on Rose, Grace and I took our time washing up by the river. I think it did me more good than Grace, talking like we did.

Somehow one thing led to another, and I found myself kneeling next to the stream with Grace—as we scrubbed the dust from our face, neck, and arms like there was no tomorrow—asking her what convinced her to marry Grady, to take a chance.

She wrung her cloth out and perched herself up on a rock, waving me to come sit next to her. "I don't recall taking much time to wonder over it," she said, chuckling. "He was there and I was there, and the minute I looked at him I was lost."

"But weren't you ever unsure?" The whole mess with Quinn and me was making me miserable, and I was looking for some sort of answer.

"I was pretty much scared of my own shadow when I was a bit younger," Grace admitted, and I looked at her incredulously.

"You?" Now it was my turn to chuckle.

"My mama bred that kind of fear. She'd come from real good people up north and just hated living in what she called 'the pesthole of the south.' It didn't matter to her that we had one of the richest plantations in Louisiana; she just knew that we were going to be eaten by some creature in the river or the swamp. And it was her life's work to make sure we knew it."

"So what changed?" I'd leaned back on the rock with both elbows, enjoying the soft roll of Grace's voice, the light in her eyes when she talked that erased some of the worry in her face, and the way she made me feel like everything would turn out all right. And her knack for storytelling was second only to Stem's.

"My granddaddy's what changed me," she said. "He was what my father called a 'wheeler-dealer,' I guess what we might think of as the black sheep. My father said he was bad for the family name, but the truth was that my granddaddy's schemes was what paid for most of our plantation.

"Anyway, Granddaddy got pretty bent up about Mama sheltering me and one day took me off into the woods to check on one of his stills with him." Grace glanced sideways at me. "By this time Mama had done a job on me, and I was scared to come out of his cabin. Granddaddy took hold of me and said, 'Goldarnit, Gracie, if ya don't ever open that door, how the hell are ya goin' to see what's outside?' "

We both giggled.

"Best education I ever got was up in the hills with that old man," Grace said amiably. "I've kept every door in my life opened just as wide as it would swing from then on. Although, I have had some slammed in my face a time or two."

"But it's been worth it, taking the chances, I mean?"

"It's a short time between birthing and burying, Callie. It's up to us to make the most of it." When she said that, it sobered me some. I couldn't help thinking of Mama and Pa, of the chances they took, the love they gave. I don't recall them ever saying anything about regrets. Not even at the end.

I'd kept silent as we walked back to camp, and Grace, sensing my mood, put her arm around my shoulders. "Callie," she said, "you're going to find life is only as tough as you make it."

"I must have a penchant for trouble, then," I said, and we both laughed. I think it was the laughing that made me feel better than I'd felt in a long while.

"Well, I guess I ought to get dinner started," Grace said, and then added, a little louder so Stem could hear, "It's a shame we don't have any good menfolk that can cook around here. Sure would help since we're doing all the work."

"Only thing men seem to do around here is gripe, fight, and spit tobacco," I said, putting my two cents in, and I saw Stem's ears perk up. "Ain't none of them good for nothing."

"Ya keep hangin' round Grace Hollister much longer, ya'll turn inta a gun-totin' cardsharp," Stem groused, with an impish gleam in his eyes, and I couldn't help thinking how blessed I was to have two such good friends.

"She's somethin' else, ain't she?" Stem said with fondness, and when I turned and watched Grace walk to her wagon, I thought of all the times she had said the right things—even if I didn't think I wanted to hear it.

"She sure is," I said.

Tuesday, August 9

Went ten miles and struck the Big Sandy River. Camped tonight along the Salt Lake City Road. Everyone's in a good mood. *Almost there*, are the whispers about camp, filled with pride and new hope. Stem struck up the fiddle, and Grace and Jack danced around the fire. Watching them brought up bittersweet memories of Quinn and me dancing together. In spite of myself, I looked for him but couldn't find him. It was when I finally gave up and was walking back to the wagons that I saw him sitting alone and I went to him.

"Stem says we've probably been through the worst of the journey," I told him, uncomfortable with the silence. "I guess we're almost there."

Quinn nodded and stared off beyond the fire.

"You should be getting excited, you being so close to seeing your dream . . . to finding your uncle's claim and all."

Quinn smiled, but no warmth reached his eyes. He rose from the fire and walked slowly away, leaving me alone.

I was writing in this journal when Rose's head popped up from the covers, making me think back to when she was just a baby and how she used to peer over the baby bed back home, just as I was coming into the room.

"Callie? Can I come lay with you?" she asked.

We both burrowed underneath the covers together, and I hugged Rose, kissing her cheek. "Are you okay, honey?" I asked.

"Yeah," she said slowly. "It was just so quiet in here. The music, the laughter, everything is gone . . . and I was feeling so alone. Sometimes, I wake up at night and I'm . . . scared. I think I'm all alone and nobody can do anything because . . ."

"Because why?"

Rose had fallen silent, and I thought she'd drifted off to sleep. But then she snuggled closer to me, burying her nose in the crook of my neck.

"I love you, Callie," she whispered finally. "Don't never forget that."

Wednesday, August 10

Riding ahead with Jack and Quinn today, we met a man traveling on foot. Quite a character. He carries a bow and arrow and informed us he lives chiefly on prairie dogs, rabbits and wild greens. After conversing with us awhile, he changed his tune a bit about his self-sufficiency and admitted to generally accepting "good-natured gifts of food" as well. Hearing Quinn's laugh, I would have gladly prepared the man a feast.

Thursday, August 11

Grace and I walked together this afternoon, and I watched with a strange, aching hunger as two of her younger boys scrambled around her from time to time, showing her things they found along the trail, arguing with each other, laughing. I had Rose, but it wasn't the same. One day, with any luck, she'd be grown and married with her own family. And then where would I be?

"If ya don't ever open that door, how the hell are ya goin' to see what's outside?" Grace's Granddaddy's words came back to me, and it was in that moment, and not before, that I knew I couldn't live without Quinn. What a fool I'd been, I thought. But then, maybe I had to feel the hurt before I could realize I'd missed every minute without him, I missed his strength and goodness, his tenderness, and most of all I missed the love that was undeniable in his eyes. How could I have convinced myself that life would be better without him?

I picked up my step, and then broke out in a run through the wagons and horses.

"Where are you off to in such a hurry?" Grace called after me.

"To do something I should've done a long time ago," I called over my shoulder.

When I found Quinn, he was standing off to one side of the trail, looking out over the jagged outcroppings of rock. I couldn't help thinking how he and the rugged country seemed to belong together. He looked so alone, I just couldn't help but blurt out that I wanted to marry him. I don't think he believed me at first. He didn't seem none too happy to see me.

I reached out for him, but he backed away. "We've made our peace between us, Callie," he said. "Let's leave it at that. I'm not sure I want to pick up where we left off, knowing there's no future in it."

How sad he looked, arms forced to his sides, as if he didn't quite trust himself to relax. I stepped closer and stared up into his troubled face. "What if there is a future for us?"

Quinn stood stock-still, as if he was trying to make sense of what I was telling him, and I grinned.

"That's just like you," he sighed finally with exasperation, pulling me into his arms, "to taunt me with marriage in the middle of nowhere, with no preacher to be found for miles."

> *Nearing Salt Lake City*
> *In transit to California*
> *August 12, 1859*

Mrs. Maggie Todd
Blue Mills, Missouri

Dear Maggie,

We have stopped to rest a bit here along the bench-land of the Wasatch Mountains before we continue on into Salt Lake City—a small group of us having broken off from the train. It has been quite a trip over these mountains—downright hair-raising at times, Mag. Earlier, as we were winding around a ticklish turn through a place called Twin Peaks, I'd spotted some broken spokes and yoke bows laying near the edge of a steep drop-off—our scout, Stem, told me that three mail-coach passengers had "tipped" and fell to their deaths here. Not a comforting thought, I'll tell you.

You might wonder at this point, after being jounced, jolted, strangled by dust, bitten by insects, refreshed only by bitter coffee and food that's not fit for hogs, why I haven't thrown my hands up in resignation. I should be in the depths of despair, but in truth, I've never been happier. Now, Mag, before you start thinking that I have lost my mind, I have a confession to make—one that will explain my newfound happiness. "Our" Irishman has asked me to marry him—some time back, as a matter of fact. It took me nearly losing him to figure out my worries amounted to just plain foolishness.

Salt Lake is where we will be married, but our reason for going there is more for Rose. The trail has weakened her, Mag. I can see it even more since traversing these mountains. She's as frail as a kitten, although she'd never admit to it. Jack says that the weather here, dry as it is, will help her regain her health—and for once, I don't doubt him. Things seem to be looking up for us in so many ways.

As I sit writing you, I have a perfect view of the city, which lies below. The air out here shows everything up sharp and vivid, ignoring distance. And what a wonderful sight it is! There's life everywhere: adobe houses with fine gardens, fruit

trees, fields of wheat and maize. After all these
months of eagerly searching for something, anything familiar to home, it's a godsend. There is
such hope that stirs in me. I feel like us coming
here might just be what we needed to start fresh
again. To new beginnings, Mag!

We're fixing to move on now. I'll write you
again as soon as I can.

All my love,
Callie

Part Five

Salt Lake City

*"Hope is faith holding its hand out
in the dark."*
—Amanda Wade

Early—We've made it into the city. So much is going on around me here, in Pioneer Square, as I sit here writing this. I can't seem to find the right words to describe what I'm feeling, but I will try my best.

By the time we made it through the last settlement clinging to the outskirts southeast of this city this morning, the excitement in me had already begun to build. I did so much neck-straining, Jack stopped the wagon to saddle Patch for me, then sent me off with Quinn. First thing I noticed was how the road had begun to be marked by posts and rails, then neat palings. Then there were garden plots and flowers—roses, tansies, and geraniums—fields of maize dwarfed by wild sunflower tops. As we plodded down the main thoroughfare, more houses sprang up, a post office, stores . . . and life! People coming and going down the wide, dusty road, everyday chores on their minds.

One lady I saw had a bolt of goods in her arms, and it made me remember Mama and the quiltings we used to have, how we used to sit for hours with our friends, sharing our joys and heartaches, stitching our love for each other with each block we pieced. I told Quinn as much, feeling wistful, and he looked at me steady, silent for a moment, then he smiled.

"Seems funny," he said, "but when I saw those

205

fields, I couldn't help thinking what I wouldn't give to feel the bone weariness of a good day's work in my back and know there was a home and family waiting for me at the end of the day."

We'd both turned to see the rest of our little train pulling in: Rose beaming, her sweet little face turned to the sun; Jack looking so handsome, guiding the wagon with an easy grin; Grace and Stem bickering good-naturedly from their perches, all the miles seeming to fade with our happiness.

"We're almost home, Callie," Quinn said, and with the tender look in those pale eyes of his, with the sound of his heart in those words, for a moment I felt like I was already there.

It looks like we'll be sleeping in *real* beds tonight! We've just now come back to the square to gather up some of our things from the wagons. After searching nearly all afternoon, trying to find a place to take us, it was Jack that got us in.

Grace and Stem had already called it quits, deciding to stay camped at the square in their rigs. The Salt Lake House—our last hope—had been a disappointment, filled solid by a rough-looking crowd of drivers and all-out idlers, most armed with bowie knives and revolvers. We'd almost given up hope as well, until Jack happened to strike up a conversation with an old-timer sitting out front of the mercantile.

While the old man scratched his head—one that hadn't seen the benefit of a comb in a while—he told Jack that we might be able to get some rooms from a Mormon lady by the name of Laura Ashby, but that he couldn't promise anything. He said, with some annoyance, that she was "snooty" and that she did pretty much what she pleased. When we took our leave, he called after us, "And for pity's sake, don't tell 'er yer from Missouri," he warned. "It'll put a bad taste in her mouth."

We all headed for the neat little house when I glanced at Quinn walking beside me, and he must've read the concern on my face. "Don't worry, Callie," he said softly, "if anyone can charm the lady, it's your brother."

Seeing the sign on the front of the house that read "Gentiles Must Pay in Advance," I admit I wasn't so sure. My hopes fell even further when Laura Ashby appeared, with her salt-and-pepper hair parted just so and her mouth set in a grim line. I saw right away she wasn't too keen on us all boarding with her—at first. But Jack changed that.

"Don't think we have room enough for all of you," Laura Ashby told us, looking over our dusty clothes as we crowded into the front entryway.

"We'll pay well," Jack offered, and the lady looked skeptical, pursing her lips.

"Well, that's all right," Jack said, beginning to turn away. "I'd just hoped to get my little sister out of the night air for a while."

"Where're your folks?" she called after him, and Jack stopped and turned back around. When I looked over at Quinn, there was a wicked smile on his face, his eyes saying to me, *"See, I told you Jack could do it."*

"Well, ma'am, they're gone," Jack was saying. He took his hat off. "We lost our ma a few years back and our pa on the trail."

He was in his element, I realized as I stood there listening to him talk. There was truth in everything he said, but it was the *way* Jack told things, friendly and simple-like—a trait that took people in right away. Mama always said he could charm the diamonds off the back of a snake, and I think she was right, because I could see Mrs. Ashby begin to waver under that "nice boy" smile of his. Rose let out a cough along then, and I saw Jack's eyes light up with newfound appreciation for our little sister.

While I tried to catch Jack's eye with a fierce look, Mrs. Ashby beckoned for Rose. As she held her hand out to her, I saw a tenderness in her that wasn't there before. "What's your name, little girl?" she asked, and when Rose told her, she said, "Pleased to meet you," real proper. She smiled at me above Rose's head, and I knew right then I liked her.

Next thing she did was take measure of Quinn, who'd caught her notice as he stood at the back of the room. "My heavens," she said, looking at him from head to toe. "I imagine I'll have to double my grocery bill. Well, there's work at the mill for any man that wants it. Big fella like you can earn your own, I guess."

We all laughed, and Mrs. Ashby nodded, like everything was settled.

Later—Mrs. Ashby just came to the room. It seems Quinn asked her about finding someone to marry us.

"Where are you-all from, anyway?" she asked, and remembering the old-timer's warning, I hesitated.

"Missouri," I told her finally. She looked from my face to Rose's and then began to laugh.

"So it was Emmet Tanzy that steered you here, was it? Well, don't you worry none, honey. I just tell that old coot I have a grudge against Missourians to keep *him* out of my hair."

Sunday, August 14

Well, actually it's almost Monday, now. The moon starting to fade outside our window here can attest to that fact. I'm up writing this I guess because I don't want the day to be over yet. My wedding day, that is.

It started off as most wedding days do, rushed and crazy and filled with laughter and tears. Rose and I had got up early—Mrs. Ashby had come to our room, her hair still all frowsy from sleep, and offered us use of the tub in her room. She didn't have to ask me twice either, not a one of us having had a decent bath since Independence.

Mrs. Ashby had the bath already drawn and ready for us when we got down to her room, and she laughed at the way Rose and I stood and stared at the steam rising from the clean water in her copper-bottom hip bath, the way we sighed over the clean, white towels.

I'd scrubbed so hard Rose giggled, saying I was taking off most of my skin. But she wasted no time hopping in herself after I was done, using the rest of the sweet-smelling soap Mrs. Ashby left us. Grace found us not long after, dressed in only our shifts as we sat next to the pot-bellied stove drying our hair.

"I can't think of anything better in life than a good hot bath," she said with a grin as she stepped into the room. "Stand on up here, Callie," she said then, her manner businesslike all of a sudden. "Let's try this dress on you."

I saw right away it wasn't just a "dress" that she held in her arms. The minute I saw the beautiful white muslin, with all the hand embroidery and lace, I knew it must've been her own wedding dress.

"It's too nice," I said, trying to protest, but she slipped it over my head anyway and helped me with the buttons. She set me down in a chair then, in front of a mirror, and Rose quickly handed her my pins for my hair, like she was in on it, too.

"You look real pretty in white," Grace said as she twined my hair up. "I'm glad it's going to get some use." I looked at her in the mirror and saw the tears standing in her eyes. "I was saving it for Lizzie . . . I used to dream of giving her a real fine wedding, with lace and bowers of roses and honeysuckle."

"Oh, Grace," I started, but she held up her hand to silence me.

"I think it would've hurt me more, sitting in that chest waiting on a day that'd never come." I hugged her and we both cried a little. We were still sniffing a bit when we met Jack down near the parlor.

"You'd think you two were goin' to a wake, the way you're carryin' on," Jack teased. "Wouldn't you, Rose?" Rose giggled, and Jack offered us each an arm, escorting us into the parlor.

"God Almighty," Stem declared when we walked into the room. "I think McGregor's too darned lucky fer his own good!" I couldn't help laughing—Stem's bantering easing the tension I felt—and I leaned over and planted a kiss on his leathered cheek. He was surprised at first but quickly recovered, lending me a look of practiced remorse. "I suspect now I shoulda given that Irish whelp a run fer it," he said, and we all laughed.

That was when I spotted Quinn across the room. He was standing next to the table of food Mrs. Ashby had set out, talking to what appeared to be the preacher. He turned all of a sudden and stared across the room at me, like he knew I'd be there. When he smiled at me, his clean-shaven face so handsome, I forgot about how nervous I was and I smiled back.

"There'll only be one woman ya'll be marryin' today, Preacher," Stem piped up from the crowd. "Sure wish I woulda had ya Mormons backin' me up when I was caught betwixt two sisters back in Santa Fe."

Our small group roared with laughter.

"Aye, Parson. One woman," Quinn laughed, "I've only the strength to handle one stubborn redhead in my life."

After that I seemed to lose all sense of time. I know Jack walked me across the room, but I don't remember it. I know the preacher led us through our vows only because I remember Quinn saying "I will" and I chimed in saying that I would, too.

I do remember Quinn sliding the gold ring on my finger, a ring that was an awful lot like Mama's, with the way the ivy and flowers were cut into the band. And I remember looking over at Jack after Quinn and I were pronounced man and wife and seeing him blow his nose hard, wiping his face like he had a cold.

Stem struck up a tune with his fiddle after the preacher left, and Jack twirled Rose around the room in his arms, her feet balanced on his as she held on for dear life, and the rest of the small crowd joined in. Quinn pulled me into a waltz, and we danced and laughed together and fed each other pieces of the white sheet cake Mrs. Ashby baked. Then, just as things were winding down, Jack came over and claimed a dance from me.

"You know, I think tonight's the first time I've looked at you and seen more than just my little sister," he said softly as he began to move me around the room. "Most of the time I still see you as a seven- or eight-year-old little gal, dancin' with me in the parlor back home."

"And you and Pa'd laugh at my sass, at how sure I was that I was going to marry *you* when I grew up," I said, and Jack laughed like he was embarrassed.

"I'd say you did a sight better," he whispered as his new spurs clanked against the floor to the time of the music.

"He's a good man," I told him, "just like you, Jack."

Around midnight, I noticed Rose straining to stay awake in the corner of the room. Quinn picked her up in his arms. "We best get her planted before she wilts," he said, and I saw Rose smile sleepily and wrap her arms around his neck.

Just as we got her in the little cot, she woke up and rubbed her eyes. "Callie, if you have a baby girl, will you name her Rose?" she asked sleepily.

I saw Quinn standing in the doorway, one corner of his mouth twitching. "Now, why would I want to do that?" I said. "We already have you."

Rose looked from Quinn to me and then settled back against her pillow. "I guess you're right, Callie," she said softly, and I hugged her tight, wondering if she was feeling left out now that Quinn and I were married.

"You know, honey, once we get to California you'll have *two* homes, Jack's and ours," I said, trying to comfort her. Rose gave me a funny look, but then smiled when I kissed her on the forehead and turned over and fell asleep.

I crept out of the room then, and as I followed Quinn slowly to our new room that we would share, I had to force myself not to turn back and check on Rose just one more time. In the silence I started feeling kind of scared and unsure, all my worries creeping in on me in the blackened hallway. I reached my hand out in the dark to steady myself and was surprised when Quinn's large, callused hand closed over my own, as if he'd known all along.

"I love you, Callie," he said, pulling me against him as his lips brushed my ear, and I breathed in the scent of him. He smelled like lye soap and leather and something altogether *male*.

"I love you, too," I whispered against his shirt, feeling a yearning swirl in the pit of my stomach. I gasped as he picked me up in his arms and nudged our door open with his boot.

" 'Tis all I needed to hear," he said, and I laughed nervously as he carried me into the room. And when he laid me down on the bed, his body shadowing my own, everything else faded away and we were out on the prairie again with the tall grass swaying all around us in the breeze . . .

I can see Grace's dress laying over the chair next to our bed from here. It shines real nice in the moonlight. The girl in me wonders if I'll ever wear something so fine as that again. But the woman in me doesn't care. I figure I'd be just as happy in a sackcloth dress, knowing I'll be able to wake up every morning to Quinn McGregor by my side.

Monday, August 15

I've just come back from the square, where our wagons are kept. I had gone down there to find Grace, to see if she and the boys would like to go picnicking, but when I got there, I was surprised to see her wagon and things gone. Worry was setting in on me when I spotted a young woman from another group of emigrants, lifting some of her things from the back of her wagon.

"I'm looking for a woman that had been camping here," I explained when I caught her staring at me kind of funny.

"Was she pretty with fair hair?" the girl asked, and when I told her yes, she smiled real big.

"That'd be Grace Hollister," she said, setting the barrel down with a thud. "Everyone knows who *she* is." She laughed. "At least most of us that's single. That Mormon fella is the most handsome man any of us has come across since we left home . . . maybe even before. If it'd been any of us that were offered an empty house to stay in next to his, we'd've took him up on it, too."

Later—I rode out to the cabin where Grace was staying for no other reason than to stick my nose in where it didn't belong. After talking with that emigrant girl at the square, I wasn't sure what I'd find. I figured whatever was going on, the best thing I could do was get it from the horse's mouth myself.

When I pulled up to the yard in Mrs. Ashby's buckboard, I spotted Grace's wagon sitting to the side of the little cabin and another buckboard out front, near the door. There were two little girls, maybe a few years older than Rose, talking to Grace's boys. They stopped talking and watched me with interest when Dane came trotting up and helped me down.

"Mama's inside with their aunt," he told me, grinning as he motioned with his thumb toward the girls.

Dane supplied me with the details on the way up the hill to the house. It seems Mr. Jared (as Dane called him) had come to Pioneer Square and asked if some of the boys would be interested in hiring themselves out. When Dane came up front with his brother, Mr. Jared took one look at Grace and offered them the little empty house on his land. I could see Dane thought this was a good thing, but in my own heart I wasn't so sure.

Grace and a strange woman met me at the door, full of smiles and welcomes. But every time I tried to catch Grace's eye, she avoided me.

The young woman, I found out none too soon, was Mr. Jared's sister. Anna, as her name was, liked to talk. I watched Grace closely as the woman talked about her life, about being a "second"—that's what she called herself—which I gathered meant the second wife.

Even though Grace was busy preparing the meal, I could tell she had been listening real close. And after the woman went on for a while, telling us about her husband, Grace finally spoke up.

"I wouldn't allow it," she stated matter-of-factly. "Not in this lifetime."

"It's really not so bad as all of that." Anna smiled. "If you had been brought up in it like I had, you would understand."

"So you believe you will be in heaven together, you, your husband and *all* the wives?" Grace asked.

"Oh, yes."

"Sounds more like hell to me," Grace said smartly.

Anna didn't appear to be offended at all. "I don't think you'd have to worry none about Jared; he's quite taken with you," she said in a way that sounded almost wistful, and it made me sad for her. Grace's eyes met mine over her head, and I could see she'd felt sorry for her, too.

I noticed, too, that Grace treated any mention of Jared with great indifference, which made me think it argued well for the two of them.

When the infamous Jared finally came in with the girls to fetch his sister, I could see right away how Grace had been charmed by him. He had a lean handsomeness about him, reminding me of Jack, and the kind of dark looks that women find attractive. He had a way of looking at Grace that seemed to make everything else in the room grow dim. He was quiet, but polite. We'd visited for only a little while when he said he had to go, and when he shook my hand and stared me straight in the eye with a shy smile curving his lip, I felt like we'd been friends for a long time.

Grace was studying me as we stood on the porch of the little house, watching them ride off. "Did you see the awful hem in those girls' dresses?" she asked after a while. Grace chuckled, shaking her head.

"Anna says that Jared sews them himself since his wife died, won't let no one else do it."

I knew then that Grace would stay; I could see it in her eyes. Maybe a little of it was her longing to have a daughter again, losing Lizzie like she did. Mostly I think she really felt needed in a way she hadn't felt in a long, long time.

"They're good people, Callie," she told me when I got ready to leave. "Their ways are a bit different, but I think I maybe could be happy here."

I know I'm going to miss Grace something awful; she's been as close as a sister to me. But I'm learning that there's no promises in life, and if Grace can have the happiness I have found with Quinn, then I think that's more than enough.

When Quinn fell into bed with me this evening, exhausted after a day at the mill, I was still thinking on Grace. I told him about riding out to the cabin, about the little girls, and about Jared.

"So what is it you're worrying over, then?" he asked, raising up on one arm.

"What if she's staying for all the wrong reasons?" I asked.

"Maybe," Quinn had chuckled, twirling a piece of my hair around his finger, "maybe those same reasons don't feel so wrong to her."

Before I had a chance to say anything else, he pressed his lips to mine, deep and hungry, and I no longer cared.

Tuesday, August 16

There was an accident at the mill today, and Jack was very nearly drowned falling into the mill dam like he did.

As we all sat together around the dinner table this evening, Quinn told us what had happened and we marveled at Jack's luck. *"A charmed life,"* I remember Quinn saying on the trail, and I'm beginning to think he may be right.

Jack's slant on the accident was a little more rueful. "The good Lord looks after fools and drunkards," he said cheerfully, and everyone laughed at that, even Mrs. Ashby—although she quickly caught herself and pursed her lips in proper reproof.

After dinner, Quinn and I went up to our room to get ready for bed. I was brushing my hair at the table, watching Quinn in the mirror as he stared out the window with a kind of faraway look on his face.

"Jack's something else, isn't he?" I'd asked, trying to fill the silence, and I saw him smile.

"He reminds me of Patrick a bit," Quinn said. "Did you see the look on some of those boarders' faces, Callie? Like they thought he'd deserved more than what had happened. People used to look at Patrick like that, too."

Quinn sat down in the chair across from me as I helped him off with his boots. "I've seen it before," I said finally. "When we were back home, I'd see envy pass over men's faces so strong when they'd watch Jack ride down the street that it scared me. At first I thought it might be because of his looks or maybe that charm of his. Jack has a way about him that makes everything he does seem easy, too easy. Actually, he works harder than most. But he *plays* hard— and that's all most people see."

"It isn't what they see in Jack that makes them mad, Callie," Quinn said, pulling me into his lap with a sigh. "It's what they don't see in themselves."

"And what do you see in yourself?" I asked. "An adventurer like the rest, a gold seeker?"

"A survivor," he answered simply. "The gold is just a way of getting what I've dreamed of since leaving the black cloud of Pittsburgh behind me."

"And what's that?"

"A home. A place to raise my children, where they can run and play and breathe fresh, clean air. Where they can dream of being more than lackeys for some foundry owner. That's what my da wanted for us— What are you smiling for?"

"I was just thinking how nice a dream that is," I said, which wasn't exactly a lie. It *was* a nice dream. But more important, it was nice to know I wouldn't have to worry over him like I did Jack. He wasn't flashy, like the men Maggie and I used to dream about. But, then, I figure he's a sight better than most any dream I could imagine. He's real.

Wednesday, August 17

Rose came strolling into the parlor this evening looking as if she'd been in a brawl. Her hair was all askew, her face, legs, and arms scratched up something awful. She smelled of wind and sand . . . and something unfamiliar.

"What in the world happened?" I'd asked, staring at her in horror, and she provided me with a wide grin.

"Oh," she replied loftily, perching her hand on her hip with the kind of dignity only a nine-year-old could manage, "Jack took me hiking out by the lake."

Judging by Jack's disheveled appearance, I'd have laid odds that it was Rose that had taken *him* for a hike. He had the look of a man that knew it would be a long while before he lived down the fact that his baby sister had run him ragged.

But what I will never forget is the secret triumph that flashed in Roses's eyes, the look that said, *"I'm not so weak as they thought!"*

I was so surprised to see Rose sitting up in bed tonight when I went to check on her. Smiling like she was, her sweet face looking so happy, made my heart swell.

"I saw her, Callie," she said then, and I sat down next to her, curious.

"Who, honey?" I asked.

"Mama," she grinned, then rushed on. "Remember

when I couldn't think of what she looked like anymore? Well, I know now! I saw her just as plain as you."

For some reason it bothered me, her talking of Mama like that.

"Sounds like a real fine dream, honey," I said finally.

"Do you ever dream of her, Callie?" she asked, but fell into a deep sleep before I could answer her.

Thursday, August 18

Stem came by the boardinghouse this morning and talked to Quinn about when we might be ready to move on for California. I don't think any of us are looking forward to the pull through the desert, but everyone had to agree it would be wise to leave soon, so as not to get snowed in on the Sierra Mountains.

Mrs. Ashby's grandson gave me a ride to the other side of town today so that I could pick up a few things before we set out for California and Rich Bar. He had no more than flicked the reins when he began telling me he was a widower and that if I was interested, he would like to pay me a visit at the boarding-house. I quickly told him I was a married woman and that my husband worked in the mills. I tried to look very fierce as I was telling him this, but then he asked, "What's his name? I know several of the men at the mills.

And when I said, "Quinn McGregor," he seemed surprised.

"That big Irishman?" he asked. When I nodded, he looked worried and wouldn't talk the rest of the way—kept his eyes to the road and I had a hard time of it trying not to laugh.

Quinn and I took turns playing chess with Rose this evening. Considered it quite a treat. Mrs. Ashby, however, told me she figured the game to be the first step toward gambling. But there was no real rancor in her voice.

Friday, August 19

Quinn and I had only been asleep a minute or two tonight when Jack came banging on our door, saying Rose was feverish. As we rushed down the hallway behind him, he told us that she had been whimpering loudly in her sleep, that when he went to see what was the matter and felt her head, it was burning up.

"I ain't never seen her this bad, Callie," Jack said. When I walked into the room I could see right away that Rose's cheeks were flushed, but what scared me was the bloodless appearance of the rest of her body.

It was when she coughed into her handkerchief, and I saw the frothy red blood that stained the cloth that I felt horror take me. Rose's eyes met mine, calm, and it made me think she'd coughed up blood like that before.

"Don't be mad, Callie," she said, and I held her to me, whispering I could never be mad.

"Jack, you best go fetch Mrs. Ashby and see if they have a doctor around here," I said finally, softly. But even that didn't stop the sound of controlled terror in my voice from escaping.

I waited until Jack left the room before I turned around to where Quinn was standing in the doorway. He must have seen the worry on my face, because he tried to smile. "Is there anything you want me to do, then, Callie?"

"Pray," I told him.

Saturday, August 20

Jack is blaming himself for Rose being so sick. He keeps saying over and over that he shouldn't have taken her out to the lake. There is such terror in his eyes I can't bear to look at times.

Quinn tried to lay Jack's tormented mind to rest. "She's been on the trail for months, man," he told my brother. "One day in the sun wasn't what weakened her."

Jack got up from the table where we sat. He never did turn back, even though I called after him twice.

Sunday, August 21

When I'd made my way to Rose's room this evening, I was startled to hear Quinn's voice coming from just inside it—I had thought he was still at the mill. I stopped short of walking in and, instead, stayed in the hall and listened, watching the two through the half-opened door.

"My ma used to light a candle much like this one," Quinn was saying. "She used to light it for her sisters that were still across the ocean in Ireland. 'They're right this minute lighting one, too,' she would tell us all."

"What about Pa?" Rose whispered. "Will he see it?"

"Aye . . . But his answer will be the brightest light you see," Quinn replied, "winking back at you every night."

Rose seemed more than satisfied with his answer. When I saw the way she gazed up into Quinn's eyes with such faith, his big hands holding hers in such a tender way, it made me fall in love with him all over again.

Tears blurred my vision, watching his large frame bent over Rose, his hands encompassing her own—it was a part of him few saw.

The door groaned a little when I finally walked in, and I saw Quinn start to turn around. The shadows that danced across the room darkened Rose's pale features, and I felt my heart constrict with fear. In the silence, all that could be heard was the horrid wheeze that with each deathly rattle took Rose further away from us all.

When Quinn's eyes met mine, they mirrored the agony and helplessness that I had been trying to hide, and for a moment I wished I could run away. But instead, I crossed the room and sat down next to Quinn.

As we watched Rose drift off to sleep, I felt one of Quinn's hands reach out for my own, and I grasped it tightly.

We sat like that for a long while, holding on to each other with the kind of quiet desperation of people who don't know what else to do.

Monday, August 22

Stem came by to visit Rose today. He held her hand in his and asked her what she wanted for Christmas— said that we were going to have a fine Christmas when we reached California. Rose held tight to that leathered old hand and smiled at him.

"Christmas is such a long way off," I heard her whisper before she drifted off to sleep, and I knew in her own way she was gently trying to pull away from the living.

When Stem met me outside the door he didn't say anything, he just reached out and rested his hand on my shoulder. Before he walked away, I saw the tear that had escaped his eye, traveling slowly down his weather-beaten face. He didn't brush it away.

Later—Rose is not doing much better this evening. Grace came by and visited for a while. After she left I went and checked on Rose again, but found she had already fallen asleep.

But I could tell she had been up and about earlier.

The candle that Quinn had given her was lit, its small flickering light illuminating her little body, which was turned toward the window, the night sky shining through.

Tuesday, August 23

The doctor came and went this morning. He told us not to expect Rose to live through the night. I hated him for how easy he could tell us that, for walking out of the room and leaving us all behind knowing our lives would never, ever be the same again.

As the afternoon drifted into evening, Jack had come and talked to Rose for a while, his face stark with pain, and I prayed hard that Rose would open her eyes for him. When she didn't, he left and walked up and down the dusty road in front of the boarding-house. Watching him, it made me think he was trying to keep busy so he couldn't think—or maybe he was just trying to keep himself from running. Quinn stood in the hallway, just outside the door, his face peppered with stubble and his eyes red—whether from lack of sleep or crying, I wasn't sure. When his eyes met mine, I saw his fear and I quickly turned to Rose, stroking her fevered hand, blocking out the memory of his gaze as I begged her to live. I heard him walk away not long after that, but I didn't call after him.

For hours I watched her face for any sign that she might come to. I looked up once and was surprised to see Quinn in the room. "She's going to meet your folks, Callie," he said softly, finally, and I felt a part of me die along with those words.

"I need her," I sobbed. Quinn nodded, his eyes haunted, and I knew he understood what I meant. Later, I noticed he'd fallen asleep in the chair beside the bed.

It was somewhere along midnight when I felt Rose stir on the bed, and I was stunned to see her watching me, her eyes clear.

"I was thinking about that time Jack'd fallen asleep in the pasture," she said, her voice raspy. "We spread honey on his face, and the old milk cow came and licked it off, scaring him something silly. He took after us madder than a bull, and you and me got to laughing so hard we couldn't run no more." She smiled at me. "I could sure run back then, couldn't I?"

"You sure could," I told her, smiling. "And you will again. You'll see, everything's gonna be fine." I took her hand, it had become cool, but her pulse was faint.

"I always dreamed of being free of my body after that," Rose said like she hadn't heard me, staring down at the blankets that covered her thin little legs, as if she were looking at someone else. "It never seemed to work real good, least not since I got sick . . . Maybe . . ."

I wanted to tell Rose to fight, that there was still a chance, but she was looking out the window, staring into the blackness as if it was the best night she had ever witnessed.

Pa had always said that Rose was our gift from God, that she was the joy we all held on to when Mama passed away. *The Lord giveth and the Lord taketh away.* Those words ran over and over in my mind until I wanted to scream.

I felt the tears begin to run down my cheeks. An unbearable anguish filled me, and I pulled Rose into my lap, rocking her silently to and fro as I stroked her damp curls. *Oh, please,* I begged God, *please not her.* Rose's eyes met mine, filled with pity for me, a kind of knowledge I couldn't explain, as her breathing became more labored.

"Don't be scared . . . I'm not," Rose whispered weakly. She tried to raise up, but slumped back into my arms, spent. It was then that I noticed her looking behind me, her eyes wide in wonder. "Do you see them?"

"See who, Rose?"

"Oh, Callie . . . they all have wings. . . ."

She closed her eyes then, and although I could still see her chest moving up and down, I knew she was slipping away from me.

I grabbed Rose closer to me, holding her tight. "Don't leave me," I cried, rocking her in my arms, wanting her to stay just a little longer. But this time she didn't answer. As I kissed her, I felt her last faint breath warm my cheek.

There was no gasp, no cry of pain. Instead, my baby sister left me with a tiny smile on her sweet face. It was a smile, Quinn said later, that would make the angels sing.

And I believe they did.

228

Wednesday, August 24

Cried all afternoon. Oh, Rose.

Nightmares . . . I was no longer in Salt Lake but on the trail standing beside Grace while the wagons rolled over and over the small grave of Lizzie Hollister.

Unable to get back to sleep, I struck out across the town to the tiny graveyard where Rose would be laid to rest. Seeing where she was to be buried, I was overtaken with a kind of madness, remembering the day Grace lost Lizzie.

I grabbed up a rusty old shovel that had been left there and began to dig. When the scoop of the shovel broke off, I dug the earth away with my own bare hands, digging and digging until my fingers began to bleed. It seemed far off in the distance I could hear the sounds of Jack's and Stem's voices, calling me to come out of the grave, but I couldn't. It was then that I felt Quinn's strong arms grip me and pull me out of the pit.

"I can't let the wolves get her," I sobbed to Quinn. "Mama's coming to take her home."

"They'll not touch her, Callie. I promise you . . . I promise."

As he held me tight to his chest, his tears mixed with my own and I felt as if my heart was shattered into a hundred pieces.

"Got to say it out loud, lass. If you don't, 'twill eat away at your soul," he whispered to me. "Don't bitter yourself to life like I did when Patrick died . . ."

He didn't wait for me to answer, instead he picked me up and carried me back down the road to the boardinghouse.

Thursday, August 25

I woke early this morning and found that Jack had already taken Rose to the parlor for the viewing. As I quietly made my way down the stairs, I saw Quinn through the open doors of the parlor. He was leaning over Rose's body when he saw me, and he straightened up all of a sudden.

In a few quick strides he was with me, wrapping his arm around my shoulder. Wordlessly, he led me outside. Wagons rolled by, kicking the pale dust up like a cloud in the heat; a bell rang off somewhere faraway; people were laughing and talking.

No one paid much attention to Quinn or me as we huddled together in heartsick silence.

I heard a commotion outside the door of our room this evening, and when I went to see what was the matter, I found Quinn helping Jack down the hallway toward his room.

I could smell the liquor strong when I moved closer. I didn't say anything; I just put my shoulder under

Jack's other arm and helped Quinn get him to his room and into his bed.

When I was helping Jack off with his boots, he reached up and grabbed my hand, whiskey and grief making his voice thick. "We can't never seem to get out from under Death's shadow, can we Callie?" he asked.

Friday, August 26

I felt as if I couldn't breathe as I watched Rose's coffin slowly lowered into the ground today. Over and over in my mind I had begged someone to wake me from the nightmare, sometimes wondering if I was going mad and sometimes hoping I would so I could shut out the pain. Quinn took my hand and I held on to his tight.

"Sometimes I wake up at night and I'm . . . scared. I think I'm all alone and nobody can do anything because . . ." A chill went down my spine, remembering Rose's words, and I felt an insane urge to throw myself into the ground with my sister. Stem and Quinn stood on each side of me, both trying to shield me as the service began.

"Suffer the little children to come unto me, and forbid them not, for such is the Kingdom of God . . . "

Stem handed Jack the shovel, and he reluctantly scooped earth onto the casket, and when I turned away, I saw that Grace's cheeks were wet.

"May the Lord show mercy on those who are still

of this world and comfort the family that so loved this child . . ." The minister's voice faded from me as more dirt hit Rose's coffin with a horrible, final sound.

Loved? I wanted to scream at the minister. Did he think my love was suddenly gone? That it was any less now than when Rose was alive?

Jack was silent as he continued to fill the grave in. When the last shovel of dirt covered the coffin, Jack's eyes met mine for a moment, and they seemed to say, *"Well, Callie, looks like the joke's on me."* I started sobbing as he dropped the shovel and walked away.

Later this evening I found Jack out by the lake where he and Rose had gone hiking. He was sitting with his back propped against a huge rock, his hat tossed to one side.

"I meant to do right by her, Callie," he said, his long body hunched over with grief. "I promised Pa as much when he died." Jack's face was so drawn it seemed he'd aged twenty years. His hands were bruised and scraped from the sleepless hours he had spent fashioning Rose's coffin and headstone . . . as if he could extract payment from his own sweat and blood.

"She was happy, Jack . . . You gave her hope. More than what she would've had if we would've stayed back in Independence." He knew the truth of this, but I could read the lingering doubt in his eyes. *Was it enough, Callie?*

Jack stood up, shoving one hand through his hair as he looked back toward the cemetery. "It ain't right to bury a child, Callie . . . It just ain't right."

I took hold of Jack's hand, just as I had done when we were kids, squeezing it tight.

Hand in hand we walked the lonely stretch of road

back into the town; neither of us said a word. There was nothing left to say.

I feel such an emptiness. When I think back, I can't remember not taking care of Rose, or having her near, always there to give me a hug or ask her countless questions . . . to tell me she loved me.

> There's many an empty cradle,
> There's many a vacant bed,
> There's many a lonesome bosom
> Whose joy and light have fled.
> For thick in every graveyard,
> The little hillocks lie.
> And every hillock represents
> An angel in the sky. . . .

It's a comfort to think of Rose as an angel. Even if I could, I wouldn't call her back to this sorry world filled with sickness and death.

ASHBY HOUSE
L. ASHBY, PROPRIETOR
Good Bath and Sample Rooms

August 27, 1859
Salt Lake City, Utah

Mrs. Maggie Todd
Blue Mills, Missouri

Dear Maggie,
As much as it pains me to write you the news,
I can't help thinking you would want to know.

233

You were always as much a part of our family as anyone, and I know how much you loved my little sister.

We buried Rose yesterday, Maggie. The doctor that saw to her said he wondered how she lasted this long, her lungs couldn't have been no more than cobwebs. That didn't surprise me none; she's always been the strong one—too good for this world.

Why is it that God takes the good ones, Mag? The harder I look for the reasons, the harder they are to find. I guess sometimes there are no answers.

Jack has taken Rose's passing something awful. When we were standing at Rose's grave, I saw him turning old before my eyes. He's drawn up somewhere inside of himself now, and as hard as I try, I can't reach him. He seems so alone. . . .

Pray for us, Mag. We're so weary, and I can't help but feel as if this journey has been a cruel joke on us all.

> *Your heartsick friend,*
> *Callie*

Sunday, August 28

Cleaning out the things in Rose's room, I found a letter from her tucked away in Mama's Bible. Just seeing her handwriting, each word painstakingly written, brought tears to my eyes.

Dear Callie,

You'll be reading this after I'm gone. I've knowd for a while that I wouldn't make it to Californy with you, Jack, and McGregor. I'm thinkin that God has other things planned for me, kinda like the preecher back home sayd. But I don't want you to cry or be sad. I've missed Pa for an awful long time, and I know that I'm goin to be with him—Mama, too. I'm a little scairt, goin on without you. Long as I member, you've always been there, holdin my hand when I needed it and comferten me when I was scairt. And makin me laf.

You've give me so much that I was feelin poorly cause I didn't have nothin to leave to you. Then I membered what Pa said about Mama leavin him all the Good times to member.

So, I'm leavin all our Good times with you, because that's what I'm wishin for you, Callie— sunshine and laughter. I'm wishin this because I know you won't for yourself. Most of all, I'm wishin for you what you gave me . . . I'm wishin you Love. I will always be

Your sister,
Rose

I read the letter and reread it, and then I tucked it in front of Mama's Bible, wondering as I closed the book if I would ever have the courage to look at it again.

Monday, August 29

I had a dream last night that I was standing in a big field of flowers and across the field I saw Rose. She was laughing and running . . . just as she'd always hoped, with no pain, no gasping for air.

The dream changed, and Rose was running to the front yard of our home back in Independence. For a moment, I saw the shadow of Mama sitting on the front porch. She became plainer to see as she stood and leaned over the rail of the porch, looking younger than I ever remembered. She smiled at me then, a warm, comforting smile, and then she turned to Rose. *"Rose!"* Mama called. *"It's time to come on home, now."*

When I woke up I was sobbing, but this time out of joy and not sorrow. A feeling of peace had come over me while I layed there listening to the steady rise and fall of Quinn's breathing. And just as the thin threads of dawn began to seep through the window of our room, I felt him begin to stir. In his sleep he reached out for me, folding me into the safety of his arms.

We all get lost one time or another in our lives, searching desperately to somehow find our way home. I guess it seems fitting that the ones that love you the most hold the light to guide your way back.

Tuesday, August 30

I was shrugging my wrap on this morning when I heard the voices of Mrs. Ashby and Jack outside my window. "At least have something to eat, Jack," she was saying. "No telling when you'll have a decent meal again."

Not believing what I had heard, I quickly ran down the stairs and out the front door to find Jack standing next to Big Black, saddled and ready.

"You're leaving?" I said.

"I left a letter for you," he said, "that and your share of money from the portion of the herd I brought in; what's left of the stock, I figure, is yours, along with the wagon and what's in it." Jack stood there unmoving as Quinn caught up with us.

"What did the letter say, Jack?" I said. "That you'd go without so much as a by-your-leave to anyone? I'd expect that from a stranger . . . but not from my own brother." Jack started to turn away from me, but I held on to his arm. I couldn't help but see how much Rose's death had changed him, making him more hard, bitter.

"Don't go," I begged, and I saw something foreign flicker across his face.

"I've seen too much death," Jack said quietly. "Hell, Callie, we lost Pa and now Rose. . . . I couldn't bear it if anythin' happened to you. It may sound like the coward's way, but I have to get away for a while . . . try to sort things out." For a moment, he'd let down the mask and I saw all the sorrow and grief that he tried to hide.

I realized too late that Jack had shouldered his pain alone. When Quinn and I had held each other in our grief, Jack had been forgotten. Always standing on the outside looking in.

"Try not to think of what might have been, Callie," he said, as if reading my thoughts.

I let go of his arm and shook my head, but no words would come. Is that what he did? I wondered, buried all the dreams of what might have been? *"The tragedy of life is what dies inside of a man while he lives,"* I remembered Quinn saying not so long ago.

Jack turned to Quinn. "Watch out for my sister, McGregor. . . . She's all I have left. Good luck in Rich Bar."

As Jack mounted up, I noticed for the first time the belt that was swung low around his hips—and the all too familiar set of pistols. Scenes flashed in my mind. I saw Grace holding the pistol the day she taught me how to shoot; then I saw Lizzie, her lifeless body cradled in Grace's arms, the pistol laying in the dirt next to them, and I suddenly felt a horrible sense of foreboding.

"He'll die out there, Quinn," I whispered, feeling Quinn's arms wrap around my waist as we watched Jack ride out of town.

"It's not death he's seeking, Callie," Quinn said, his voice deep with understanding. "It's life."

Late tonight I opened the door to Jack's room and found it empty. I lit the lamp then and sat on Jack's bed, searching for some sign that he'd been there. All I found were my memories.

We were kids again, laying beneath the willow tree back home.

"What do you want to be when you grow up, Jack?" I'd asked, watching him chew on a piece of grass as he gazed up into the sky.

"Happy," he'd replied, but his young face had been grim, as if he might never find what it took to get there.

Oh, Jack . . . I pray you find what you need wherever you're going. And I hope with all my heart it will be enough.

Later—Quinn just told me that we would be leaving in the morning. In my mind I know it's probably wise for us to go on to California now, before the snows come to the mountains, but in my heart it seems so wrong to leave Rose so soon. Stem will be coming to stay in Rich Bar with us.

Wednesday, August 31

Good-byes are hard most anytime, but this morning I felt as if my heart were being torn from me when I said good-bye to all. Mrs. Ashby has developed quite a liking for us, and I could see she was having a time of it, like I was, letting go. She told me she thought it was a mistake, us going to California this late in the year, while she bustled about her kitchen, stuffing little "extras" for us into a large basket. "But I suppose you think you're unbeatable," she said, and then shrugged. "Oh, well, it's a vice that generally fades after youth—if one lives that long." Her reproach seemed to fade once we were outside by the wagons, and I saw she was sad. When I hugged her, there were tears standing in her eyes, and she sniffed, greatly annoyed. "Sometimes I get the feeling we women are destined to laugh by the inch and cry by the yard," she said, then turned and fairly ran back into her house.

Later—Grace and Jared were waiting in his buckboard at the end of the road that led out toward the cemetery. Their engagement wasn't a surprise.

It was Grace's idea that we should walk together, and it seemed fitting that we should—we'd walked side by side through so much. I saw Jared frown as Quinn and Stem pulled out. "Walk?" he said. "It's nearly three miles to the cemetery."

Grace looked at him in the way of a woman who loves a man in spite of his shortsightedness. "I imagine three miles is something Callie and I could do in our sleep by now," she said wryly, and linked her arm in mine, and we started off down the road. We talked in spurts as we walked, finally falling into a long silence when we neared Rose's grave.

Quinn, Stem, and Jared seemed to sense our need to be alone and kept near the wagons as we both sank down to the ground next to the little grave strewn with wild roses. The pain of knowing I had to leave Rose behind seemed more than I could bear. Over and over I still felt her little arms around my neck, still saw her smile so clear. How could she have been here one moment talking, breathing, and the next gone? "It seems such a horrible mistake," I said after a while, "God taking Pa and Rose and leaving me behind."

"It's not a mistake, Callie," she said. "I don't reckon any of us will ever figure out God's choices, but He does seem to have a way of righting things." Grace's face softened. "You and Quinn McGregor finding each other . . . Now, that's no mistake. Best thing you can do is take what happiness you can." Grace hugged me tight, and when she let go, I had a strange feeling come over me, like I wasn't standing there with Grace anymore, like I was already gone.

"I'll miss you," I said, and she smiled in spite of the tears that streamed down her cheeks. It was best not to say any more, mostly because I didn't think I could. Why, I wondered, does it have to be this way? Having no answers, I stumbled on, blinded by my own tears as I ran toward our wagons. I turned around only once and saw Grace still standing there. For a moment I caught a glimpse of the young girl she must have been, when life had yet to take so much from her. Her face changed then, and she appeared more angry than sad as a chilled wind whipped the shawl she'd been clutching off her shoulders.

"Don't ever look back, Callie," she called urgently. "Don't ever look back."

Thursday, September 1

Passed by farms that marked the last of civilization for a while. Once again, I am leaving behind a piece of myself. As our two wagons moved along, the oxen faithfully following the team in front, I felt the distance begin to yawn wide between us and our last ties to Rose, and I gritted myself against the pain of it. Quinn glanced up at me once as he goaded the animals on, and I saw that he felt it, too.

I didn't cry this time, although I wanted to.

And unlike Quinn and Stem, who stopped for a moment, staring back over the miles that separated us and Rose, I never looked back.

Just woke from a dream—Rose and I together again. When she hugged me it felt so *real*, so wonderful, but then I woke up, and the pain of her passing was worse.

She's in heaven, the voices whisper, voices of my mama and my pa. Somewhere in my soul I know it's true. Yet here *I* am, with my loss, my shattered hopes. I wonder if grief is for those we lose, or better, those of us who have lost?

Friday, September 2
Great Salt Lake Valley

So low in my mind as we crossed the Weber River today, I can't remember if we had a hard time of it or not. The whole morning seemed like a dream. I sat on the hard seat, hearing the sounds: the rush of water as the wagon dipped down in the current, the stock protesting as they were prodded out, Stem and Quinn whistling and shouting. It was as if everything moved on but me, and I recall thinking it wasn't right, that it was too cold and orderly, everyone going on about their business as if Rose never was. When Quinn looked over at me, I wanted nothing more than to step down from my perch and run into his arms, but I didn't. Seems impossible to be strong and grieve at the same time.

Made it as far as Ogden. Came across another group of weary travelers, consisting of two men and one woman. One of the men, a gentleman from Kentucky by the name of Lije Harding, spoke for the small group. He told us that they would be obliged if we let them join on with us. He said that they'd already lost a child and his wife was in the "family way" and was having a hard time of it. He offered to do the hunting for us if we would agree to let them come.

"Me an' my brother, Sam, we don't need much," he said, his face screwed up painful with embarrassment, "but I was hopin' you might have some food to spare for my wife."

I remember Mama saying that a surefire cure to help you forget your troubles was to jump into someone else's. I guess I went in both feet first, rushing around, gathering up beans and jerked meat, filling a little basket with some of the dried peaches Mrs. Ashby gave me. My mind went forward, thinking of a new friend—a woman I could confide in, someone who'd lost and had to move on just like us. I'd headed for the wagon while the men stood around, talking, but when I got there, I couldn't find anyone in sight. After calling out a greeting once or twice, it struck me that maybe the woman didn't *want* company.

Disheartened, I left my offerings and turned to leave

when out of the corner of my eye I saw a frightfully thin face peer out the back curtain of the wagon, dark eyes shifting from side to side until they rested on me for a moment. "Mrs. Harding," I began, and the face retreated, reminding me of a ferret ducking into its hole.

It was when I moved away, heading for my wagon, that I saw Lije Harding standing not far from me, a sorry look on his face.

"Carrie ain't herself, Mrs. McGregor," he said, looking down at the hat in his hands. "She don't talk much, nor get out of the wagon, for that matter."

Any other time it would have been a little thing, this strange woman shunning my company. For some reason it hit me hard. Before the man could say any more, I turned away, tears filling my eyes, so that I couldn't see what was before me. I didn't realize Quinn was standing at the back of our wagon until I nearly ran him over.

When Quinn said, "What is it, lass?" a part of me yearned for nothing more than to give in to my grief, but another part was afraid if I let go that I might never find my way back, and if that happened then Pa and Rose dying would be for nothing. Then he pulled me into his arms, and I felt a piece of the wall I'd built around me since leaving Rose start to crumble. But I patched it up quick.

I stepped back from him, put on my best face, and smoothed over the wrinkles of my dusty, tattered skirt. "I best get the meal started," I said.

"Are you sure you're all right?" he said, and I could hear the worry.

"Just foolishness," I said. Then I walked off before he could see the untruth of it in my eyes.

* * *

Later—Finding it hard to fall asleep. I dozed for a while but woke with a start. Thinking of Rose again, of Pa and Jack. Seems the longer it is without them, the harder it gets. When I look to the heavens, the only question that comes to mind is "Why?"—such a small word, *why*. If only He knew how much His answer would mean to me. . . .

Saturday, September 3

Evening—I think I learned today what Mama meant when she told me that the calm after a storm gives peace to weary souls. We've just finished setting up camp for the night—the only sound that might be heard is the gathered sigh of relief after the long day we've endured. Trouble came with the dawn, before we could get the sleep out of our eyes. The hail struck just before full light, battering against our wagons with such fury I was sure the canvas wouldn't hold up. Quinn, Stem, the Harding men, and I went right to work, lashing the wagons down to picket pins as the hail stung our faces and hands. We no sooner had that done than the stock ran off—horses would've, too, if Quinn hadn't tied them to the wheels. With the storm worsening, we had no choice but to take to the wagons until it died down and pray we'd find the animals after.

It wasn't until Quinn and I were sitting huddled together, with our wet clothes and water pooling around our feet, that the feeling of hopelessness struck me full force. Quinn wrapped his strong arms around me, trying to ward off the chill, when I began to shake. Then the tears came and the angry ragged sobs, sobs of pent-up grief and frustration that poured out to rise and fall with the wrath of the storm. Through it all, Quinn held me as I railed over the unfairness of everything, as I tried to bargain with God—then begged. When I finally fell silent, Quinn turned me to him and touched my face with his large, callused hands, and he kissed me. When he finally pulled away, his eyes held mine and I felt a peace come over me, an understanding that sometimes there aren't any answers in life, only acceptance.

"Don't give up on life, Callie," he said then. "Don't give up on us."

It wasn't until we heard the sound of hooves pounding past our wagon, heard Stem and the Harding brothers whistle and shout followed by the bawl of cattle, that we realized the storm had passed.

Later—I left Quinn sleeping only a short while ago to come out here and write, to try to sort out the feelings I can't seem to speak. For a time tonight I came alive again in his arms. Lately, grief is the first thing I wake to and my last thought before I sleep. But the memory of our love, of Quinn's touch, is strong in spite of the chill that this fire doesn't reach.

I was in the wagon when he came to me, when he took this journal from me and laid it to one side so he could pull me into his arms. There was none of the slow deliberateness he usually has with me, just urgency, and I felt I was being carried into the storm once more. The way he touched me, running his hands down my body. The look in his pale eyes as he hovered over me, and then when I met him with the same yearning, the happiness on his face. For a time the world was pushed aside and it was only he and I.

I watched him sleeping for a long while after, surprised, in a way, that I could feel such strong love seeing the sleep-smile that creased his tanned face. It was when I brushed back the black lock of hair from his forehead that the thought struck me that the choice was there, to take the good with the bad. *It's up to you, Callie,* I found myself thinking; *after all, how would any of us feel joy if we hadn't ever felt sorrow?*

How I wish I could keep my feelings separate. Is it possible to feel love and heartache at the same time?

Oh, Lord, if you hear me, give me the strength to be a good wife, help me through this journey—help us all through. Let me feel the sun on my face again and hear my own laughter.

Sunday, September 4

Sabbath—but no rest for the weary yet.

We had just struck the Bear River when Indians appeared. I'd been walking, prodding the oxen along at a steady pace, the other team plodding behind, when I noticed the Harding wagon slowing down in front of me. That's when I saw them, fourteen or fifteen braves, scraggly-looking but armed. As they rode closer to our little train, blocking the trail ahead, I had the insane urge to laugh, and shout, *"Death, hailstorms, now Indians. What next, Lord?"*

I heard Stem mutter under his breath then, reining in next to me as Quinn rode up to meet them. I guess it was more the look on Stem's face, than anything else, that scared me at first. Stem, who seemed to take everything as a common occurrence, who wouldn't waste ink on anything less than a full-scale battle with the Sioux, was genuinely worried.

"What do they want?" I asked.

"Them's *Digger* Indians, Callie," he replied. "They'll take about anythin' they can git." Keeping one eye on Quinn, he went on to tell me that he'd run into them before in his travels. He said that they mostly did their work on the sly, hiding along the trail to pilfer from gold seekers or to tomahawk a lone traveler. "These young'uns are bolder than most."

Something caught his attention. He squinted for a moment and then began to laugh. "Yessir, bold but stupid. There's a trader out there laughin' himself silly—Those guns are older than I am."

"So, they're no good?" I asked.

"Ain't worth the effort ta carry 'em," he said.

The relief I felt was soon washed away as we heard a woman's scream come from the Harding wagon and turned to see one of the braves sticking his head in the back curtain, playing tug-of-war with Carrie Harding over the basket I'd given her. Before any of us could say a word, Quinn whirled his horse around from where the leader stood, rode up, and cracked the brave over the head with the butt of his gun.

In the silence that followed, no one seemed to quite know how to react—especially the Indians. They drew together, talked for a bit, scowled, and then argued amongst themselves, pausing long enough to look back at us—at the Harding men, Quinn, and Stem, who had their guns leveled their way.

"Move on," Quinn shouted, and much to our surprise, they did just that, leaving their fallen comrade, still sprawled facedown, in the dust of their departing ponies.

"Quinn must've noticed the guns, too," I said then.

"Maybe," Stem said. "It were still a jackass thing ta do, them outnumberin' us and all. Well, Jack said once the good Lord looks after fools and drunkards. I know he ain't drunk. Either he's a fool or jes damned lucky."

Later—Crossed the Bear River easy enough, it being not more than four rods wide and still. Three more miles and we came to Malad, a miry stream with enough mosquitoes to drive off a city, but evidently not enough to drive off the Indians. Three women and a child came to camp there not long after we had set up for the night.

I'd no more than got the fire going when I glanced up and was met by four pairs of eyes whose owners looked as sorry as I felt—tattered shreds of cloth hanging limp on too thin bodies, faces pinched with hunger—as they stood a ways back from our camp. It was the little boy that affected me most, his dark eyes following me like those of an old man, waiting for his last day. That hit me hard, for in his face I saw all the little ones whose innocence was stripped from them by hardship. Before Quinn or Stem could stop me, I gathered what food I could spare and waved for them to come closer. The youngest of the women stepped forward, proud in spite of the leaves and sticks that clung to her matted hair and the layer of dirt that covered her body. She gave me a scornful look, grabbed the food, then turned and handed it over to the others. In less than a minute, they were gone, swallowed up by the dark.

"Yer courtin' trouble, Callie," Stem said, and I was surprised to see the gun in his hand before he holstered it once more.

Across the fire, I saw Quinn search the distance. "It's Sam's turn at guard tonight," he said, almost to himself. "Maybe I should tell Lije to stick close to him." When he turned back to me, his eyes told me he understood, but he was worried, too.

"Three women and a little boy—what could they do?" I said. "They're beat."

"Beat or not, they'd jes as soon kill ya fer that piece o' calico yer wearin' than not," Stem said, calmly. "I wouldn't doubt if'n those braves put 'em up ta it. Where there's one, there's bound ta be more."

More worried then, I watched the little group until it grew dark, their figures blocking the glow of their fire as they moved about near the stream. I never saw anyone else. But just before I turned away, I made out one of the women as she knelt down next to the little boy, saw her pat his head affectionately, and I felt my heart go out to them.

How can Stem believe these pitiful creatures will cause us trouble?

Monday, September 5

Early—What fool-headed thing did I write last night about trouble? Funny how life has a way of proving you wrong when you're convinced you're right.

I'd been so busy cleaning up after breakfast and packing that I'd almost forgot about those Indian women—until Stem came to the wagon with a grimace on his face. Sam Harding trailed behind him, leaning against Lije, an angry-looking gash on his forehead. The "squaws" had lit out sometime last night, Stem told me, taking one of our pack horses with them. He said Sam was lucky they were good-natured enough to leave him behind alive, that it was probably due to them being in a hurry.

"It's a fair guess what they'll be eatin' tonight," he said then, and I was struck hard by those words—not at the thought of them eating the mule—but because I *knew* before he'd even said it what they intended. It occurred to me then how much the journey had changed me, how back home I couldn't't've imagined folks being so hungry as to butcher a mule, let alone understand it.

"Are you going to go after them?" I asked finally, and much to my relief Stem shook his head.

"Ain't worth the time we'd lose," he said, putting his shoulder under Sam Harding's arm. When they walked off, I felt a little like a child that had been chastised. Though I felt good that we weren't going to go after them, I felt to blame for Sam Harding's injury, that it was my fault, inviting them into our camp. Quinn, who had been quiet the entire time, wrapped his arms around me then, his voice quiet.

"Don't blame yourself too much, Callie," he said. "If what he says is true, they needed that animal far more than we do." He put his hand under my chin and raised my eyes to his. "But don't be thinking you can save the world, lass. Sometimes it doesn't want to be saved." His expression was one of painful understanding. *You can't make up for Rose,* was what it seemed to say.

How well he knows me.

Later—Quiet night, all of us being worn to the bone. Drove thirteen miles—up a hill, through a valley, then on to climb another hill, finally reaching Blue Springs only to find the water warm and brackish. So it was on the move again, fourteen miles further, where we found a good cold spring (Hensell's Spring, I think) and are now camped. The Hardings asked Stem about the Sierras this evening. He said, "Got ta cross the desert first, boys. Best ta git out of one fix before ya figger another." The silence that followed spoke volumes.

Still no sign of Mrs. Harding. I wonder what she is thinking, if she's longing for home like me. I wish she was more amiable. Hearing another woman's voice would be a comfort.

Quinn has just called for me to come to bed. More later.

Tuesday, September 6

Cool today but dusty. Rode out with Quinn first thing this morning, before we reached a wide valley filled with sagebrush. We were forced to go another sixteen miles before finding any good water to speak of, finally stopping at a place called Pilot Springs. Quinn laughed when I shamelessly hitched up my skirts to run into the stream, splashing water on my face and arms, scrubbing for all I was worth. " 'Tis good to see you cheered," he said. "I think I'd end our journey here if I could take some of the sadness out of your eyes."

I'd straightened up and looked at him. Standing on the bank like he was, smiling, with the sun and the cedar-blanketed mountainside behind him, I couldn't help thinking how *good* he was. When he held his hand out to me and helped me up the bank, the urge to be close to him came over me, and I gave in to it, resting my head against his chest as he held me tight.

"I love you, you know," he said, and I held quiet, waiting for the grief to come, the pain to put the moment to an end, but for once it didn't.

"I know you do," I said. "Although sometimes I wonder why."

"We've come a long way together, haven't we, lass?" he asked, but before I could answer our scraggly little train began to file in; Lije and Sam Harding first, their voices muffled under the sounds of wheels grinding over rock; Stem trailing behind in a haze of dust as the stock caught the scent of water, breaking into a weak trot.

Later—Camped here on the first bench of a mountain. Cold. Fire is dying, so I must save my thoughts for another time.

Wednesday, September 7

Long, tiresome day today—dust and loose rock once again, wearing nerves thin on both man and beast. Passed through scenic country though, low ranges of mountains in sight nearly all day, capped in snow. Traveled nearly twenty-eight miles, the last leg of it through the head of an immense valley before camping here, along Trout Creek.

Carrie Harding absent, as usual. I'd have a hard time believing she was real if I hadn't seen Lije leaving her a bucket of water at the back step of their wagon this evening—if I hadn't seen her wait until his back was turned before she tipped it over.

Later—Went to check on Quinn this evening as he was corralling the stock. When I finally found him, he was leaning against a tree, watching the animals intently.

"I thought you were going to round them up," I

said, and when he turned to me, I was surprised to see the reluctance in his eyes.

"I haven't the heart to pull them in just yet, Callie," he said, and I realized he was seeing *us,* hemmed in and caged within this jail of our own making, bound by miles.

We stood together for a long while after that, watching the herd as they grazed freely over the rolling slopes, watched as a few young calves ran at each other playfully, feeling their abandon as if it were our own.

Thursday, September 8
City of Rocks

Left off early, traveling only four miles before we crossed Raft River, then along the stream for some ways, inching up a trail not much wider than the wagons before we nooned here opposite the City of Rocks. Rocks are huge, white as marble, and some several hundred feet in height—beautiful in their own rugged way.

I've just come back from a walk with Quinn. It was when we reached the ridge of the canyon that I was struck again by how deceiving the beauty of this land can be. Down below, at the base of the rock, there are two wagons, or what is left of them. Seeing them has unsettled me.

* * * *

Later—Camped at Goose Creek this evening, washed-out and weary.

Traveled hard after leaving the City of Rocks, some of the steepest, rockiest hills I've ever seen. My feet, swollen and bloody as they are, are proof of that. Quinn just brought me my shoes—he managed to patch the soles with some canvas.

Friday, September 9

Another long day. Drove hard; didn't stop for noon, as we spotted Digger Indians in the area. Passed through a narrow canyon until we finally camped here, at Rock Spring, where the road leaves Goose Creek. Huge rocks flank our camp, covered with bright yellow lichen. My feet, being as sore as they are, stopped me from taking a closer look. It wouldn't have done much good, anyway, poor mood that I'm in.

The men aren't in much better spirits. After dinner, when I climbed out of the wagon for a breath of air, I saw them standing around the fire, the four of them, hands shoved into their pockets, as they spoke in low tones. Lije appeared troubled, his face haggard as he glanced toward his wagon.

"I'm worried about Carrie," I heard him say, sounding tired. "She ain't handlin' things well. I wish this journey was over already."

Everyone fell silent. It was a wish we all held somewhere down deep, but one that we couldn't afford to have come out—or at least it *shouldn't* have come out. Not with all the miles yet to go.

"Wishbone ain't no substitute fer a backbone, Lije," Stem said, sharp, and the way he looked around to all of us makes me think the advice was meant for more than Lije.

Saturday, September 10

Cool day, trail long and arduous. Drove thirteen miles over a very stony mountain, made the mistake of passing a spring without taking water and ended up finding nothing drinkable for another twenty miles. On and on we went; high wind kicking up so much dust I tied a kerchief over my face and donned Pa's old hat. I walked most of the day until reaching Thousand Spring Valley—in spite of Quinn's protests. Our poor oxen didn't look as if they could take much more.

I'm having a hard time believing *I* can.

Sunday, September 11
Thousand Spring Valley

Sabbath—the first one in a long time that we've been granted a rest on—or at least a spell from the trail. Quinn and I worked most of the morning, riding side by side, helping to drive the loose cattle to the springs that fill the valley. As sweaty and sore as I was from our labors, it felt good to be near him, felt good not to have to think of miles or wonder what is over the next hill, even if only for a day.

Tuesday, September 13
Humboldt River

Funny how little things can sometimes make all the difference.

Everything started easy enough as we began this morning, over hills and through valleys once again. But the stock got "wrathy" as Stem called it, as each spring we came to turned out worse than the one before, poisonous and smelling like the strongest lye. Then dust, dust, and more dust, so deep it appeared ashlike, thickening the air and clinging to our ragged clothes as we plodded on and on.

"Ain't much further ta the Humboldt, folks," Stem called, trying to get us to take heart. But the next few hours wore on us, the sameness, mile after mile. I watched Lije Harding's shoulders go rounder and lower by the hour, as if his burdens were becoming too heavy. Then I saw him glance to his wagon, defeat clear on his face, and it was all too familiar. I remembered that same look on Bess Mercer's face not so long ago, and what I'd said: *"We're all scared,"* I'd told her. *"But these little ones need you. How are you going to help them if you can't help yourself?"* I peered up then to our own wagon seat where Rose had sat so often, and the pain of my loss sliced through me fresh: *But who needs me?*

Like an answer to a prayer, Quinn appeared, reining in alongside of me, sleeves rolled up to show those big work-strong arms of his. His pale eyes seemed to take in everything. "River's not but a mile more," was all he said, but when he smiled I felt a part of something, a togetherness that had been hiding somewhere in the shadow of my grief, and a renewed strength came over me.

When he rode away, I squared my shoulders and hawed the team on, as I walked beside them, determined not to let the trail beat me.

Later—I'd got the fire going and started cleaning the fish Quinn had caught when I happened to glance up and see him watching me work. I started for the scraps and sticks I'd gathered earlier, but Quinn moved quicker, adding more kindling to the blaze before turning back to me.

"You're pushing too hard, Callie," he told me gently. "Working yourself until you drop, until you have no time to think, to *feel*. One day soon this journey will be over. What will you do then?"

I answered as honest as I could.

"Figure it out when I get there," I said, looking up into those eyes of his for a moment before turning back to my work.

Wednesday, September 14

The trail is getting rougher. We had a hard time of it, pushing and prodding, finally double-teaming to get up the steep inclines. No relief when we made it over, though—twenty miles and no water save for two or three muddy springs. Then more hardship; on and on through the dust and heat, alkali stinging our faces as we were jarred over wagon ruts so deep the sides of the trail met the tops of our wheels.

Camp wasn't much better, the water being foul, and I watched as the oxen slumped to the ground, still under the yoke, their large eyes following Quinn as he replaced the yoke and chained them to our wagon.

"Why can't we let them go free?" I asked, feeling their bondage like it was my own. Quinn was quiet as I dropped down next to them. I took my little casket of water and bathed their parched tongues with a wet rag.

"No choice, Callie," he told me finally. "Even as tired as they are, if I were to let them loose, they would take off for water and we might never get them back."

Poor beasts, even they yearn to escape this Godless country.

September 15–22

I haven't written in quite a while, not for lack of words, but because of the sheer drain this leg of the journey has been on us. Lately, it's been all any of us can do to keep our feet moving until Stem calls us to camp. The days have been long and monotonous, the next worse than the one before; deep sand, the river so foul and muddy that we've been forced to go sometimes a full day before finding good water or passable food for the animals. Dinner is hurried; dried meat with bread baked days before, and the strain to get through it so we can go to bed.

Even as I put this to paper, my body aches to lay down, for me to shut my eyes and drift off into nothingness before the next day dawns.

Yet a voice in me whispers that I must write, if only to remember who I am.

> *Along the Humboldt River*
> *In transit to California*
> *September 23, 1859*

Mrs. Maggie Todd
Blue Mills, Missouri

Dear Maggie,
   Home has been so much on my mind tonight that in spite of my weariness, I felt obliged to

write you—and to remember. Memories of home are hard to come by lately and tougher to share, what with Jack gone, taking off on his own soon after Rose was buried. Sitting here, I couldn't help thinking that the things I once took for granted now mean so much, like family laughter on a front porch, a cool shade tree, a good bath or a soft bed to rest in . . . a friend to tell your troubles to—things that seem as far away from me as God Himself out here in this barren land.

There is a woman traveling with us, but my hopes of sharing anything with her were put down shortly after she and her husband joined our outfit. She rarely shows her face, let alone speaks. I can't say I blame her; she's lost one little one . . . along with her hope.

When we first started out, I used to wonder how folks did it, how they moved on in spite of all of their losses. Now I know. The trail is a greedy thing, Mag; it takes and takes for the miles it allows you. With nothing left of your past, there's no choice for some but to march forward. And so I have, all the while praying for strength—and finding it in the love in Quinn's eyes.

The shame of it is that fighting to go on, to survive, is taking its toll on me, and I worry I have nothing left to give to him in return, Mag. Already, I have felt a change in me, a hardness that wasn't there before, and although Quinn doesn't mention it, I know he's seen it, too.

In the waning light here in this wagon, I can see the proof of my past; Pa's old hat, Mama's rocker and Bible, Rose's dresses, her dolls. Daughter, sister, friend . . . I've been them all.

*But now I am a wife, and I find myself scared
and searching for proof of a future.*

*Life is a lot harder than I dreamed. But then
isn't that why we call them dreams? I have to go
for now, so that I don't use up all our light. It's
probably just as well, this letter is a poor greeting
to a friend.*

> *With much love*
> *Your troubled friend,*
> *Callie*

Saturday, September 24
Great Meadows

We have reached the meadows this afternoon,
weary, our clothes stiffened with sand. The men
loosed the animals shortly before we reached the
river—a good thing, for once they caught the scent of
the water, they scrambled, plunging in deep until all
that showed were their snouts. I told Quinn I was
tempted to join them, and the men laughed. The strain
has faded a little from the faces of us all—at least
for the time being. We've just finished cutting grass,
cooking, and preparing for our drive across the *desert*,
some of which will be done by the light of the moon.

Later—I am worried about Carrie Harding. Lije just
confessed he thinks her time is soon.

* * *

Creaked through twenty miles of sage and dry river-beds before reaching the Humboldt sink tonight. Tired—but had no more fallen into bed when I heard the crunch of stone against sand, hard footsteps outside our wagon, and a scared voice came just outside our curtain. "Mrs. McGregor?"

It was Lije.

"It's my woman," he whispered. "I think the baby's comin'."

I was up and dressed in no time, quickly following behind Lije to their wagon. Moving around inside proved to be a chore, though; clothes and linens were piled everywhere, half-eaten food. In the middle of it all lay Carrie Harding, squirreled beneath dirty covers, her face just poking out. As she went to speak, a spasm of pain gripped her and she writhed beneath the covers, then her face went slack. After I'd sent the men off, she seemed to come to quick, her eyes locking with mine.

"I just want to go home," she said. "I don't care no more about California, the gold, or the baby, for that matter." She didn't speak a word after that, not even a moan when the labor became hard, when I fought to keep the bleeding down.

The little one was born about an hour later. A tiny mite of a boy, with a thin cry that reminded me of the brother we lost. As much as Lije and I pleaded and cajoled, Carrie refused to look at him, let alone nurse.

Lije, who appears so much older than he had that first day I saw him, took the boy up in his arms and asked for me to show him how to make a sugar tit for the babe.

Sunday, September 25

I think poor Carrie Harding has gone mad, and I wonder if I'm not close behind.

Her little baby boy died this evening, along the time we came to Boiling Springs. If I could ever imagine hell on earth, it was there, surrounded by deep pits of boiling water and steam, the strong stench of sulfur overwhelming us as Lije and Sam filled the tiny grave and marked it with a crude cross fashioned from the sideboards of a wagon.

We were forced to move on shortly after, and I was surprised that Carrie didn't cry or ask to stay a bit longer. She just marched out behind her husband's wagon as if nothing had happened, her back straight, her steps sure through the deep sand.

I think it was only an hour later when she started saying awful things, loud, so that it carried in the smothering desert heat as we plodded on, drowning out my quiet "haw" to the team, the jangle of chains, the hoarse bellows of the stock.

She said she was glad that the baby had gone on, she didn't want the trouble of it, she never loved it anyway. She said when it looked at her, struggling against death, she was a little sorry, but real glad when it finally died.

Then she laughed, and suddenly I felt as though the last thread that held me intact had snapped.

In all our journey no part had ever felt so heavy,

so hard to bear. On and on I dragged through the sandy waste, images going through my mind, memories of Pa and Rose—especially Rose. I saw her back home, laughing, then on the trail, her sweet face looking at me with such trust; next I saw her as she died, her eyes filled with such pity when I told her things would be all right. Unable to bear it, I dropped to the ground, my hands digging through sand as I began to sob. In the pale light of the moon all I saw was death. Strewn around me were the remains of the shattered lives of so many: abandoned wagons, tools, clothes, the bleached bones of animals and men alike, lining the trail like unearthly guards.

Then our wagon passed and I saw the team follow blindly behind the Hardings', their night shadows stretching across the ground, and in my madness I wanted them to leave me.

I was sure I was mad then, for when I lifted my head I swear I saw Rose standing just out of my reach. She seemed so real! A hundred questions went through me, but for the life of me, I couldn't find my voice. I watched as she touched a small gold cross that hung from a chain around her neck and then smiled at me, like everything was going to be okay. I cried out, reaching for her, but she was gone and everything went black.

The next thing I remember was Quinn carrying me back to the wagon, which is where I am now, writing this.

Later—Tonight, when I began telling Quinn about seeing Rose, of the cross she'd been wearing, he sat bolt upright in bed.

"My ma's necklace," he whispered hoarsely. "I put it on her at the wake."

I ran my hands across his chest, around his neck, feeling like a blind man who had been handed a cup and wasn't sure if it was full or empty. "What does it mean?" I asked, and heard him let out a long sigh, felt him fall back against the mattress.

" 'Tis our journey, now," he said after a while, and I knew he was thinking of Patrick.

It's my tears that are washing these words away. I can't forget what I saw. Oh, if only I could believe . . .

Monday, September 26

Lije and Sam bid us farewell this morning as we were doling out the last of the feed to the animals. As unthinkable as it is, they've decided to turn around, to go *back*.

With a face coarsened by sand and sweat, Lije told us that he feared Carrie was failing and that she refused to go on through the Sierras. He thought she might have a chance if they can get her to Salt Lake.

"Are you daft, man?" Quinn said, incredulous. "At least with us you'd have a chance, *we're* almost to the Truckee River. There's nothing but death waiting for you back there in that desert." The words were hard enough, but the silence that followed seemed worse.

It was at that moment that Carrie Harding chose to step unsteadily down from the wagon, still dressed in her soiled nightshirt, her eyes bright with fever. "Ya comin', Lije?" she said, her voice wavery.

Lije looked to his wife then to Quinn—either way he was lost, and the misery on his face said he knew it. "I gotta do *something*," he said softly. We watched him walk off then, clothes hanging on his too thin body, his shoulders hunched over with the burden of it all.

"Do you think they'll make it?" I asked Stem, and I saw a grimness on his leathery face as we watched them pull away, puffs of dust spewing up as Sam Harding pushed their feeble stock on behind the wagon.

"No," he said, plain, then, "Well, let's move out, McGregors. Got a few big hills ta climb, and I reckon waitin' won't make 'em any smaller."

Truckee River

We've just now reached the Truckee River, so large and clear, a true godsend after the scorching heat and foul water we've had to endure for so long.

To look across and see the shady bottomland, the fine open country, and watch the stock that was loosed some time back straggle ahead of us down to the water takes some of the soreness from me. To see Stem's old eyes take in the land in a way that speaks of memories and Quinn's with new hope brings up a fierce sense of pride that I can't deny.

A different feeling from when I first saw the Platte

or the Laramie, better somehow and earned by our hardships.

Stem and Quinn have just brought the teams back. There's a ranch about a mile and a half down the river Stem knows of, and we're to make camp there.

Came to "the ranch" by late afternoon—more an Indian village than a ranch. Paiutes are camped all about the place.

Stem introduced us to a real fine weathered old fellow by the name of Ned, whose speech was spare, but intentions good. We had no more set up camp than he sent his oldest, a strapping boy nearly the size of Quinn, to help lead our animals to good pasture.

Then Ned's wife, a small-built Paiute woman, came and served us up some little fish the size of sardines and some bearberries—a treat, especially after the past two days of living off of soup made from boiling an old ham bone and some flour.

Before she left, she gave me some balm for our faces, which have been chafed raw by all the sand and alkali dust.

Later—Why is it that I can never find peace for long? While Quinn and I were alone by the fire, I'd got out the balm the woman had given me and began to smooth it over the tender places on his face—all very matter-of-fact until he grabbed my hands and drew me to him. "Let's go inside," he said, like we were home. Then without another word, he picked me up easy and carried me back to our wagon and layed me gently on our bed.

There was no shyness. When he moved over me, I pulled him into my arms. In spite of all that we'd been through, or maybe because of it, my love for him, my body's *need* for him, was strong, and there was nothing else but Quinn's lips on mine, Quinn's powerful hands moving down my body. I drank in the strength of his love greedily, hoarding it away somewhere deep inside like I couldn't have enough.

And for a while, I'd almost forgotten where we were. For a time, in the dark of the wagon with all our things around us, I could almost imagine we were *home*.

It wasn't until Quinn had drifted off to sleep and I'd rolled over to face the sideboards of our wagon that the memory of the marker Lije made for his little boy reared up, slicing through my moment of peace, and I remembered.

Tuesday, September 27

Layed over at the ranch another day to rest our weary animals, as well as ourselves.

I have to admit, I'm feeling a bit stronger after a good night's sleep. Quinn is as well. As we stood together tonight, gazing off to the mountains we would soon face, he wrapped his arms around me and said, "We're going to make it fine, lass. You'll see. Before you know it, this will be a memory . . . something to tell our children when we're old and lost our senses."

There was such warm conviction in his voice, in his eyes, that I felt my heart give in as well, willing it to be true.

"Many waters cannot quench love, neither can the floods drown it": Song of Solomon 8:7.

Wednesday, September 28

Started out once again, lighter than when we came. Quinn and Stem sold off some of the stock that, to quote Stem, were, "Too weak ta fend off a chigger." A wise decision, I imagine, as the roads turned rough early out, climbing higher and higher into mountainous country. Noon was spent winding through a steep trail, great masses of rock towering above us, while below to the left, a deep gorge with the Truckee River at its feet, flowing past willows and cottonwoods.

We've just come to camp here at the river, worn to the bone. Whatever strength we gained laying over at the ranch seems spent already.

Thursday, September 29

Windy today. Passed up and down again over steep hills, jagged rocks—constant fear of upsetting the wagons. Crossed the Truckee, good ford but so *cold*. Then through a meadow and on past a large marsh that took us a full afternoon of hard driving to get around.

I've refused to ride except for brief rests. The animals are threatening to give out altogether.

I know this time will pass, but tonight it's hard to imagine. This sorry land seems endless. Camped near the river again this evening.

271

Friday, September 30

Woke this morning to hear Quinn whispering soft, crooning words to one of our oxen, and I knew by the rattle of the chains and yoke that he was trying to get it to step into line. As I joined him, I saw the ox sink to the ground, and I felt like crying for the poor beast that had served us so faithfully.

Loaded up. On and on we went, and I watched the outlines of heads and horns droop further and further from exhaustion as we crossed the river, striking into the hills once more. Sixteen miles before we reached the valley and more disappointment, finding the lake alkaline.

Struck Springbrook and camped.

Not soon enough, it seems. We lost another of our oxen tonight.

I can't help but feel a grim shadow of worry hang over me this evening. In the distance I can see the Sierra Mountains, the threat of winter eating at the peaks with snow.

"If thou faint in the day of adversity, thy strength is small": Proverbs 24:10.

Saturday, October 1
Pass at the Sierra Nevada

Reaching the pass today, we saw three large wagons in the distance and thought we'd overtaken another company, but as we rode near we realized the wagons had been abandoned, their oxen, still yoked, dead in front.

Stem figures they packed what they could and hurried on through the mountains by foot.

Later—Seems we have met the same fate as the company whose wagons we saw this morning.

We made ten miles before losing another of our oxen this evening, his poor body finally giving out to exhaustion. Quinn's face was drawn with worry. Before he could say anything, I quickly cut in. "Let's pack what we can," I said, and I saw the look of gratitude in his eyes. Together, we went about unloading what we could put on the pack mules tomorrow.

Sunday, October 2

We shared coffee over the fire this morning in silence. While Quinn and Stem were busy packing up the rest of our supplies, I hurried to the wagon, quickly grabbing up the Bible with Rose's letter tucked inside and the friendship quilt Maggie had made for me, shoving Pa's old hat down over my head. When I got back to where the mules were hobbled, I saw Quinn and Stem watching me as they watched over the animals, their faces somber.

"Just a few things," I told them, quickly stuffing the quilt under my saddle. I tried to smile and not think about the rest of the things that were still back in the wagon, parts of my life I would never see again.

I climbed up in my saddle and turned Patch toward the mountains. "I'm ready," I said.

But the dead sound to my voice scared me.

Summit of the Sierras

I don't think I'll forget this climb as long as I live; the sounds are still ringing in my ears: the crack of whips, the groans of the feeble stock and heavy-loaded pack mules, the clatter of gravel. I kept tripping over my skirts as I led Patch, the going too steep to ride. Rocks and more rocks, tearing through my worn boots, into my hands. Narrow ledges with death waiting below. "Just a little further, Callie," Quinn would call. Another step, another breath. "Ten feet more an' we're there," Stem said finally, and we fell into camp, the weight of it all bearing down on my shaky legs.

It's too dark now to see much—except for the mountains, looming up large in the night sky of California.

Bittersweet victory that it is.

Later—Quinn tried to comfort me the best he could tonight as he saw the sorrow settle in on me, but it was no use. Over and over the pictures fill my mind, pictures of Mama's rocker, the dishes Grandma Wade gave us, even the personals that Pa and Rose left behind—all gone.

"Don't turn your back on me," Quinn whispered in the dark of our tent, "on us."

I got up from our bed and walked outside, hating myself even as I did it, but not able to stop myself just the same. *It's the living that matter,* the voice inside of me whispers.

Then why isn't my heart inclined to listen?

Part Six

~~

The Sierra Nevadas
and Home

*"No matter how hard the winter,
the spring always comes."*
—Amanda Wade

Tuesday, October 4
Rich Bar Mining Camp
North Fork of the Feather River

We've made it to Rich Bar! I'm snatching a moment to write this while Quinn and Stem are searching out a place for us to stay. It's been two days of hard travel to bring us here, through valleys and up jagged mountainsides, then over long stretches with nothing but low white shrubs and dreary waste. Finally the descent down into Rich Bar, five miles long and steeper than anything we'd been through.

The first thing I laid eyes on as Patch stumbled through the muddy street was the tiny graveyard fenced with wagon tires and long chains; then I saw the homes: wagons, tents, plank hovels, down to shacks pieced together by pine boughs and calico shirts.

It's so hard to put words to my feelings, good and bad. Good to know we made it, to know the days on days did have an end, the bad water or no water at all, the dust . . . the death. Bad to look around and think that this place stands for all that has been taken from me, and that no matter what it might give in return, I'm not sure it will ever be enough.

Later—after we settled what was left of our stock, Quinn and I reined in our horses in front of the Murphys' old house, my first thought was it looked like a broken-tooth comb; all kinds of different-length boards and strips of wood nailed together. I saw the lady of the house appear at the door then, and in spite of all of my misgivings, I couldn't help but like her.

Mary Murphy, strong and sturdy as a small oak, laughing eyes and a tumble of children peeking out behind the folds of her skirts—her warm handshake made a little of the hardness in me melt. She smiled at me like she understood and led us off to a shack with a porch in front built not far from the "big" house.

It was when we stepped into the tiny cabin and she saw the horror on my face that she patted my arm.

"Try not to look too close at first, honey," she told me. "Not till you're more settled. I remember us moving into this very shack, and I looked around thinking, I came through dust, dirt, mud, and sickness for *this*? If I'd had a gun, I think I would've shot my husband right on the spot."

As much as I tried, it seemed too bitter a pill to swallow. Not long after Mrs. Murphy had excused herself, I sank down next to the trunk that Quinn had carried across the Sierras and ran my weathered hands over the battered box before I opened the lid.

There wasn't much inside: one of Rose's dresses wrapped around a few dishes, Mama's wedding picture . . . I pulled the quilt Maggie had made me from my things then, and for just a moment, I held it to my breast and shut my eyes, pulling in the warmth and the memory of friends, family, and home.

But then I forced my eyes open again.

A lit rag dipped in a tin cup filled with tallow sheds a low, dirty light about this room. A thin deerskin flap is stretched over the hole in the wall that's the window. Weak light shines through the cracks in the logs.

All around me is dull brown. No color. How Rose would've hated this place!

When Quinn came and stood beside me, his face was full of emotion. " 'Tis not forever, you know," he said.

I tried my best to smile, but couldn't.

Wednesday, October 5

Quinn has just left. He and Stem were hired to work for the Feather River outfit. The money was good, he told me. He would be able to buy tools to eventually work his own claim. But if he doesn't return, it's because of me.

"Eight dollars a day, Callie," he told me excitedly. "Can you imagine it? I'm thinking it won't take too long before Stem and I can work my uncle's claim."

I don't know why, but I felt hollow inside as he went on telling me that he and Stem were to leave, that it wouldn't be so bad for me, with Mrs. Murphy living so close and all.

It was when he stripped himself of his shirt and leaned over the washbowl that I closed my eyes and tried to imagine the days and nights I'd endure in the tiny house without him, and I felt a fear like I'd never felt before begin to bubble up in me.

"What is it, Callie?" he'd whispered, and when I opened my eyes, I saw that the excitement in his face had dimmed and he looked uneasy.

I knew, even as the thoughts went through me, that

it wasn't right—that I was being foolish and selfish. But the fear inside of me was bigger than I'd battled before. That's when I started thinking that we shouldn't have ever left Salt Lake, where at least there was some shred of civilization, of life—where Rose was buried and the memory of her was real and fresh. That's when I told Quinn we should go back.

"Back where?" he'd said, looking at me incredulously.

"Salt Lake," I said. "You could find work—"

"No," he said, firm. "I intend to stake my uncle's claim, to finish what Patrick and I set out to do. I thought you wanted to build a life with me out here, Callie."

"I do," I said. "But so much has happened. Don't you see? I'm not sure I have the strength to start all over again, to make new memories. I feel like everything has been drained out of me."

"And it would be better in Salt Lake?" he asked.

Something inside of me seemed to give way then. I wanted to hate Quinn, to blame him for all that was gone. But I couldn't, no matter how hard I tried. If nothing else, my love for him remained.

"Go then," I said dully.

He got up and crossed the room, tried to pull me into his arms, but in my selfishness I stiffened.

Quinn sighed. "I can't save you from your own will," he said quietly. "And I'll not ease your conscience this time."

He turned his back to me then and opened the door. When it closed, the finality of it scared me and I sat down and buried my head in my hands and sobbed.

Thursday, October 6

Woke this morning feeling poorly. At first, laying in the bed, I tried to tell myself it was just a bad dream, but when I opened my eyes, it was all still there, the cold starkness and the loneliness. Quinn sent word before he and Stem left that he'd been checking with some of the travelers coming through. There might be someone who I can ride back to Salt Lake with.

Too tired to write. Can't eat, just get sick. The potatoes and boiled wheat lay on our table untouched. I must be coming down with something.

Later—Got a note from Jessie Bell this evening. Mrs. Murphy passed it on to me. To say I was surprised to find she has made her home here in this very mining town is putting it mildly. She's been cooking for miners, making a brisk business at it, and is planning to open a laundry service with Mrs. Murphy, as well. She wrote that she saw Stem, that he told her of Rose's passing, and she said how sorry she was. She added she'd promised Stem she'd look in on me. No mention of Quinn at all.

Friday, October 7

Mrs. Murphy brought me a visitor today. Jessie! I can't put into words how happy I was to see her, how much just being able to look upon her good face and hear her laughter made me feel like a part of me I'd left on that trail, a part of my past, had been given back somehow.

They both bustled into the shack, Jessie watching me real close with those world-wise eyes of hers as Mrs. Murphy prattled on about how it was probably just as well that I'm going back to Salt Lake, that she must be crazy for coming out here herself. She tried to get some tea and crackers down me, but I got sick again.

"Oh, you poor thing," Mrs. Murphy cried, and looking over at Jessie. "I am thinking I should call for the doctor."

Jessie smiled.

"I think you best wait a spell," she said finally.

"How long?" Mrs. Murphy asked, staring at Jessie as if she'd lost her senses.

"I imagine nine months," Jessie replied mildly. "Give or take a few."

"I'd been so busy . . ." I trailed off weakly, feeling foolish and naive.

"I guess you have," Jessie laughed. Mrs. Murphy tried her best not to.

* * *

My hand shakes even as I write this. Before Mrs. Murphy and Jessie left, I asked them not to mention to Stem or Quinn, if they should see them, that I might be expecting. I told them I wanted to sort things out in my mind.

"Birth is a wonderful thing, Callie," Mrs. Murphy said, patting my shoulder as she and Jessie walked out the door. " 'Tis nothing to fear."

Funny thing is I expected *fear*. What I'm not so prepared for is the funny sense of hope and promise I feel for this tiny life within me.

Saturday, October 8

Mrs. Murphy came to check on me again. She seemed pleased to see me up and about. When I told her, in a fretful voice that irritated even me, that I guess I didn't have much choice in the matter, she just smiled.

She looked at me for a long time, then she said to me, "We women are a lot tougher than we allow ourselves to imagine, Callie. It seems to me we have the most exasperating trait of being able to survive the worst and go on, whether we like it or not."

I saw a bit of Mama looking back at me in the mirror tonight. The reason I say "a bit" is because Mama wouldn't have allowed herself the red-rimmed eyes or the face tight with fear. *"Fear's just a lazy person sayin' I can't,"* she always used to tell me. Even from her sickbed she'd laugh and go on, like dying was more of an annoyance, some pesky fly to be swatted out of her way.

"Don't be a quitter, Callie," that little bit of Mama said to me. I saw a spark of the fighter that Mama had been shining through my eyes then, and I welcomed it.

Sunday, October 9

It had been raining all morning, the water splashing down the chimney, so that the mud and soot splattered the floor. I was halfheartedly trying to clean the mess up when Mrs. Murphy came to the door with a tight look of dread on her face.

"We have to move to higher ground, lass," she said breathlessly, " 'Tis all we can do. Once the streets start flooding, the houses are sure to go soon after. I've seen it before."

I grabbed my shawl, starting to follow her, but something stopped me. I looked around the tiny shack, at the fine quilt Maggie had made me, the Bible with Rose's letter still tucked inside, and Pa's floppy old hat. Not much left from my life before. But it was enough.

"No trees to hold the soil anymore," Jessie told me grimly as the three of us stood outside in the rain, our eyes scanning the hillside behind the town that had been stripped of lumber. I saw some other women huddled in a group, watching with weary, resigned looks, and I suddenly felt something begin to build inside me, something that made me want to scream *No!* to the heavens. It was too much to take from me, from *us*.

"We're not leaving," I said firmly, and Jessie looked at me like I'd lost my mind, until I explained to her that we could dig ditches around the houses, ditches that would lead the water *away* from us. Her eyes became sharp then, studying me.

"We'll need some shovels," she said simply.

Soon Mrs. Murphy, Jessie and I went to work, along with the rest of the women, digging trenches around our little shacks, fighting to save the very homes we all hated so much.

I dug and dug, until my hands bled from the splinters, but I kept on. It was for Pa and for Rose that I worked like such a madwoman, for all the dreams they'd never see, for Jack, who was haunted by things he could never change, and for Quinn, for all that he gave, never asking for anything in return. But most of all it was for *me*.

Tears filled my eyes, mixing with the rain, as we stood back from our work, watching and praying. As the water sloshed away from the little huts, a cheer went up from the other women, and I looked around, really looked at these women for the first time.

I saw women with babies—or thick with the beginnings; I saw old women and young, their faces still gaunt from the trail, but in their eyes was a new strength and promise—hope, just as sure as I felt it myself, swirling within me, making me feel alive and *strong*.

"I'm thinkin' now, the bloody 'Elephant' will never show himself to the likes of *us* again," Mrs. Murphy said with grim satisfaction.

Jessie looked at her for a long moment and then tilted her head back and began to laugh, long and hard, her dark eyes shining with tears.

We all joined in, laughing and crying and hugging each other as the torrents of rain poured down over us.

Monday, October 10

Busy today. I hung Maggie's quilt over the fireplace to give the place some color and braided two rugs from the rags that Jessie brought to me. I think I can make some decent curtains from the gunny bags left from our journey, maybe a tablecloth if I'm careful.

Fixed up, the little house isn't so awful looking.

> *Rich Bar Mining Camp,*
> *East Branch, North Fork of the Feather River*
> *October 11, 1859*
>
> *Mrs. Maggie Todd*
> *Blue Mills, Missouri*
>
> *Dear Maggie,*
> *I hope you aren't angry with me for not writing you in so long, but I was determined not to write to you until I was more like my old self again. Funny thing is, I came to realize that we both would be waiting for something that wasn't likely to happen. Looking in the mirror this morning, I found myself staring back at a young woman whose*

eyes told a different tale from that of "Callie Wade from Independence, Missouri's." These new eyes spoke of struggle and tears, of laughter, of love, and of triumph. I knew then I would never be the same as before. But you know what? I'm glad.

A very good friend once told me that sorrow hurts worse out here, but that it heals quicker, too. I guess I've found out how right she was this past week I've spent here in this little mining town. In some ways I think I had to learn to live all over again, Mag. I've been baptized by fire, you might say, but that fire has forged a strength in me, a resolve I never knew I had, and I know I'm better for it.

Now that I've come to see things more clearly, I just hope I'm not too late to mend things between Quinn and me. I did a foolish thing, Mag, and I'm not too proud to admit it. In my grief and fear I struck out at Quinn, the one person who had always been there for me and probably is the best friend I've ever had besides you. Mama always used to say that we hurt most the people we love because we never have to fear them leaving us. Well, this is one time I'm not so sure.

I have learned my lesson well, I guess. And if I get a second chance? From now on, I am going to grab the good times with both arms, Mag. I am going to walk outside and feel the sun on my face and learn to laugh, really laugh again. Most of all, I am going to take the love that comes my way and hold on to it for dear life. Sometimes we don't need new scenery, just new eyes.

Love,
Callie

Wednesday, October 12

When the news came today that some of the men at Feather River had been injured in a mud slide, I knew in my heart that Quinn was one of them.

Mrs. Murphy confirmed it when she came to my door this afternoon.

"It's Quinn," she said, out of breath. "They're bringing him here."

Minutes seemed like hours as Mrs. Murphy waited with me at the door of the cabin. I was told that when some of the men went to check up on a dig they had just set up, a slide had begun from the heavy downpour of rain. She said that Stem and Mr. Murphy had been washed down into the ravine. Quinn had gone after them. Quinn was hurt, she said, but alive, as were Stem and Mr. Murphy.

It took three men to carry Quinn into the cabin. I felt as if my heart would burst when I saw him, unconscious and looking so helpless. After they laid him in our bed, they told me there was nothing else I could do but sit and wait, as the wound on his leg had been cleaned and bandaged. So, I pulled the little stool up and sat there, holding Quinn's hand and comforting him, just like he had done for me so many times before.

Around two in the morning, he finally started coming around. His eyes focused on me, looking surprised to see me. He reached up and touched my face. "Tears?" he said, and I swiped at my face.

"You nearly scared me to death, you know," I told him, fussing around him, checking on the wound on his leg. Quinn grasped my arm and pulled me to him, gritting his teeth a little from the pain as my fall jarred his leg.

"We'll go back, Callie," he rasped in my ear. "Together. I'll take you to Salt Lake, to Independence if that's what you want."

"I'm not going," I said simply.

"What?"

"I'm not going. I'm staying here with you. Where I belong."

Quinn hugged me tight against him, and I smiled, even though he nearly squeezed the air out of me. "We'll have the best life together, Callie," he said. "I promise you that. I promise you. I'll build you a fine house—"

"With a nursery?"

"And . . . What did you say?" Quinn said, looking shocked, but when he saw my smile, a sudden realization broke over his handsome face. "A baby . . ."

I saw a gentling of the lines around his eyes, like something inside of him had been given back, like there was hope after all. He closed his eyes for a minute, and when he opened them again, I saw they were filled with emotion.

"A baby," he breathed in wonder. "Well, don't that beat all."

He held me tight to him again, like he might never let go.

I hope he never will.

Thursday, October 13

Stem and Jessie came tonight for dinner. The two have been thick as thieves since Stem returned. It was a good evening, with all of us gathered around the fire, snug in our little cabin as the drifts of our first snow hugged the Bar. I was thinking to myself that it couldn't get much better when Quinn and Stem announced that they had a surprise for me.

When the two went out and then tromped back into the cabin with Mama's rocker in their arms, I thought I was seeing things.

"We salvaged it sometime back." Quinn grinned, and I knew he saw the tears in my eyes. "Kept it at the Murphys' house until we could get it fixed up for you."

"It's a fine rocker, Callie," Jessie said, and I hugged Quinn around the waist as we all stood back to admire it. I noticed Stem was looking kind of good and pleased with himself, standing off to one side, and I went to him and hugged him, too.

"Well, if I knew ya were goin' ta do that, I'd a carried the whole derned wagon down here on my back," Stem teased, but I could see that he was touched.

"You best watch yourself, Justice Dawson," Jessie said, winking at me. "I don't take kindly to men with roving eyes."

"Justice?" Quinn and I chorused.

"Oh, didn't you know?" Jessie grinned, in spite of the scowl on Stem's face. "I guess his mama had a sense of humor, too."

Friday, October 14

Quinn and I went for a walk today. In spite of all of the snow it was quite warm, and as we climbed the little trail, I felt the beauty of the mountainside take my breath away.

Finally making it to the top, we stopped to rest, sitting down next to each other on a large boulder that jutted over the gorge, and we both grew silent, looking out across the mountains.

The thick white blanket of powder that covered everything seemed to wash away all the dirtiness of life, and I felt renewed in a way. All the sounds of crying and despair that had haunted me from the trail had faded, and instead I remembered the excitement, the laughter, and the eyes that had been filled with eager hope.

"I sure wish Pa and Rose could've seen this," I said to Quinn after a while.

Quinn took my hand in his. "Maybe they do," he replied.

Later—Quinn was standing out on the porch this evening after dinner when he called for me. I stepped outside to see what was the matter, only to find him gazing up into the night sky.

"Look, Callie," he said, pointing up to the dark dip of sky that seemed to hang so low over us we could touch it. "I'd say heaven's as near to us here as anywhere else we could ever find, wouldn't you?"

"I guess I would," I said.

Saturday, October 15

Quinn rose early this morning, and as he was stoking the fire in the woodstove, he began to talk in earnest about the things we should do before he and Stem headed out for his uncle's claim. I got so tickled watching him, standing there in his long underwear with such a serious look on his face, that I began to laugh.

It wasn't so much the laughter that shocked me, but the *sound*—joy sounding so real that I clapped my hand over my mouth and we both stared at each other.

"We made it, Callie," Quinn said, smiling, and I saw the unshed tears in his eyes. "We made it."

March—1860

As I watched Quinn and Stem ride out today, my thoughts traveled back to the months we'd all spent together on the trail. Quinn told me once that no matter how many twists and turns life's road takes us on, we seemed destined to follow it together.

In a way, I think our lives really began back on that trail leading out of Independence. The hardships we had, we shared, as we do with our memories now.

Although the spirits of Pa and Rose remain with us, there are nights now when we laugh, remembering some of the silly things Rose and Lizzie used to do, and how we smile with pride remembering Pa. These are memories I don't think I'll ever be able to let rest, and maybe that's the way it's supposed to be. I guess memories are kind of like gifts left behind after the struggle.

This time, when I watched Quinn ride away, I didn't worry about never seeing him again, for in my heart I know I will. I find myself smiling even now, remembering how the baby kicked as I waved good-bye to them both, and despite the low wispy clouds that hung just over the green foothills as Quinn and Stem faded into the distance, I felt no fear.

If there is anything in this world that I have learned, it's to reach for the clouds and never, never fear the rain.

Dawn Miller

Rich Bar,
North Fork of the Feather River
Plumas City, California
June 17, 1860

Mr. Jack Wade
Julesburg, Colorado

Dear Jack,

I hope this letter sees you safe. I don't imagine
you'd think that I might worry after you, tromp-
ing all over God's half acre, but I do.

Well, it looks as if Quinn's uncle's claim has
paid off after all. I'll tell you, there wasn't a happier homecoming than the day Quinn and Stem
came riding back into town. "May not be the
'Mother Lode,' Callie," Stem laughed, "but I
reckon we have enough here so's I could buy a
mother if I was inclined ta have one."

Quinn has bought a nice piece of land that we
can work and added some livestock to replace the
ones we lost. Stem has bought the parcel next to
ours, telling us that he can't leave us "green and
primed fer any trouble that might come our way."
The morning after Quinn and I were finally settled into our new home, I gave birth to a beautiful
baby girl.

Oh, Jack—if only you could see her. It seems
like all the hardships that we left behind and all
of the dreams that are yet to come are in this
baby's eyes. She's the best of all of us, Jack, of
our past and our future. The doc from town paid
us a visit. He told us that it was a miracle that I
didn't have any problems, her being such a big

*baby and all. Quinn told me later that he figured
it was God's way of balancing the scales.*

*We all miss you something awful, Jack. I wish
you would reconsider Quinn's offer to go into
partnership with him. In spite of what you say, I
think cattle ranching would give you plenty of
room to roam. While I agree with you that life is
a "gamble," I think professional gamblers hold
more hazard cards than the rest of us. Promise
me you won't take any unnecessary risks. I pray
that God will keep you safe until we see each
other again. With much love from Stem, Quinn,
baby Rose, and*

*Your loving sister,
Callie McGregor*

Author's Note

There are memories in our lives that never fade, given to us as gifts, I believe, to keep us going even in the toughest of times. The memory of my great-grandmother was one of my gifts and the true inspiration for this story.

Nellie Mae Harper was born in the 1800s on a small farm in Missouri, and like so many women that forged west, she was to endure more than her fair share of hardships. She saw floods and storms that could wipe out in a day what had taken them months of sweat and toil to cultivate. She saw death—more than any one person should—losing three sisters and one brother in her arms. The scene of Rose seeing the angels, by the way, was a true account told to me by my great-grandmother who had held her sister Rose in her arms to the end. But more importantly she *survived,* she taught us all to laugh in spite of what fate dealt us and to love each other all the more because of it. And this same wonderful spirit is what helped to settle the West.

Unfortunately, history has left out many stories of the women who went west. But because of their letters and journals that survived, telling of their courageous trek across this country, their memories will never fade.

So, Callie's story is my gift to you. To the many women who, like our ancestors, have toiled, loved, laughed and cried and who fought against the odds and *won.* My hat is off to you all.

Dawn Miller
Hanover, Maryland